PLAYING THE FIELD

A BROTHER'S BEST FRIEND SOCCER ROMANCE

LA DEVILS

STACY TRAVIS

FAST TURTLE
PRESS

PLAYING THE FIELD

~

STACY TRAVIS

Cover Design: Val at Books and Moods

Editing: Jenny Sims, Editing4Indies

*For every woman who worries that one failure is the endpoint. It's not.
It's the beginning of something better.*

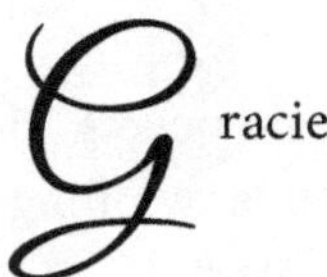
racie

I'm not exactly a sports fan. I know, I know. It's blasphemy in a sports town like Los Angeles, but let me explain.

For my entire teenage life, I spent my evenings and weekends sitting on the sidelines of some sport or another. My parents were diehard basketball, baseball, football—you name it—fans, and to them, "family time" was hours spent tailgating and watching games. Or eating nachos at home and screening play-offs on TV. Or asking me to pick up my younger brother from his sports practices once I had my driver's license.

For a while, I tried to join the party, rattling off game stats I calculated in my head. "He's not going to score. He goes wide off a breakaway 87 percent of the time."

I also kept track of behavior. "Watch how he takes that second touch right before he passes left. Someone should be guarding that side."

It worked a little too well. My family members began showcasing my knowledge like a party trick. Instead of feeling like I was in on the joke, I felt like the butt of it.

So I tucked my knowledge away and started bringing a book wherever I went, generally a romance novel or a scientific journal because I knew my macho dad and brother wouldn't talk to me about that.

It worked.

I read from starting whistle to ending applause, even if I couldn't invest in the reluctant duke or the heartthrob earl because I didn't identify with the female character. Her life would never be mine. I lived firmly planted in a reality supported by statistics and numbers, and nerd girls from small towns didn't generally seduce royalty. But as long as I was with my family, attending counted as bonding.

When I moved to college, I declined the student tickets to Stanford football games, even when we were on a winning streak. I clung to the reading pretense when athletes strutted into the dining hall in their practice jerseys, just as everyone else clambered around them like groupies. I ignored the occasional Super Bowl invitation and delighted in a library.

It's worked out just fine.

Until now.

"Dev-ils, Dev-ils!"

Now, I'm sitting at a Los Angeles Devils soccer game against a Houston team in heaven knows which league. Only now, I'm thirty-three and going hard on the numbers because this may be my new job—watching pro soccer players, compiling their performance data, calculating their odds of future success—in a town I don't understand because half the people here are too beautiful to be real.

In the time since my plane landed, I've seen tanned limbs, pouty lips, impossible bodies, and social media-perfect hair. Maybe it just happens from living here. Maybe it filters in from the infernal sunshine. I'm not used to it. San Francisco fog is legendary, and I'm at home in the cool, damp weather.

The scientist in me is curious about how things work in LA. This fashion-backward wallflower is intimidated.

I forget all about that for a second because there's drama on the field. Fans are standing. People are yelling.

I crane my neck for a better view and see a Houston player charging ahead with the ball. He dribbles up the field and passes to another who makes a run toward the goal, with no one in his path.

Unless the keeper stops it, the point is all but guaranteed for Houston. It would put them ahead with only minutes left in the game.

The fans are going nuts, yelling unintelligible things that blend into a collective roar. The player takes one step too many before trying to pass the ball, and he's cut off in his tracks by a Devils defender. And not just any defender. This one I know by his statistics and reputation as one of the most aggressive in the league.

Hunter Reyes.

He was my brother's best friend growing up, but I haven't seen him since he was a gorgeous teenager with an attitude in our kitchen. Probably just as well.

Playboy off the field, hothead on it. He has one of the worst penalty records in the league, more red cards than almost anyone, and more defensive victories. Fans can't get enough of him. And, if the rumors are true, women can't either.

Coaches, not so much.

If I take the job as head of analytics, one of my first tasks is to run data analysis to decide whether the Devils should keep him or throw him out on his tight, muscular rear end.

That is why I have an iPad in my lap and I'm adding data to the trove I already have on Hunter and his teammates. I need to be thorough and impress my potential future bosses, even if I'm ambivalent about taking the job.

On the field below us, Hunter attacks like a missile, slide tackling a Houston player, deftly sweeping his legs out from under him, taking possession of the ball, and kicking it away to end the play.

Houston fans shout their disapproval at the reckless move. Devils fans cheer for the expert defense.

The Houston player lies on the ground, gripping his ankle and writhing in pain. Hunter paces in a circle like a wound-up animal. Every muscle flexes in preparation for the next fight. From my center field seat, I see a sheen of sweat fly off him when he kicks his toe into the ground. More beads of sweat launch when he flips his damp hair off his forehead.

He's like a stallion stalking the field, all lean muscle and almost frightening power. I have no idea if he's as menacing in person as he looks down there, huffing angrily. Fortunately, I can do my job better from a distance, so I enter my notes quietly as the fans around me continue to go nuts.

Marching over to Hunter, the ref blows his whistle, pulls a red card from his breast pocket, and holds it high in the air. The Houston fans in the stadium cheer for justice, but the overwhelming number of Devils fans let out a loud, collective "boo!"

A guy next to me hurls his arm with a pointed finger at the field. "You suck, Ref."

Hunter gets in the ref's face and yells, pointing at the injured player and gesturing madly. I may not love sports, but I don't think there's ever been a ref in the history of sports who's changed a call because a player copped an attitude. But all that testosterone is hard to wrangle, and apparently, Hunter has more than the average male.

He comes just shy of decking the ref, who shakes his head and points him forcefully to the sidelines. Hunter stomps off to a chorus of more loud booing, but the damage is done.

The Devils are now down a player for the rest of the game. He may have scored a goal, but he's made it harder for his teammates to compete. If Houston scores on them, Hunter will take some of the blame for leaving the team weakened.

I watch Hunter storm to the team bench. His coach says something to him that makes him blow up again, pointing at the ref. But it doesn't change the fact that he's out of the game.

TWO HOURS LATER, I'm stuck at the airport. My flight back to San Francisco was delayed by weather in the Pacific Northwest, leaving me with time to kill.

My brother Kyler is away on business, and I don't know anyone else in LA, so hanging out at the airport seems like a good plan. I can always put on my headphones, catch up on work, and mull whether I can see myself moving to LA.

Not like I have much of a choice, thanks to a little meltdown in my former boss's office at AIFund, a huge Silicon Valley tech company, which finances all the biggest artificial intelligence startups. I'd gone to bat for a qualified candidate without bothering to mention that he was my boyfriend. We'd only been dating for a couple of months, but I loved him, and I wanted to help him.

He got the job, and shortly thereafter, he ratted me out. Then he broke up with me.

Turns out the job he really wanted was mine, and now that I'm gone, he has it. That's right. I may be the only woman in history who slept my way to the bottom.

And because I signed a non-compete agreement, I can't work at any other Silicon Valley tech firm for two years.

I learned my lesson. Work and romance don't mix, a hill I will die on. At least, if being the chief data analyst for a sports team is the same as death, which is how it feels.

More sports. More soccer. More hotheaded Hunter Reyes. Ugh.

I grab a seat at the Sip 'n Fly restaurant bar, where the menu includes one of my all-time favorite dishes—stuffed potato skins. At least things are looking up on the dining front.

I order the potatoes and fish my iPad out of my overstuffed purse. I have at least a dozen unread books queued up, plus I can recalculate my analysis of Hunter Reyes with the new data from the game. New data is my happy place.

Soccer highlights play on one of the TVs over the bar, and I roll my eyes at it, not interested in seeing any more post-pubescent displays of macho behavior. I've had enough for one day, thank you very much.

My diet soda arrives, and I take a healthy sip while cuing up the first chapter of a new novel set in eighteenth-century Scotland. In moments, I'll be swept off to the Highlands to lose myself in a guilty pleasure about a strapping young Scot who's good with his hands.

I'm so single-mindedly focused that I don't notice anyone sidle up on the stool next to mine until a gruff, rumbling voice disrupts the images of heather fields and icy lochs in my mind.

"This seat taken?"

By the time I turn to acknowledge the man next to me, he's already seated, so I wave him on and go back to my book. I hear him order a beer, then cancel it. "Just sparkling water, actually," he says, sounding annoyed.

I should put on my headphones and tune him out, but I'm also a people watcher, so I chance a look in his direction, wondering what bug crawled up his britches.

I'm met with a face in deep distress, forehead creased, and mouth turned down in an irritable frown. But that does nothing to dampen just how spectacularly gorgeous he is.

Dark, wavy hair. Broad shoulders under a navy hoodie. High cheekbones, hard jaw, a week's worth of beard that barely softens the angular beauty of his face. I'm not used to being this close to a man who looks like he belongs in a movie—a romcom in the Scottish Highlands, if I'm being specific. His eyes, a deep gray flecked with green, look stormy as they focus on the TV screen above our heads. Reflected light flickers in his eyes.

The bartender delivers his drink, and his long fingers wrap around the glass. I stare at them, mesmerized as he takes a long sip. For a moment, I fantasize about the feel of his fingers on my bare skin, and I shift my gaze, mortified at the idea he could read my thoughts. I return to my diet soda and my book.

I'm sure the odd hum of electricity I feel in the space between us is my imagination. I feel self-conscious, thinking about how a stranger must see me, sitting ramrod straight on the stool with my ankles primly crossed and my iPad on the bar.

"Must be a good book." His growl crackles in the air between us, and I don't need to look up to know he's talking to me. I'm the only one anywhere nearby, which makes it all the more strange that he took the seat right next to me when there were six others.

"I like it." I glance in his direction, not expecting to see his unfettered gaze bearing down on me. Having those gray eyes raking over my face would be frightening if it didn't also warm me down to my toes. I swallow hard and try to calm my racing heart, hoping he can't see the effect he has on me. Glancing up at him through my lashes, I can tell by his smirk that he can.

"Care to share?"

Is he asking me to read to him?

"Um…"

"The title. I could use something new on my bedside table."

He must be making fun of me. I use a large font so I don't need my reading glasses, and *The Highland Bachelor* at the top of the screen leaves little question about the content.

"You—you're a big reader?" I don't mean to sound skeptical, but my question comes out in a deadpan tone that makes his eyebrows jump.

"Among other things." The smug half smile leaves no question about those other things. My face heats like I'm back in high school, gawking at a football player who deigned to talk to the shy girl holding her books against her flat chest by the lockers.

The smirk looks good on him. Too good. This must be his game, making unsuspecting women go red in the face and weak in the knees for sport.

It's hot in here. I take a sip of my soda, willing it to chill me from the inside out.

He looks familiar. Probably an actor. This is LA, after all. It's why I'm eager to get back to the safety of nerdville in Northern California, where most of the people I know are computer coders.

But wait…is he…? Have I spent too long watching soccer players, or does he look a bit like Hunter Reyes, whom I spent a good part of the day watching from thirty rows up?

No. What are the odds? He's just one of many hot LA guys with charm to burn.

"It's, um, a regency romance. About a Scottish duke." That'll get rid of him.

He nods, grinning and flashing a dimple in one cheek. "Scotland, eh. I read the Diana Gabaldon series. Couldn't get on board with the time travel aspect at first, but I came around."

I blink slowly, trying to decipher if my brain has gone haywire from the heat. Is he telling me he *reads* period romances?

"Be interested in trying something else if you feel like letting me in on the title of yours."

Yup, he still seems to be talking about romance novels, so I oblige. "This one is particularly generous with setting. I really feel the Highlands atmosphere—the steep craggy hillsides and the stormy lake waters—makes me want to take a trip there someday… Anyhow, the heroine owns a farm and tends sheep there, but her property and her family name are threatened by this duke, who inherited the title but has no real love for the land. At least, not yet. And then there's—"

"Excuse me…" A young woman with an apologetic giggle inserts herself between us. All I see is a mane of blond-streaked hair, and I inhale the sweet scent of floral body wash. "I'm such a big fan. Could I get a picture?"

The man grunts his approval, and I scoot over to make space for her to move in and snap the usual array of selfies—the sideways peace sign, the puckered lips, the arms around his neck with a heel kicked up in back.

"Okay, I'm tagging you. Follow me back, or just follow me. Footiefangirl68." She points an accusing finger with a manicured nail at both of us. I'm so unnerved that I nod and obediently enter her social media handle, which I plan to delete later.

She thanks him profusely right as I'm fumbling through a streak of mortification, wondering if he really is Hunter. Gorgeous face, muscular build, dark hair… The outputs are too numerous, so I quickly survey what I can see around us, looking for a visible luggage tag, a business logo, an obvious sign like his name spelled out in block letters on his forehead.

Nope, nothing except his face grinning in amusement at my obvious distress and the fact that I'm gawking at him. Arms folded across his chest, he looks like he has all the time in the world to enjoy my awkward stare.

Mercifully, a voice drones through the PA system with the first boarding announcement for my flight. "That's me, gotta go," I say, digging into my wallet for some cash to throw on top of my check. I'm leaving a 40 percent tip, but this guy has me too rattled to wait around for change. I'm off the barstool with my carry-on over my shoulder in seconds.

"Too bad for me. I was enjoying the view."

I chance one more look at him, certain he's gazing out the plate glass windows at airplanes or something, but his eyes are roaming over my body in a way that's sexy, not creepy.

Does he mean…me? It doesn't compute. It's not that I don't think I possess *some* female charms, but they're mostly limited to the occasional good hair day and ways I can impress people by adding three-digit numbers in my head.

Neither is happening here.

Popping a too-large bite of potato, bacon, and cheese into my mouth, I slide off the barstool and shove my e-book into my purse. When I finally swallow, I find his gaze trained so hotly on me that I feel pinpricks of sweat on my skin and a surprising clench in a G-spot I didn't know I had.

If this man can do that with a look, I can't imagine what he could do if he actually touched me.

I want to find out.

At that thought, I jump nervously away, afraid he can read my thoughts.

On my way to the gate, I feel the first hint of excitement over the new job that may be my future for a while. Having a hot guy flirt with me while eating potato skins? Maybe LA has something to offer after all.

I swipe open my phone to get my boarding pass and land on a social media app, where Footiefangirl68 has already posted her selfie and tagged Hunter Reyes. Of course she has. She knows a playboy soccer player when she sees one.

I'm just the dope who thought he liked me for my reading list.

CHAPTER 2

$\mathcal{H}$unter

One Month Later

THE LAST FEW reps hurt the most, but not because my muscles are giving out. Quite the opposite. It's the feeling of knowing I'm done with my workout that makes every synapse cry the blues. My mind is only calm when I'm in motion.

Fortunately, I make a living moving around a soccer pitch and training my body to perform within an inch of its very existence. That's when all the outside noise quiets, and I feel at peace with the world.

"Nineteen," I grunt, pushing several hundred pounds of metal with my legs. They shake as I bring the weight back down, visibly shuddering at the load. "Twenty." It's all I have, at least for tonight. Tomorrow is another day.

"Good set." Jimmy, the team trainer, is the only one in the

gym, mainly because it's after eight and most of the guys have gone home to their wives or girlfriends. I have neither, and I like it that way.

No complications, no distractions.

I grunt, knowing Jimmy doesn't need more acknowledgment than that. "You wanna get a beer?"

He looks at me warily, no doubt remembering what happened over a year ago when he okayed a trip to a Hollywood bar. Before we'd even ordered, three women had draped their arms around me, posing for selfies. Two drinks in, I had one of them on my lap and was making out with her friend. Not a good look, according to the team's publicist.

"Better not. Natalie will choke the life out of me if I let you near more empty carbs." Oh. Right. There's also that mandate from the team nutritionist. Clean diet: high on protein, low on scandal-causing carbs. Check. It's the reminder my body needs because my brain wants to be numb.

I nod. "Okay."

Jimmy smooths his mustache with his thumb and forefinger before fiddling with the string on his gray hoodie. He's lean and a couple of inches taller than me, which makes it impossible for me to intimidate him at my mere six-three. His basketball career ended before it began with an Achilles' tendon tear in high school, but he's still an athlete in his mindset. It's why he works us all to the bone but stops just shy of injury. He's careful, thoughtful, and a mean son of a bitch when he needs to be.

I sometimes forget that he's the team trainer and not my friend. Thus, no Hollywood bar.

At this point, my friends on the team are few and far between. I know I've alienated a lot of people with my aggressive playing style. Some of my teammates forgive it when it gets results, but there are a few—Jamie Plank, our starting center midfielder, to name one—who'd like to see me get canned.

It makes his job harder each time I get a red card because we play one man down for the remainder of the game. And depending on the penalty, I might be required to sit out a game.

None of that is good for continuity, not to mention that it's harder to win when we're down a player. But the fans love it. A little drama on the field gets them revved up, and that energy helps the team too.

I'm not about to argue that unnecessary slide tackling is smart, but it's how I've always played. A fierce rage triggers when I'm on the field, a reaction to something my unhappy drunk of a father said a decade ago. "You succeed as an athlete because your temper drives you. You'd fail anywhere else. That's how life works—it gives you one asset to compensate for all the deficits."

At the time, I was in the heart of my push to get recruited to a professional team, so I leaned way in. And once he died, I clung to those words because they were all I had left of him.

It doesn't matter that I have a calmer side. When I'm challenged—either on the soccer pitch or in the face of some asshole who pushes my buttons—I see red. I might as well be a bull unleashed from a holding pen. It's all power, unrestrained energy, and killer instinct.

It's everything wrapped up in a will to succeed, and anger at my dad for not being a better man. A perfect storm that drove me to career stardom.

And now, it will probably get me traded.

We walk back to the lockers, where I shove my zippered warm-up jacket into my bag and grab a fresh towel from a stack in the corner. Mopping the sweat from my brow, I gather the rest of my shit to go home.

"You still have that meal prep place delivering to you?" Jimmy asks, raising an eyebrow. He always pretends to be jealous of my bougie lifestyle, but his wife is a trained chef, and I know he's going home to something a helluva lot better than my box of pre-measured proteins and greens.

"Yeah. Tonight's either fish or fish."

He laughs. "And then?"

"Porn marathon on pay-per-view," I joke. Jimmy is one of the few people I trust enough to reveal what I really do at night. He waits, tapping a finger against his bottom lip and stretching to his full height. It never ceases to amaze me how a guy that wiry can look menacing. "Fine. I'm in the middle of *Emma*. Jane Austen."

Jimmy squints. "Don't think I read that one, but I did read some Austen at some point in school."

It's one thing we have in common—a love for books. I dig reading in general, but a good classic is always in my rotation.

There are bound to be guys on the team who'd give me shit for being a bookworm. I like having some aspects of my life that aren't available for public consumption. Another takeaway from my dad—let people think I'm a grunting athlete and nothing more because it's a lower bar to maintain.

"Thanks for sticking around for my late sesh," I say, feeling a little guilty about keeping Jimmy away from his wife and kids. But not guilty enough to skip a workout.

"Not a problem. I'm on dish duty anyway, so I'm not missing much. Except the girls' bedtime routine, and I'll roll in at the right hour to screw everything up, not to worry."

Jimmy and I leave the sports facility and walk to the parking lot, which is empty except for our cars and tall streetlamps The sky is that periwinkle color that happens when day gives up and night pushes in. I have to make a special effort to keep my head down when we have night games so that color doesn't distract me.

So far, it never has.

Soccer is my entire life, so I'm not about to jeopardize it. I've already done a bit too much of that, putting my job on the line right as the transfer window swung wide open. I'll probably be moving out of LA soon enough to some town with worse weather.

"How does one screw up the bedtime routine of five-year-old

girls?" I'm legitimately curious, especially since I won't be daddying it up anytime soon. If ever.

He can't suppress a guilty smile. It comes with another finger tap on his bottom lip. With the trucker hat Jimmy popped on when we walked outside, he looks even taller, like a eucalyptus tree stuck in the breeze. "Hannah does the dinner and bath and gets them settled in bed. Then I rile 'em up, tickling them and stomping around like Bigfoot. Hannah looks at me like she'll murder me, but I can't bring myself to stop. Pretty much a daily occurrence."

I chuckle at his shamelessness, and for a second, I feel something strange. It's a tiny pang behind my ribs, and I wonder if there's something wrong with my heart. Maybe I went too hard on the cardio before I dug into leg day. Because it certainly can't be a feeling of wanting what Jimmy has. The last thing I need in my life is a woman waiting to yell at me and kids waiting for me to do something else.

So I give Jimmy a bro hug and a slap on the back before throwing my bag onto the passenger seat of my Range Rover. When the engine turns over, its hum vibrates through my bones. The power and strength of the car override whatever errant stuff just happened in my heart and direct me down the narrow road between the soccer complex and the freeway.

That's when my phone connects to my car and tells me through the speakers that I have new messages. The first is from Gerald Moder, the club CEO who holds my fate in his hands. He'd never tell me I'm getting transferred in a voicemail, but hearing his voice sends a chill down my spine nonetheless. "Reyes, it's Gerald Moder. Let's get you in my office this week. Much to discuss."

There's no point in replaying it, looking for signs of what he wants to discuss. Better to drink some whiskey on my own at home to make sure I fall asleep and don't spend the whole night spinning out. My fate will be revealed soon enough.

The second message is from my closest friend, Kyler, with the "good news" that his sister is coming to work for the team. I roll my eyes even though no one can see me. I remember his older sister, Gracie, and it won't be hard to find her at Devils headquarters if memory serves. She'll be the one with bangs hanging halfway over her thick glasses. She'll be roaming around in pajama pants and a baggy shirt.

She'll be the one who's too brainy and too cool to talk to the likes of me. At least that's how I remember her. Nothing I did impressed her, and by the time I was drafted to the English Premier League at nineteen, she wasn't around to be impressed by that either, off earning her graduate degree.

I can't imagine why she'd be working for a professional soccer team, but my phone buzzes, and the breathless voice on the other end wipes any thoughts of Gracie away. "Hunt, it's Emily from next door. The firefighters are here."

"What? Where? What are they doing?"

"They're at your house. Something caught fire. I'm so sorry."

"Sorry" is not a good thing to hear when it comes to fire. "Sorry" can only mean one thing: my house is going up in flames, along with my soccer career.

CHAPTER 3

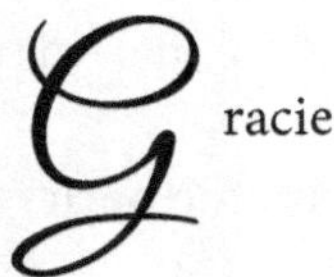 racie

"WAIT, *WHAT* HAPPENED?" I need to be sure I heard my brother correctly. Maybe he's talking about a different Hunter Reyes. Any Hunter Reyes, except the one I convinced myself I'll never run into because my job is in the corporate offices and his is on the soccer pitch.

Apparently, a person will convince herself of anything to make it through another day. And this day started with me wrenching myself out of bed an hour earlier than necessary so I could stress bake a batch of chocolate-chunk cookies and eat four of them with my coffee. It's my first day at work with the Devils. My stomach is roiling, but at least the house smells good.

"His house caught fire last night." Kyler flips a pancake higher than necessary, and its uncooked side lands perfectly in the center of the griddle. I want to know how he learned to do that, but first things first.

"How?" Sitting on a barstool pulled up to the granite counter that separates the kitchen from the dining area, I rub at my temples, where a perpetual headache is brewing. "I mean, wow. That's terrible." I shake myself out of the blur that momentarily stole my humanity. "Was he inside when it happened? Is everything okay?"

Kyler shrugs with his back to me as he loads frozen berries into a blender. I watch him add protein powder and coconut milk, then secure the lid and turn it on. When he's whipped the mixture into frothy purple submission, he reaches for the cabinet above my head and takes out two glasses.

He has the energy of a jackrabbit and has always been a morning person. Growing up, the scene looked similar, with Kyler already having worked out and showered by seven, and me dragging myself to the kitchen for orange juice to fuel me through the process of getting ready for school.

Only now, Kyler is an adult with a job, and I'm still too bleary to finish buttering my toast.

I stare out the window of the Hollywood Hills bungalow that he bought a few years ago and renovated from top to bottom. The place is an architectural beauty, all wood beams and floor-to-ceiling glass windows that make it feel like we're in a tree house. The view at night is spectacular, facing a canyon on one side and the city on the other, with a panoramic view of twinkling lights and a dark sky. It's so quiet here that I find it hard to believe we're in Los Angeles, home to twelve million people.

"All I know is that he got a call last night, and by the time he got home, the fire was out, but the place is unlivable. Half burned, and the rest is so smoke damaged that it'll take a while to sort through and see what's salvageable."

"That's horrible. Does he know what caused the fire?" I don't mean to sound insensitive, but my science brain seeks answers, data. It's almost a defense mechanism to protect me from worrying about emotions because once I start down the road, a surge of empathy makes it hard to process anything else.

Kyler shrugs, his brow creased. "No idea. He video-called me in a panic from his front yard. The house was still smoking, but it mostly looked like a gaunt shadow behind him. He's on his way over here now."

"He's...what? Right now?!"

It's not like I expect my brother to run every decision he makes by me, especially since he's being kind and putting me up while I see if my new job has legs, but it's seven in the morning on a Tuesday, and I'm barely awake enough to process information. Any information. Let alone the idea that Hunter Reyes is coming over here.

I never mentioned to Kyler that I ran into him at the airport a month ago. All part of my attempt at denying it ever happened. Like maybe if I wipe the episode from my mind, it will be wiped from the annals of time.

My grasp of physics was never the best, which is why I turned toward computer science. It's probably more than I can hope for that Hunter won't recognize me from our brief interaction, but here's to hoping.

A stream of memories comes barreling forth. Not the days when my brother was in grade school. Back then, I was in high school and barely aware of what my younger sibling did.

I'm thinking about when I went off to college, and my hormones finally woke up from their epic slumber. Back when I finally noticed guys and felt desperate for them to acknowledge me, yet I had no idea how to make that happen. Not when I was only a nerd girl who could help them ace a calculus test or a stats problem set.

I came home from college wholly unprepared for the sight of Hunter Reyes, who had grown into a chiseled rock of muscle with a face that made me blush on sight. It was so embarrassing to be the older sister who couldn't look a teenage soccer player in the eye without staring at his muscles while salivating. It's why I didn't come home the summer after my junior year at all.

Sitting in Kyler's kitchen now, I cover my eyes as though it can block the images from intruding on what was, until this moment, a decent cup of coffee.

Scenes of me wearing a lab coat, which hung from my non-curvy body like a tent. Memories of teenage Hunter stifling a smirk when I couldn't help but ogle how muscular his soccer thighs looked in his practice shorts. Hunter and Ky sitting at our kitchen table, and Hunter averting his gaze like I was toxic to his eyes.

I felt like an older, leering spinster to his rugged high school athlete.

"It's hopeless," I mutter.

"What's hopeless?"

I realize I spoke out loud. "Nothing. I was worried about Hunter's house. It's terrible."

"Oh. I thought you were talking about him."

"No. Of course not. Why would I do that?" My attempt at a casual laugh sounds like the croak from a marooned seal. Kyler tilts his head at me quizzically and slides a glass of purple smoothie my way. I grab it and chug half of it down, using the excuse to block the bloom of pink that hits my cheeks. Immediately, the freeze hits my forehead, and I slam the glass down. "Ack, brain freeze."

I close my eyes and press a fist against my forehead.

"That looks painful."

My eyes pop open at the jarring, deep voice that does not belong to Kyler. I whip my head around and have such a confusing combination of reactions that my brain can't decide whether to laugh, cry, or hide. My hands fly to my face and cover my eyes, then slide down and cover my mouth.

The man standing in Kyler's kitchen is muscled and lava hot. A complicated web of tattoos snakes around one forearm, emphasizing the ropes of muscles.

Just as hot as he was when we spoke at the Sip 'n Fly airport bar a month ago. I fan my cheeks when I recall him chatting with me about Scottish romance novels. Judging from his stunned expression, which is quickly turning to a smirk, he remembers. But he covers it much better.

"Nice to see you, Gracie." The growl of his voice does that same spine-tingling thing it did at the airport, only now I have no illusions about whether he's flirting—he's not. He doesn't do that with me. But apparently he does let himself in without knocking.

I feel a wet slurping against my thigh and jump away when a large, golden retriever nose-bumps me, trying to get my attention.

"You afraid of dogs? I can try to find somewhere else for Bogie—"

"No, I'm good. I just didn't see him, and he caught me by surprise."

Bogie goes to the middle of the kitchen floor, circles twice, and lies down with his back feet splayed out behind him.

Hunter stares at me as if trying to discern something. Maybe he thinks I'm lying about the dog. Maybe he's having trouble reconciling me with the woman he was talking to at the airport. Finally, he shifts his steely gaze to Kyler.

"Thanks for letting me crash, man." He hugs my brother with a clap on the back.

"Of course." If he thinks I'm acting strangely, he doesn't say. "You remember my sister, obviously."

I suck in a sharp breath at the sheer size of him—over six feet and muscled from shoulders to calves. He's even more beautiful than I remember. I swear I can see the contours of his pecs and abs right through the fabric of his long-sleeved Devils jacket. His track pants do no better at covering what looks like an anatomy textbook of muscle below the waist.

And...my eyes linger there until I hear a low chuckle. I tear my gaze away from Hunter's physique to glance down at my enormous but also threadbare sleep shirt. It billows around my waist and hides whatever curves have managed to develop since my teen years. Over that, I have on a stretched-out gray cardigan with Minnie Mouse on the back and a pair of black shorts. My feet are stuffed into bunny slippers, complete with actual ears.

Because this is my brother's house.

Because I'm not expecting strangers to walk in. I can only hope that he's less angry and aggressive than he is on the soccer pitch. Otherwise, I'll be spending a lot of time hiding in my room.

My head feels like a pool table with thoughts rebounding and knocking other ones out. *Butter the toast. Yell at my brother. Stare at the muscles. Act aloof and unaffected by said muscles.*

Fortunately, common sense finds its way through the conflicting bat signals in my brain. "Hunter, I'm sorry to hear about your house." I force my gaze past his muscles and all the way to his face, where I stare at his unblinking eyes.

After a while, he waves a hand, and I realize I have no idea how long I've been eyeing him like a psychopath. I blink several times and smile nervously.

You'd think that all of this ineptitude around athletes means I have no business working for a professional sports team. But the issue isn't people. Or men. It's this man.

Twelve Years Earlier

The kitchen is my safe space. Or at least it was. Then I left for college, and Kyler took over the house, which is why he's hunkered over a sandwich at the table with Hunter Reyes, his muscly sidekick who barely acknowledges my presence. All the better since I'm nestled in gray sweats, hair in a pony, glasses on my nose so I can read a blueberry coffee cake recipe from one of my mom's cookbooks.

He may not notice me, but I'm very aware of him. I feel like a lecherous older woman, ogling a teenager when I'm twenty-one. I don't realize how long I've been holding a mixing spoon and staring at Hunter's strong shoulders and biceps until he picks his head up, gray eyes pinning me in place. His lips twist into a smirk, and I realize he knows I've been looking this whole time.

"What'cha baking?" he asks.

"Um, cake."

"I like cake." He grins like I've asked him to have sex.

"Blueberry. It's a blueberry cake. The eggs are too cold, which will make the batter stiff."

"Stiff?"

My cheeks heat, but I can't stop my scientific blather. "Yes. Cold eggs are more viscous. They don't mix as well with fats, and that makes the cake dense and potentially lumpy. I need it light and fluffy, and I can't heat the eggs, and I don't have time to let them warm on their own. It's... a quandary."

"I'll bet." Hunter's nod makes me feel even more like a dork.

Kyler looks up from his plate and rolls his eyes, accustomed to how my brain works. But Hunter can't seem to wipe the grin off his face, which somehow makes me insecure and turned on at the same time. I dash from the kitchen and abandon the cake.

NOPE, nothing has changed.

He gestures to a large piece of luggage and a black gym bag emblazoned with the Devils logo. "Where should I dump this stuff?"

Kyler trots over and grabs the two bags. "I'll put 'em in the guest room. Well, the other guest room, since Gracie is set up in my spare bedroom. You okay with the fold-out couch in the den?"

Hunter puts his hands together, gratefully. "Are you kidding? I appreciate the assist." He gestures to the heavier bag. "Didn't even unpack from a game on the road and I've had enough of hotels, so you're really doing me a solid."

"Stop. You're like family." Kyler's voice trails off as he goes down the hall toward the den.

Hunter rakes a lock of hair away with his long fingers, reminding me of how I ogled his hands at the airport a month ago. I shiver with mortification.

"So that was you at the airport." His voice is low and gruff but teasing. His eyes dance, and the corner of his mouth pulls back, revealing that damn dimple.

I look in the direction where Kyler went, but he's not on his way back yet. "Sorry I didn't say something when I figured it out."

"Figured what out?" Kyler pipes in, suddenly back.

"Your sister was telling me about how a guy was flirting with her at the airport last month, and I was saying she probably gets that all the time." He grins.

"Um, yeah. Happens all the time," I mutter, hopping off the stool and going for more coffee. I feel like there's an obvious implication that no smoking-hot athlete would be flirting with me. Kyler seems oblivious to the tension.

"So what happened, man?" Ky asks, pulling out the stool next to mine for Hunter to take a seat. I scoot mine over to create some distance while my brother pours more of the purple smoothie into a glass. "It's all fruit and some protein powder."

Hunter reaches for the glass but stops short of touching it. "Milk?"

"Coconut."

"Awesome." Hunter takes the smoothie and slugs down half of it in one gulp. "Smells like a bakery in here."

"I baked cookies."

"Breakfast cookies?"

"Nope, regular old cookies."

I swipe my knife through the block of butter in front of me and slather it on my cold sourdough toast, on top of the healthy layer of butter that's already there.

When I look up, I catch Hunter smirking at me. "What?" I ask.

"Nothing."

I point at Hunter's smoothie. "What happened to regular milk from a cow?" I ask.

"Cholesterol," they say in unison. I decide to drop the subject before I pull out some Wikipedia fact I've filed away in my brain, lest I reveal how much time I spend researching random things.

"Wow. It's like I've moved to a foreign land. Where's a refrigerator full of Yoo-hoo when you need one?"

"Yoo-hoo?" Hunter asks, raking a hand through his dark wavy hair. He causes more disorder, and now his locks look like they've survived a windstorm and are better for it.

"Chocolate milk. Never mind," I say.

His brow creases in long lines, and I can see the heaviness in his eyes, which look dark in the overhead kitchen light. "I can't fucking believe this happened. They think the sunlight hit that stained glass mandala at some weird angle and burned a hole in my sofa, which flamed up and torched the house from the inside out. You know how much wood furniture I had in there. Plus the logs. That house was basically kindling." He shakes his head, seemingly blaming himself.

"Sounds like a freak accident," I say. "I can't imagine you had that much wood." I've never seen his house, so I have no idea how much timber we're actually talking about.

"Wood's never been a problem for this guy," Kyler says, smirking. My face flushes again.

"It was styled like a log cabin built into a hillside. Wood, top to bottom." Hunter sighs with such sadness that I turn to see if he's okay. He rubs his eyes with his knuckles and shakes his head. "It's been a hell of a twenty-four hours, that's for sure. Devils CEO calls me in for a meeting to discuss my contract—probably means they're trading me to god knows where. And I find this out five minutes before hearing my house is on fire. I mean, what the actual fuck?"

Hunter nods back at me, but he looks bleary, and I'm not sure if he's really processing the information.

I shuffle across the kitchen in my slippers, ignoring the feeling that Hunter is watching me. My back and legs feel hot like his gaze is setting me on fire, but it must be in my head. He lost his house, and I'm barely on his radar. I refill my cup and go to the refrigerator for the half-and-half tucked away on the top shelf.

When I walk back to my stool, I hazard a glance in Hunter's direction to find him staring. Not just looking my way, but staring.

For a second, I worry my shorts have fallen to my ankles because his eyes are glued to my legs.

My hand goes to my thigh, where I can feel the fabric of my shorts covering at least the top couple of inches of flesh. He's probably marveling at the fashion faux pas that is my sleepwear. Well, I'm comfortable. He can shove it.

"I have some time today between meetings. I can help you get into it with your insurance company," Kyler says. It snaps me out of my silly self-consciousness. This isn't about me.

"Me too," I say. "I can lend a hand."

"Thanks." Hunter's eyes look glassy, emotional. He's probably been up all night. I decide right then and there that I need to woman up and stuff my old insecurities away. I will make this work. Living under the same roof as the guy I once crushed on won't send me back to prepubescent levels of insecurity and mortification.

I'm a professional. This will be okay. I mean, probably not, but a girl can hope.

CHAPTER 4

*H*unter

"I DON'T HAVE to say it, right?" Kyler asks, eyeing me over a bedsheet folded into a crisp square. It almost looks like he irons them, but instead of asking about that, I puzzle over his question.

"Say what?"

My oldest friend looks at me like I'm a vermin that threatens to invade his pristine house. And by the way, when did he become such a neat freak?

I remember his room in high school—a mess of vinyl records next to a vintage turntable, stacks of skate wear catalogs, and piles of surf wax and tools for fixing his never-ending accumulation of sports equipment, none of which included a soccer ball.

When we lived together in college, he wasn't much better, but the mess shifted to clothing strewn around our dorm room and girlfriends' hair ties left on the bathroom counter. I was the neat one of the two, and that's saying something. I came home most nights after training drenched in sweat and too tired to microwave a bag of popcorn. Fortunately, back then, the sports teams had a plush dining hall where a nutritionist looked out for our health better than we ever could.

But now, I'm getting hives. "It's like an OCD fever dream around here," I grunt as Kyler unfurls the sheet and tucks it over the fold-out couch mattress in his office.

"Thanks."

"I swear, man, if you start making hospital corners, I'll put you in a chokehold."

He finishes the bed and tosses two plaid pillows to the top. "Back atcha if you creep on my sister."

"Oh, is that what you meant before? We're not exactly in high school here. Don't you think we're a little old for 'hands off my sister'?"

"It's not that. She's…been through some stuff, and I feel a little protective, is all."

"Well, now you've got my attention."

He picks up a skateboard and stacks it in the corner on top of two others. I have to hand it to the guy. He's made a living out of being the same adrenaline junkie he was as a kid, only now he makes millions fulfilling the dreams of a new generation of skate and surf kids.

"Not gonna give you specifics. But she's had a bad breakup or two, got her heart crushed. Most recently, it cost her a job. She tends to get overly invested and doesn't see the signs. At least, that's how she used to be."

"Yeah? The woman is in her thirties. Give her some credit." I don't know why I'm defending her. Maybe because she seemed into me a tiny bit at the airport, and I want to believe she has good judgment?

I plop down on the bed and push a hand through my hair, shaking my head in disbelief. "And chill the fuck out. Do you think I'm some sort of animal who can't control himself? Jesus."

"No, but your track record speaks for itself."

I fight a smirk because he's not wrong. I haven't exactly limited myself to indulging in the lineup of fangirls who approach after every game. "I can't help it if women come up to me at hotel bars after games."

He nods warily. "No judgment. I'm saying my sister isn't like that. She's wife material, not fling material."

I hold up my hands in protest. "Hey, message received. Relax. I'm focused on my shitty circumstances. I won't have time to bother your sister."

Well, that's not exactly true. I'll bother, but that's only because I've always found her nice to look at. The highs of being a high school athlete were only blunted when Gracie came back from college periodically and ignored me. Wouldn't give me the time of day, while I stared at her like she created the sun and moon.

After finally getting that image out of my head, seeing her brings all those old urges back.

And now, she holds my professional future in her unmanicured hands. My worst nightmare come to life. If she's the team's chief data analyst, she now controls the levers that will determine whether I have a future with the Devils. It maddens me because I've worked my ass off to earn my starting center back spot on the team, and I don't want it tanked because she doesn't like sports. Or me.

I remember how she barely gave Ky and me a passing glance when she came home from college, clearly aware that her brains outmatched our weightlifting and hormonal high school antics.

I also don't want to curry favor with her and influence her decision. Well, maybe I do.

I'd do pretty much anything.

Okay, that's not true either.

I've turned down my coach's suggestion that I do intense anger management work with a therapist. I've turned down the team doctor's suggestion that I take meds to control my impulsive behavior on the field. And I've flat-out rejected the idea of blunting my social media presence if it can influence people to eat cleaner and take better care of our planet.

"You have everything you need?" Kyler stands in the doorway holding a pile of towels. I set them down and sink into the mattress with my head in my hands. The pity party is real.

"I don't want to sound like a whiny asshole," I say.

Kyler chuckles. "It's me. I already know you're a whiny asshole. Just vent." He crosses his arms and leans against a dark-stained bookshelf with framed photos of him surfing in Hawaii and Santa Cruz. I have a moment of envy for that time on the water, where his only job is to wait for a good wave.

Then I snap back to reality.

"I know it's my own damn fault that I'll probably get traded, and maybe my house burning is some kind of a sign. It's time for a fresh start."

"Maybe so. You know I believe in that shit." He picks up a pillowcase and stuffs it with a fat pillow. "Then again, maybe it's a couple of setbacks and you're gearing up for some other kind of karmic bump."

"I'm not sure getting thrown out on my ass is the big score you think it is."

He laughs, seeming unconvinced of my dire situation. "Well, you're welcome here as long as you need. And Gracie likes to stress bake, so that's something."

Something, indeed.

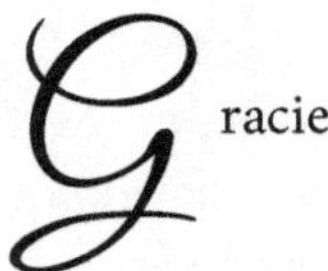racie

I HUFF my annoyance into the steam coming off my coffee with a splash of good old half-and-half as I rush down the hallway for my first official meeting at the Los Angeles Devils corporate offices. I came in the wrong way, and now I'm navigating a warren of halls to the executive lobby.

The team logo—a fierce-looking angel with devil horns on a dark red jersey—is emblazoned on the elevator walls and the floor of each landing. I've already seen three people wearing long-sleeved shirts or hoodies with the Devils logo. I own exactly zero fan gear, and I'd be swimming in any of Kyler's swag.

My brother would make more sense in the corporate offices of the LA Devils soccer club. The guy eats, breathes, and sleeps sports, at least when he's not at his own job running a skate and surf lifestyle brand. I'm not exactly sure what that is.

For practical purposes, it means he gets to travel all the time and visit "epic" surf towns the world over. He's an expert at peopling, whereas I should be quietly ensconced in a techie cubicle farm wearing sweatpants and headphones. Not clip-clopping along in heels, navy slacks, and a cream-colored blouse. I hope I look like an appropriately dressed data analyst.

I'm right on time, which, to me, means I'm late. I like to arrive at least fifteen minutes early. It gives me time to prepare—mentally.

And this meeting requires more than fifteen minutes of prep. I need to calm my nerves and push away the lonely feeling I get when I don't yet feel comfortable in my new surroundings. I'm like an animal, needing ample time to circle in one spot and sniff my way through to finding a landing place.

Ugh, I hate being on time.

Sweat dribbles between my boobs as I totter down the hallway in these heels. I only need one interim job to get my legs back under me before I can go back to my safe haven of Northern California. I still have my house there on the edge of an open space preserve, where undisturbed forest is all I can see.

That was the image in my head as I navigated freeway exits and urban sprawl on my way to the Devils offices downtown. I passed by the garment district and a patchwork of cheap-clothing stalls at an outdoor market that went on for miles. Ten shirts for ten dollars, fifteen pairs of socks for twenty bucks, baseball hats and track pants for a steal.

I tuck a stray lock of hair behind my ear, annoyed at myself for agreeing to a new layered cut when my hairdresser proposed an "LA do." At the coffee place I visited earlier, none of the gorgeous women glowing from hot yoga had an "LA do." Their hair was perfectly messy, piled on top of their heads like a matching set of crowns. I tuck a wavy tendril behind my ear, and it immediately springs free.

Sigh.

"Hi, I'm here to see—"

"Gracie!" The mountain of a man appears in the well-appointed lobby. I barely have time to take in the cream-colored leather sofas and spotless glass tables before my hand is enveloped in the strong handshake of Gerald Moder, the CEO of the Devils franchise.

He looks like a TV sitcom dad, with a chiseled face aglow beneath a wide smile, an expertly trimmed mountain-man beard, and close-cropped dark hair. He has the large frame of a former athlete who still keeps himself in peak condition into his fifties, and I know from research that he spends his vacation time white-water rafting whenever possible. He's the sliver of light that makes me think I can fit in at this male-dominated organization—a guy who likes his time on the river and isn't going to kick me out for talking about something other than soccer.

"So nice to meet you in person, Mr. Moder," I say, wishing the feeling of belonging would last. As soon as he lets go of my hand, however, the loneliness creeps back in.

"No, no, none of that. It's Gerald. Come, come, let's get you situated." He beckons me down a long hallway that surprises me with the bright light flooding each office we pass. Floor-to-ceiling windows comprise two walls of his corner office, and he lowers the blinds to shield me from the direct glare coming from the east.

Taking a seat opposite him, I run my hands over the metal armrests and lean against the oatmeal-colored pillow on the low-slung, brown leather chair. It manages to give off both modern and western cowboy vibes, and I wonder if Gerald had anything to do with choosing it.

He smooths his hands over the leather pad on his giant glass desk and taps his fingers a few times like a warm-up. "Let's get right to it, shall we?"

I must look like a deer in front of a set of high beams because he chuckles and opens a folder containing a stack of pages. He studies me instead of looking down at the papers. "I believe the kind of thing you do is the future of this sport. And I intend for this team to be on the cutting edge of it."

"Sounds good." I meet his stare.

He slides the folder across the desk toward me.

Inside, I find the set of preliminary calculations I emailed him a week ago. "Oh. Okay. Is there anything you want me to clarify?"

Gerald points at the page and leans back in his chair. "I circled it." His brown eyes, which looked warm and friendly a moment ago, now look darker and more challenging.

Flipping through the neat stack, I find a circle on the third page. My heart drops to my stomach because next to the name he's circled, there's a large X. I don't have to read it twice to know the name is Hunter Reyes.

"I know he's had a pretty challenging season." I hope my gaze looks just as unflinching, but after a moment, I glance down at the sheet of paper, double-checking that he didn't circle a different name. Nope, still Hunter.

"I'd say. Some here in management think he should go. He's expensive, and we could get some fresh talent with that money."

"He's undervalued, even at his current salary," I assert.

Gerald keeps tapping his fingers, but instead of seeming jolly, now they seem impatient. His smile looks stiff. This is where people start to lose faith in me before they know how hard I hammer the numbers to get results.

"Look, I like him, but I'm between a rock and a hard place when he's so volatile," he says.

"I can see where you'd have doubts." I need him to know I spotted every detail. "There are other options in case you think his, um, baggage is too much to deal with, but I disagree."

It's no secret that Hunter holds the distinction of having the most red cards in the history of the sport, even after a lot of hotheaded players preceded him. Red cards don't mean he's not a good player, but his off-the-field antics are legendary as well, and it's no secret Liverpool wants to poach him.

"Fans love a hothead. He gets people riled up. That can be a good thing, a very good thing. At the end of the day, pro sports is a business," he says.

On one hand, I breathe a sigh of relief. I'm glad Gerald isn't questioning my methods. It would be a bad start to my new job.

"But Reyes is polarizing. Some teammates can't deal with his antics, but that's their problem. If you can convince me his talent outweighs the rest, I'm listening. I like that you're a contrarian. That's what made you stand out among the other candidates, frankly," Gerald says.

My data doesn't lie. If I'm sure of anything, it's that I know how to do my job.

Unfortunately, my analytics show that, by far, the team's best move is to sign a new contract with Hunter Reyes, the player with the worst attitude in Major League Soccer. I can only hope that means he'll find a more permanent place to live.

Until then, I'll stay holed up in the corporate offices looking at game tape and statistics. He'll stay on the soccer pitch doing what he does best—racking up penalties and keeping opponents from scoring.

And I probably won't ever see him. Fine by me.

CHAPTER 6

unter

Two days since the fire, and it feels like a lifetime.

I'm wearing Devils gear because the team equipment manager had a box waiting on Kyler's doorstep this morning. Right now, it's all the clothing I have to my name, other than a suitcase full of stuff that still smells like smoke after three washings.

The worst part is that I lost the majority of my books. They went up like kindling—no surprise—so I bought myself an e-book reader. At least I can load that up. The ease of downloading books is the one bright spot since Monday. Well, two if you count seeing Gracie Albright again—and I do.

The sight of her fresh-scrubbed face has kept me from circling the drain in despair over how my life is crumbling, and now I'm here at the corporate offices to weather the final blow from Gerald Moder, who has warned me several times that I may be traded. Guess today is the day to make it official.

Moder looks pleased as he slides a sheaf of papers across his glass desk and gestures for me to read it with a nod of his head. "It's for three years. Terms are similar to your last contract, except for salary. Your agent can begin negotiations on that, but we've floated a preliminary number."

I can't believe what I'm hearing.

"You…you're reupping me for three years? I thought I was on the trade list." I can't help stating the obvious because it's been rattling around in my head for so long.

Moder nods. "I know. We've been considering all possibilities, but this is where we've landed." It's code for the fact that I'm lucky as hell to be here.

"I assume there are conditions. Keep the penalties under control…"

"I'm not saying that. I mean, sure, the fewer PKs we give the opposing team, the better, and we want you on the field, not sitting out games because of red cards, but groomed correctly, your playing style is still the biggest value add we have on the pitch. It's all in the numbers."

There's a round clock on the wall without numbers on it. Small black letters at the top read, "The time is now." I watch the second hand tick all the way around while I let his words sink in. He's not asking me to change anything. I'm not here for a beatdown over past mistakes.

Moder shuffles some papers around the surface of his desk, moving them from one side of a leather desk pad to the other and reading something. I can't tell what he's looking at from where I sit, but it looks like statistics. Numbers. *Analytics*.

Second time in two days that word has come up, and I struggle to convince myself it's a coincidence.

I say nothing, letting him guide the meeting wherever he wants it to go. I'm still damn glad to have a job with this team. But after a few more moments of silence, I can't stand it. I need to know.

"So when you say value add, you mean you're studying my stats," I confirm. "Looking at me, mathematically?"

"That's one way of putting it, yes. There are a thousand different inputs that involve analysis of hundreds of hours of game footage across the league and spreadsheets from here to Kansas."

"Analytics."

"Exactly."

"I thought that mostly was used for finding undervalued talent. New guys. Players who can be developed over the years for a potential jackpot. Isn't that the whole point?"

"Undervalued talent, exactly."

The reality finally dawns. "That's how you see me? Like a freshman scrub who doesn't know what he's doing, but if I'm 'groomed correctly,' you can find my untapped potential?" I keep my voice even, but it's all I can do not to pound a hole in Moder's glass desk. I've been playing this sport since I could walk, and I don't think there's any more potential to tap.

"I wouldn't put it that way. Obviously, you're seasoned. This is a good thing, Reyes. Where other teams might see baggage, we see potential. The stats and analysis prove it. What if you haven't even hit your stride yet?"

"At twenty-eight, you don't think I've hit my stride?" I'd like to hit something, but it ain't my stride.

"That's what the data shows. And we want you here with the Devils when it happens."

"And you're sure of this data." I have a sinking feeling in my stomach, far worse than at the thought of sharing a kitchen for the foreseeable future with my buddy's bookish older sister, who doesn't seem to realize she's wearing booty shorts.

"Yes, we have a new hotshot heading up that area, and she's laid out some very convincing data. I'm excited, frankly. Feels like the shot in the arm this team needs."

He doesn't say it, but he doesn't have to. Gracie Albright saved my job. As it is, I'm doing everything in my power to blunt my attraction to her, but now I'm in debt to her brainy computer skills.

"So does that mean the players will be spending time with the data analysts, or will they do their job in the background?" *Please let them work in a separate office. Preferably in a different zip code.*

"Mostly the latter, but it's not my call. Best thing I can do is let the analytics team do their job and do it well."

Moder rubs his hands together like an excited little kid in front of a hundred candy bins.

So I call my agent and agree to three years of knowing I have a starting spot on a team I love. Knowing I'll be able to stay in LA. Knowing I can rebuild my house and spend the next offseason training in Lupine Valley.

And I'll try my damnedest to avoid staring at Gracie Albright every time I see her.

I let out a long exhale and think about the next three years. My deal with the Devils. Literally.

CHAPTER 7

racie

One Week Later

I'm grumpy.

Not the usual grumpy before I've had my coffee. This is next level.

"For how long?" I ask.

"A week, maybe two. Depends on whether I come home between meetings. But if I can set one more in the middle, I'll stay on the road."

Kyler has thrown me my first curveball. Well, second, if you count Hunter living here and walking around shirtless—a minor daily distraction I try to avoid. I get up early for work, and he trains late and comes back after I'm safely ensconced in my room with a book.

We don't really impact each other, and that's fine with me because he still makes me nervous. Part of it is his sheer strength and size, and the other part is my lady parts staging an all-out coup. Talking them down is a little nightly ritual I've added in alongside teeth-whitening strips and an avocado moisturizing mask.

Kyler sprinkles granola on his yogurt parfait, which is topped with organic strawberries and spirulina powder. How he and I are from the same gene pool, I'll never know.

I dig my box of frosted cornflakes out of the cabinet and shake it into a red ceramic bowl. Kyler raises an eyebrow but doesn't say anything. When I add whole milk, he opens his mouth and closes it again. Clearly, he values his life.

Filling a coffee cup for me and pushing it across the countertop, Kyler thumbs through messages on his phone for more information and shakes his head. "Not sure yet, but I'll be in Spain at least a week. It'll be good for you. You'll have the place to yourself."

"Not exactly."

I squint at his incorrect information, and he waves a hand. "You mean Hunter? He'll be at the training facility night and day. You'll never see him. I promise he won't cramp your style."

"Ha. You say that as though I have style to cramp. We haven't spent much time together lately, little brother, but an exciting night for me consists of a takeout cheeseburger and a national parks documentary on TV."

Kyler bites his cheek, and I know he's trying hard not to comment on my so-called life.

"It's fine, you can say it." I sigh. "It's not like I don't know I'm a homebody."

He shakes his head. "It's not that. It's just…" He grimaces and waves a hand. "Never mind."

"No way. Now you have to tell me."

From the crease in his brow and his downturned mouth, he looks like he's suffering, or like that green smoothie he made really tastes as bad as it looks. "You're a catch, Gracie. You should act like it, is all."

He kisses me on the cheek and hefts his backpack luggage over his shoulder. I'm still stunned at the unexpected compliment from my normally stoic brother. It's why I don't have time to make fun of all the pockets and gadgets on his bag before he goes out the door. But I make a mental note to do it later.

Who needs so many eyeglass cases, carabiners, tool kits, and bandannas?

For a few minutes, I sip my coffee quietly in the kitchen that I'll have to myself in the mornings for the next week. I need to leave for the Devils offices soon, but for now, I like the peace and quiet.

"Morning." The deep baritone of Hunter's voice shatters the silence like a wrecking ball.

And…there go the lady parts. My core aches, and my nipples stand at attention like Navy SEALs.

At least now I'm dressed for work and somewhat buried under a cardigan sweater. I've eaten a few spoonsful of my sugary cereal, so I can dart out of the house without having to make too much small talk.

"Good morning," I mumble. Taking a sip of coffee, I swivel on the barstool and immediately spray the mouthful onto Hunter. In my defense, he's standing there in a pair of low-slung navy sweatpants, and that's it. Dammit.

He's a walking anatomy lesson, his abs rippling and his chest looking like it was carved from marble.

Mortified, I leap from the barstool and grab a kitchen towel, but my attempt to mop up the spray only emphasizes how incredibly hard and sculpted those abs are. My mouth fills with saliva, and I swallow hard. "I'm so sorry. I wasn't expecting… you."

Hunter shoves a hand through his hair, which makes it stand up before flopping over his forehead. He looks younger than his twenty-eight years, and I suddenly feel much older than thirty-three. He lets out a deep sigh.

"You okay?" I ask.

"Just heard from my contractor. Even if everything goes smoothly with the insurance company, it's going to be at least a year before I'll have a house to move into."

He looks so lost that I want to wrap him up in a blanket, tuck him into a corner of the couch, and make him hot chocolate.

Instead, I rush over to the coffee pot. Coffee fixes everything. Pouring the hot liquid into a yellow mug from some surf brand, I hand it to him wordlessly and go to the fridge for the coveted oat milk.

"Thanks," he says, holding the cup in one hand and the carton of milk in the other, looking confused about what to do with them. I take the milk out of his hand and pour a splash into the cup. Darting around the kitchen, I return the milk to the refrigerator and mistakenly open three wrong drawers before I find a spoon.

Still standing frozen, he takes the spoon and drops it into his cup. As he absently stirs, the muscles of his tattooed forearms flex.

"Um, do you want to sit?" I ask.

He looks down and notices his feet rooted to the floor. "Sure." His stride is so large that it only takes two steps before he reaches the barstools and drops into the one next to mine. I sweep around to the other side of the counter and look for something else to do.

Kyler's kitchen is massive, with a skylight letting the sun glint off twenty stainless-steel appliances. There's enough space between the butcher block island and the refrigerator for three people to do yoga. Fortunately, Kyler hasn't unloaded the dishwasher, so that gives me a task.

"Did you sleep?" I ask.

"Not really," Hunter says. I look up, and he takes a sip of his coffee, closing his eyes and exhaling the way I do after that first life-giving sip.

"Are you like me, need a cup of coffee before you want to interact with other people?" I see him staring into his cup, but he almost smiles.

"Not normally. I'm a morning guy. I'm...it's a lot with the house. And, you know, I'd pretty much accepted that I was in the transfer portal, so...I guess I still haven't reset my expectations. Suppose I oughtta thank you for the next three years of my career. You're like my own personal Tinkerbell, flitting down to sprinkle fairy dust on my long list of penalties and somehow make them look good."

Seeing this strapping athlete, who's so confident and fierce on the field, looking downright lost stirs something in me. I want to help him more than I want to run and hide from his audacious abs.

"I'm hardly a fairy. Data isn't magic. It's objective science." I put my cup down and walk over to the counter that separates us. "You should not thank me for that. All I did was analyze the data, and it all pointed to you being the best possible option for the Devils defense. That was all you, not me."

The hard line of his jaw softens, and he nods. "Well, all the same, I appreciate your data, Tink."

Warmth floods my body. It's not just the nickname, which is cute, but the fact that data is my love language. "That may be the nicest thing anyone's ever said to me."

He barks out a laugh. "Seriously? People should give you better compliments."

"Nah, that one was next level."

He nods. "Nice to know how to get on your good side." Despite the shirtless glory in front of me, Hunter seems like a regular guy, not a stormy, impulsive star athlete. Maybe I should know better than to judge a person's personality off the field by what I see on it, but I haven't met that many people who surprise me.

This man, with his fiery, impulsive decisions during a match and his golden retriever mellowness right now, is a puzzle. I don't understand how he can be both ways with equal fervor, and I chastise myself for lack of insight.

I'm curious about him, and it sets off a little spark of joy in me because information is the lens through which I see the world.

I want to learn more about him and shore up the small details I already know about his interest in books and...wow, I really don't know much else. I've been so distracted by my reactions to him physically that I've pushed my normal curiosity aside. It's good to have it back.

At least, until I notice Hunter's eyes travel south from my face. I follow his gaze to where my silk blouse is unbuttoned one too many and my bra is clearly visible, along with a healthy amount of cleavage, as I lean forward on the counter. Baby steps, apparently.

Feeling my cheeks heat, I stand quickly and move toward the sink, where I dump the rest of my coffee. "I need to get to work."

He nods. "I'll be around later. Maybe we can have dinner together or something one night this week. Catch up on old times."

"Oh. Okay. I guess." I shift from foot to foot, wondering if I should come up with an excuse to be busy every night this week. The problem is, I don't know anyone in LA.

Hunter laughs. "Don't want to freak you out or anything."

"No, no, I'm not freaked out. I thought maybe you'd want to eat with your teammates or whatever."

"I can eat with my teammates or whatever anytime. I thought one night I'd eat with you. Since we're living together and all."

My stomach flips, and a small thrill runs through my veins. I've never lived with a guy. My brain knows we're both in a temporary situation that has nothing to do with real cohabiting, but my body apparently doesn't understand the difference. I swallow hard and tell my body to get it together. And quick.

"Sure, Hunter. Dinner sounds good," I say.

I tell myself it's going to be okay, us "living together and all…"

Then I sprint from the room.

CHAPTER 8

$\mathscr{H}$unter

TRAINING FEELS DIFFERENT THIS WEEK. For the first time in months, I'm here without the specter of being traded hanging over everything. This team is my home for the next three years.

Unless I fuck it up.

"Hunt, you're up." Coach Carroll grunts instead of speaking as he stalks the sideline and watches us handle the ball. I appreciate the break from travel during the offseason, but I miss the energy of playing matches.

My teammate Ritchie Bloor dribbles the ball toward me, and I pivot from side to side, facing him down. I won't let him get a shot off, even in training. If I have to slide tackle him, I will, but I'll go easy so neither of us gets injured. People think I'm so hotheaded that I can't control myself, but that's not true. Mostly.

I'm not about to be reckless during practice and risk hurting myself or a teammate. But it's a whole different story during a match. I'll go hard, do whatever it takes, and throw everything I have into stopping an opposing striker from taking a shot on goal.

It's second nature. The roar of the crowd fires me up, and my ultra-competitive streak fills in the blanks.

Bloor gets close, and I corner him, running faster as he tries to dribble past me and cutting off his shot the second the ball comes off his foot. I aim toward the center, keeping the ball on the ground, where we have the most control over it. It's like breathing. And today, I breathe a little easier knowing I'm here with a secure starting spot.

"Nice one," Bloor grunts.

"Almost didn't get there," I say.

"Right."

"Bloor, you know Hunt's gonna cut off your ground game. You need to be more creative."

Bloor tips an imaginary hat with his index finger, but he'll make the same mistake again. We'll keep working this drill until he stops. That's what Coach has in mind, and I'll keep doing my part.

As I jog back in line for the next run, I glance up at the corporate offices that sit right beyond where Coach stands on the sideline. It's not like I expect to see Gracie standing at one of the plate-glass windows watching our practice. But I like the idea that she saw something in me worth keeping around, even if it's based on data I don't really understand.

It feels good to sweat and breathe hard, so when Coach has us take a few high-speed laps around the field to end practice, I lead the pack, feeling the blood pump in my legs and the burn in my lungs. I hadn't realized how much I've been holding inside until the energy comes pouring out.

Whether Gracie thinks of it that way or not, she did save my job.

The least I can do is make her a decent dinner.

~

Two hours later, I push open the front door to Kyler's house with my foot. I have two full grocery bags in my arms because I couldn't decide what to cook, so I ended up with way too many options—pescatarian, vegetarian, and full-on meat. No idea what Gracie is into, and from the silence that pervades the house when I walk in, I'm not going to find out anytime soon.

I could call Kyler and ask what his sister eats, but he's in a different time zone and probably asleep or enjoying some Spanish nightlife.

Spreading out the groceries on the ample granite countertop, I survey my options. Somehow, while I was in the store, the combination of ingredients made more sense. I scroll through my phone's recipe app, where I bookmark things that seem interesting. Admittedly, I've made exactly zero of them. It's what happens when I spend most of my day, and well into the evening, with the team or the trainers, and rely on a meal delivery service to fill in the gaps.

The first thing that becomes clear is that I'll do better with a drink in my hand. I know better than to go for the empty carbs in the form of beer, but a scotch never hurt anyone, and I know Kyler has a nice collection of bottles.

I grab a single malt and bring it into the kitchen. I'm banking on the idea that I can cook on the grill outside while I work on sauces and glazes in the kitchen.

I debate the phone call I'm tempted to make, knowing I'll face more questions than answers if I do it. But I don't want to burn down another house, and I'm running out of time. So I dial.

"Hi, sweetie. How's my favorite son?" My mom answers the phone after one ring as though she's been walking around with her cell in hand, waiting for my call. She never varies her greeting, and she always sounds delighted to hear from me, even if it's only been a day since we last spoke. In this case, it's been a week.

"I'm your only son."

"Potato, po-tahto. I didn't want to bother you, but I heard you're staying with the Devils in LA."

"Never believe everything you hear. Who told you that?"

"Betsy." I already know Mom's sports source is her mahjong friend Betsy, who follows sports news like it's her job.

"Tell Betsy she shouldn't spread rumors. But between you and me and the oak trees, I'll probably be in LA for a while. I'll tell you more when I have all the details."

I hear the splatter of water in the background and assume my mom is gardening, which is how she spends most of her time in the evenings while it's still light out. Her vegetable garden is legendary, and her organic farming practices have influenced the way I eat. Kyler likes to take credit, but we both know it's the way I was raised.

Rattling off the list of ingredients I have on hand, I wait for my mom's approval. I know she'll like the emphasis on seasonal produce.

"I'd roast and puree that celery root and put that on the plate as a base. Add some arugula and a mustard vinaigrette—I'll text you the recipe. Don't mess with the salmon too much, just put it on the coals in foil with some maple butter… Grill the squash and add some lentils…"

She rattles off the recipes as though she's had a week to prepare. I make a few notes on my phone while she talks and divide the ingredients into piles.

I tell her I love her and promise to call once my contract is finalized, so she can give Betsy all the details.

"Love you, Boo." My mom clicks away before I can protest a nickname no one else could get away with. I set to work chopping, dicing, and pureeing, then rifle through Kyler's cabinets for dishes and silverware to set the table outside.

It's not an attempt to curry more favor with our new research analyst or stoke some long-simmering heat into a flame. If I wanted sex, there are plenty of women who've made it clear they're available. I'm not interested.

I merely want to thank her for whatever she saw in her spreadsheets that saved my job. I hate owing anyone anything, and this will make me feel like we're even. A simple dinner with a bunch of options to make sure there's something she likes. This is normal, good roommate behavior. It has nothing to do with buried feelings I've had for my friend's sister for nearly half my life.

Yes, I said it.

Gracie rocked my world back when I was a freshman scrub on the varsity team, and all I could do was flex and grunt in her family's kitchen in an attempt to impress her. Small wonder I failed.

That woman is head and shoulders beyond me in intellect, not to mention the beauty she tries to keep buried under layers of clothes. I'd find it adorable if it didn't frustrate me so goddamn much. The other night, I could barely keep from reaching out and running a hand up the milky skin of her legs in those little shorts of hers. Since then, I've only seen her in work clothes, which is just as well.

And now that I've given the thought a little room to breathe, I shove it back down where it belongs.

One dinner. Two old friends are eating because it's a human necessity. Basically, I'm keeping her alive. Starvation would be rude. No reason to make anything more of one dinner.

Then we'll go back to our separate worlds and our separate lives.

CHAPTER 9

Gracie

THE ONLY THING my brain can acknowledge is the phenomenal smell coming from the deck of my brother's house. It won't let me detour or even put my purse down before following the scent out to the back patio, where a ribbon of smoke heads toward the dusky blue sky.

It's probably Hunter trying to impress a date, and I should leave them alone. But the delicious smell of roasting chicken beckons me forward, and I have no choice but to follow.

I feel slightly relaxed after the half glass of wine I had with my new analytics team. "It's tradition," Mick Eldrige told me, grinning as he hung in the doorway of my office. "We're all chuffed to have you here."

Mick joined the Devils two seasons ago from Manchester City, and he's my number two. I'm relying on him to keep me abreast of insider club knowledge, so if drinks with him and our four-person team is tradition, it's tradition.

It meant I stayed near headquarters later than I expected, but with Kyler out of town, I didn't think anyone would notice. I didn't see the team on the practice field when I left, so I figured they were in the dining facility or doing whatever players do in the evenings.

When I slide open the screen door, I find Hunter fanning the smoke with an oven mitt shaped like a trout with mascara on its eyelashes. With his other hand, he bosses around a couple of chicken breasts on the grill, along with what looks like a steak, squash, and something in a foil pouch.

I glance around the deck for the woman I'm certain I'll find lounging on a chaise with a glass of wine in her hand. She'll have manicured nails, expertly applied makeup, and hair worthy of a social media video. Of course, he's allowed to entertain here. He's a guest in his best friend's house, and Kyler would definitely approve of Hunter enjoying himself.

But I see only two empty chaise lounges with blue striped cushions and three chairs around the wooden table.

"You cooking for someone?" I raise my voice so he'll hear me over Taylor Swift's *Red* album. I want to make sure he knows I'm here before he inadvertently trots a scantily clad date out here, and I feel mortified.

When he turns, I notice the green apron over his Devils practice tee and a pair of athletic shorts. I know this is Southern California, and the weather's nice all the time, but the man never seems to cover much of his body. That's only a problem because I seem to have no control over my eyes, which run the length of his legs two or three times, committing each muscle group to memory.

Seriously, you'd think I've never seen a man's legs before.

But these are spectacular in a way I'm unfamiliar with—large, strong quads and well-developed calves that practically scream their need for speed. But Hunter seems to be in no hurry, methodically turning the chicken and meat over before he points the spatula in my direction.

"Nope. Cooking for you."

Some sort of garbled combination of nonsensical vowels spews forth, and he waits until I regain control, a smirk forming on his lips.

"You're…what?" I think I heard the words, but a synapse must have misfired in my brain.

"Cooking dinner. For you." He looks at me expectantly, but then he seems to notice the two bowls and one platter already on the round, wood table nearby on the deck. "And me, obviously."

"Wow. That's so nice." My voice sounds like it's echoing through a cavern, and I wonder if I'm about to faint. I can't recall the last time a guy cooked for me. No, wait. I can't recall it because it's never happened. The men I've dated in the ten years since college took me out to dinner here and there, and we ordered plenty of takeout. Even during the relationship I had for over a year, there wasn't a day I came home to the scent of meat grilling or even a piece of bread burning in the toaster oven.

This is truly unprecedented.

"Glad you approve." Hunter goes back to tending to the meat on the grill, where it drips and spits onto the charcoal briquettes below. I ate half a grilled cheese sandwich from a food truck earlier today and didn't realize until now how hungry I am. But my senses are on overload, and I'm not sure if my mouth is watering because of the delicious aroma or the delicious man. "It…looks amazing." I can barely form words because they cut down on the deep inhaling I want to do.

The corner of his mouth tips up like he can't decide between a smirk and a smile. "Thanks."

I spy the bottle of scotch and the glass next to it on the table. When he catches my roving eye, he nods toward the bottle. "Can I get you a glass?"

"I…I'm not sure I'm a scotch drinker."

The rumble of his laughter is oddly soothing. "Never know until you try."

He puts the spatula down next to the grill and closes the hood. Then he moves past me, leaving a lingering scent of pine soap and firewood. I take a deep inhale without meaning to do it. When he returns, still wearing the trout oven mitt, he holds out two glasses in his palm. One has ice cubes, and the other is empty.

"Not sure if you want it neat or on the rocks."

I shrug. "Not sure either."

"Maybe try it both ways and then you'll know what you like."

He wriggles out of the oven mitt and pours two inches of dark brown liquid into each glass. I take the first one from him, doing my best not to touch his hand in the process. "Inhale the scent of it first and get used to the strength. Then take a tiny bit in your mouth and swirl it over your tongue." The deep growl of his voice mixed with the sensual instructions has my toes curling in my shoes, not to mention a straight shot of lust that rockets down to my core.

I do as instructed and try not to wince at the first, frighteningly strong sip of scotch on the rocks. A smile plays on his lips as he watches me swallow.

I blink away the tears forming in the corners of my eyes. "Okay, that wasn't too terrific."

"You don't have to—"

I hold up a hand. "Hang on." I swirl the scotch against the ice to chill it and boldly take another small sip. It goes down more easily this time. No tears. And I actually sort of like the taste. It almost has a maple syrup aftertaste, which probably means I have no idea what I'm tasting. "Better."

"Yeah?"

"Yeah. Lemme try it neat."

"Look at you. Now you're a pro."

Smiling for real now, he holds out the second glass. Our

fingers brush as I take it from him, and a tiny jolt of electricity runs up my arm. I kind of knew it would happen because he makes me nervous—the excited, good kind of nervous. Still, it catches me by surprise. It's crazy that the barest graze of his skin causes such a reaction.

If I lean into the science, I can try to make sense of it. It's purely biological. We react to the opposite sex because, otherwise, no procreation would occur, and the species would die out.

Okay, forget all that. There's nothing clinically scientific about the way Hunter causes a flutter in my chest to rage into a butterfly army when he comes near me. This is otherworldly magic, and I'm not about to ruin it by turning it into a textbook explanation. I'm going to enjoy it quietly and hope he isn't aware of how fast my heart is beating.

I don't dare look him in the eye because I don't want him to know how hard I'm trying to control my breathing. He can't know. The thought of him laughing about my obvious crush is enough to shock the feelings from my body. Within seconds, I return to my calm, collected self, and I take a tiny taste from the second glass.

The room temperature liquid goes down smoothly, and I venture a slightly larger sip.

"I feel proud. Popping your scotch cherry."

Holy crap.

I choke, liquid dribbling out the corner of my mouth while an awful burn follows the scotch down my respiratory tract. I cough scotch from my lungs, and it takes me a minute to regain my composure. Hunter looks sympathetic but also amused.

"Oh my god, please don't say things like that around me." My voice is a croak when I can finally form words.

Hunter fails to suppress a smile, his eyes twinkling with mischief.

"Oh no, Tink, seeing that look on your face just sealed your fate. From now on, it'll be impossible *not* to say things like that around you."

"Great," I mutter, looking away. This is not what I need right now, the distraction of a roommate who wants to rile me up as I'm finding my footing.

I take another sip. By now, I'm feeling the warming effects of the alcohol, and I welcome the assist to unravel my jangled nerves around Hunter.

I never would have called myself a scotch drinker. I'm barely a drinker at all, except for a strawberry margarita or a mojito on a girls' night out. And here I am on my second drink of the night. But something about the way the scotch burns my throat and warms me from the inside out is very soothing.

The company isn't too bad either. Somehow, drinking the same thing as Hunter makes me feel connected to him in a tiny way. That makes me happy.

A few birds perched high in an oak tree beyond the house seem to be in a competition, each trilling a different set of notes and waiting for a response. For a moment, I get lost listening to them and almost forget where I am. This is the first time since I came to Los Angeles that I've been aware of nature in the way I am back home. It's also the first time I acknowledge the thought that I could like it there.

"I have a question. Where did you learn to cook?"

"Back in middle school. I'm from a big family. My mom corralled us all into different cooking duties out of necessity. She couldn't come home from work every night and cook for five hungry guys without a few sous chefs. So we all pitched in. I liked it, so I did it more than some of my brothers."

And now I like him even more.

This is silly. He's a guy. You have a brother. It's the same.

Except it's not the same because he's as hot as molten lava and sets fire in your veins.

Letting out a long exhale, I wrangle my self-control. "I really appreciate you cooking dinner. I was about to microwave a baked potato, which qualifies as gourmet fare for this girl." My voice sounds normal again, and I remind myself that I'm a capable woman with a masters degree in computer science who can certainly handle one dinner with my brother's friend without going to pieces.

The next inhale cements that idea, and I finally start to relax. I dare a glance at Hunter's face and find him eyeing me.

"What?"

He shakes his head. "A baked potato?"

"Oh. Yeah. Does that not meet with your approval, soccer star?" I don't know where the teasing tone came from, but it's too late to edit once the words are out.

"It's not much of a dinner. Side dish, maybe."

"Only maybe?"

"Depends what you put on it."

I don't think before answering. "Butter, sour cream, and bacon."

His smirk widens into a full smile, but he doesn't comment.

"And what's wrong with that?" I ask.

"Sounds delicious. But I'm in training. Can't do the sour cream and butter."

"Never?" I'm aghast. "And it's worth it to you?"

Now, he laughs. "Worth it to be paid to play soccer? Yeah, I can make the dairy sacrifice during most of the week."

I give him a side-eye. "Most of the week? What happens during the other part of the week? There's still a chance you can redeem yourself."

"There are cheat days. I'm not a saint."

I nod as he opens the grill hood, and the full effect of his cooking floods the deck. I can't help closing my eyes as I inhale. "If your cooking tastes as good as it smells, I doubt you'd need to cheat much. Don't tell Kyler, but I might even be willing to make an exception to my meat and potatoes ways to try something else."

"I swear, not a word." He mimes locking his lips and tossing away a key. "If you answer a question for me."

Panic hits me because I hate agreeing to answer a question before I know what it is. "Um, sure."

"Relax, I'm not going to try to unearth your darkest secret." He chuckles. I relax a tad. "Yet." I panic again.

"Fine, whatever. You can ask, not saying I'll answer."

"What were you looking for when you came out on the deck?"

My shoulders drop. "Oh. I figured you were here with a date. You know,

trying to impress a girl."

"Who says I wasn't?" His eyes are kind, softer than they get when he's talking about soccer. I like it.

And there it is again, that twinge low in my belly that turns to full-on fire at the idea that he's talking about me. But, I reason, he told me he's cooking as a thank-you for the help he thinks I gave him. This is dinner between roommates. My hormones need to chill the heck out.

I take another sip of scotch, trying to extinguish it like a tiny flame, but it roars up even larger. I push away the feeling that I want this man for more than a nice dinner because dinner is all I can have. We work for the same organization. And given how my last relationship cratered my job, I do the smart thing and shut down the fantasy.

CHAPTER 10

$\mathcal{H}$unter

FEEDING people has always given me a sense of satisfaction, mainly because it fulfills a basic need we all have. But watching Gracie devour the plate of food I've set before her is next-level sensory overload.

The way she delicately places a slice of steak on a shard of sourdough and dribbles it with peppercorn sauce. The way she licks her fingers to get every bit of sauce from the steak. The way she moans when the first bite of mashed potatoes hits her tongue.

I don't think she's doing any of it to torture me. She's just enjoying my cooking. I should feel flattered. I should not feel like hauling her onto my lap.

"So, Gracie, when's the last time we saw each other? Has to be sometime when Ky and I were in high school."

"You mean, the last time before the airport?" She gives me a guilty smile. "Sorry I didn't recognize you right away."

"Why're you sorry? I didn't recognize you either."

"I'm probably the only female in Los Angeles who hasn't seen your face all over social media."

Leaning back in my chair, I put my hands behind my head. "How do you know my face is all over social media?"

Her cheeks flame. Caught. "I may have done a little digging once I realized who you were. I work for the team now. Data is important. Specifics."

She's so earnest that I'm not sure if she has a passing interest in me or if she's just telling me how she does her job.

"So, okay, fill me in on the time between college and the airport. Is that specific enough?"

"Sure, but it's a long period. Anything in particular you want to know?" There it is again. I can't tell if she's flirting, challenging me, or asking a question. I can't help reading into everything. I want more from her. I shouldn't, but I do.

"Well, hey, if you're giving me free rein, tell me about the best sex you've had."

She chokes on a bite of bread. Her eyes bug out, and she grabs a glass of water to wash down the sourdough. I feel like the same teenage goon I always was around her. "Seriously?" She wipes her eyes and regains her composure.

I shrug, undeterred. "You said 'anything.'"

"Didn't realize you'd take that and run."

"Specifics are important," I remind her.

"Fine," she grumbles. I catch a hint of amusement that I've recalled her comment from earlier. "You can ask anything, but I won't guarantee I'll answer."

"So that's a no on the sex question? Just confirming."

"It's a no."

"Okay, relationships?" I could banter like this forever. It often gets me into trouble, sure, but I get the sense that Gracie won't fall for my charms. Never did when we were younger, probably too smart now.

"Not in one at the moment."

I wait, expecting her to give me at least a few details. She stares me down, lips sealed shut.

"Vow of celibacy? Yeah, I get it."

A flicker of a smile tickles her lips. I'm itching to get under her cool facade, and I sense progress.

"Focusing on work. Same difference."

"Ouch. Come on, Gracie. Surely there's room for romance. I saw what you were reading at the airport. Tell me you don't believe in being swept away by a duke."

She scoops a bite of lentils, and I feel like I can see the pleasure centers light up in her brain as she savors the bite.

"I mean, sure. If you know any dukes, send 'em my way."

"So that's a categorical 'no' on relationships except for dukes. So we're clear."

"Correct. Why do you want to know so badly?"

"I'm just trying to figure you out, Gracie. Ky tells me you hate sports. I'm curious why you took this job."

Caught, her eyes go wide. "I don't…it's not that I…"

I chuckle, watching her face go pink straight through to the tips of her ears. "It's fine. Not everyone's a fan."

"I don't hate sports," she corrects, smoothing the napkin on her lap. "I'm not a diehard, but things change. I do like the job so far. It suits me."

"You didn't answer the question. Why the move?"

"Um…" She chews her bottom lip. "I got fired."

Staring at her lap, she seems ashamed, and I hate that I'm the instigator of it. "Hey, listen, everyone gets fired at some point. It's a bump in the road, not the destination."

"Fine. You want to know about my romantic life? Here's the deal. I've had relationships. They were good until they weren't. In particular, my last one was with a guy in the Bay Area. I recommended him for a job, made a bad judgment call, and ended up unemployed because of it. No job, no relationship."

"Sounds like bullshit to me."

"Thanks for your opinion, but the company had a strict policy on relationships." Her lips pull down in a frown, and I can see how hard she's taking this perceived failure. It makes me want to pummel her former boss and anyone else who ever made her feel small. "Anyhow, I won't be making that mistake again." She sits up straight like a grade-school student, proving her seriousness. I can see this is important to her, and I can't help finding her prim insistence adorable.

"Sounds like you checked the fine print over at the Devils organization before signing on."

"I didn't have to. I'm only going to be here as long as it takes to earn back some respect and wait out the non-compete. Then I'm headed back to a better job in the Bay Area tech world. Relationships are not going to be a thing because I'm here to work. Running analytics for the Devils is my life. That can only benefit you and your team, so you should be thrilled. Do I get to ask a question now?"

Her sudden outpouring of candor catches me off guard, and I lose focus. I want to digest each kernel of information she spewed on its own, but she's so fired up that I don't want to sleep on the moment. The power of her stare throws me.

"Um, sure."

"Relationships? Fiancées? Hookups? What's your jam? Who can I expect to run into in the kitchen in the mornings?"

"None of the above. No one."

"Haha." She tilts her head and waits out the lie. But it's not a lie. "Please. I should believe that?"

"Why wouldn't you believe it?" I lean back and cross my arms, challenging her to admit to what she's googled and why. Even if whatever information she found is old and giving her the wrong impression.

"You're a soccer star, you're extremely attractive, and you're single. You…you must know you have a reputation for, um, dating a lot of women. Or whatever."

"Sorry, I'm just stuck on the words 'extremely attractive,' but what's this 'or whatever' business?"

"Hooking up with anything that moves. You're telling me you won't be doing that here?"

"I'm guaranteeing you I won't be doing that here. In fact, I'm guaranteeing you that you'll be bringing a guy here for a hookup long before I will."

She laughs and extends a hand. "Care to make it interesting?"

"What do you have in mind?'

"I bet that you'll hook up with a woman before I hook up with a guy."

I grasp her hand and try to ignore the shot of electricity that slams into me at the feel of her skin. "Easiest money I'll ever make. What's the bet?"

She thinks for a moment, eyes darting around like she's trying hard to come up with something good, something she really wants. "Don't work too hard. You're not going to win."

She smiles. "The loser has to cook dinner for the winner."

"Really? I already did that."

"I know. And it was delish. So I'm looking forward to winning this bet and doing it again."

"Good luck to you. And when you lose, you'll need to do better than a baked potato."

"Noted."

Our plates are scraped bare, so there's no excuse for me to keep her out here longer. And I don't plan on losing this bet, so I guess I won't be cooking for her again.

She gets up from the table and starts carrying our dishes into the kitchen. "Thank you again for dinner."

"Thank you for saving my job."

"You don't have to thank me. You did all the work. I'm purely a data analyst, trying to get ahead." She doesn't emphasize for a third time that she needs to do well so she can get the hell out of here and go back to the life she likes far better than this one. I've been an athlete long enough to know I should take the win on dinner and tune out the rest.

"Sleep well, Gracie."

"G'night, soccer star."

I turn away so she won't see how much I like it when she calls me that.

racie

THE TIMER DINGS, telling me the batch of muffins I popped into the oven forty-five minutes earlier is probably done. I should check them and hover nearby until they're perfect.

I like them a little soft in the middle, and I hate it when the bottoms get too brown.

The oven light doesn't tell me anything, so I ease the door open, inhaling the delicious cinnamon scent of eight giant apple muffins. The recipe is for a dozen, but I think they're best when the muffin top bulges out of the tin and spills over. The top is the best part, so why not make it as big as possible?

The toothpick I insert in the center comes out clean, so I decide they're done. One more whiff of the heavenly smell as I pop the tray on a rack to cool. I know better than to eat them when they're too hot. Burning the roof of my mouth is a rookie mistake, and I'm no rookie.

Padding back to the storage area I've turned into an office, I make a bet with myself. I think I can get through one week of training data and upload the numbers into my software program before the muffins are cool enough to eat.

Game on.

I've been working for the past three hours, and somewhere along the way, I drifted into the Zen zone, that place where time stands still, and I lose myself in numbers and data. A herd of elephants could dance in the next room, and I wouldn't notice.

The house is so quiet. Even though Hunter passed me in the kitchen earlier and raised an eyebrow when he saw that I was making muffins, I haven't seen or heard him since. I'm sure he has a life with his teammates or the women he dates, and there are many.

Yes, I took a little time last night and did a social media search, all in the name of research. It's only good sense to know all sides of the players I'm dealing with, and even though I have assistants who run reports with similar information, it couldn't hurt to do a little checking myself.

Okay, fine. I'm nosy.

I'm also smitten, despite my best instincts that tell me to stay far away from players with attitude. The best way I can think of to stanch that budding flame is to pour cold water over it before it can grow. In other words, I searched for any and all information about Hunter and women—the more compromising pictures, the better. I didn't have to work very hard.

I found breathless posts showing Hunter with his arm draped over the shapely bare shoulders of models, actresses, and even a few people's wives. When I finished rolling my eyes over his lack of scruples, I saw enough cleavage and curves to cure me of any illusions that he could ever be interested in someone like me. My curves are courtesy of Ben and Jerry's, thank you very much.

Cold-water dousing achieved. Check.

It's yet another helpful reminder that I'm new at my job, and the last thing I need is to compromise my integrity by appearing to favor players. It's bad enough that people have gotten wind of our temporary living arrangements, resulting in a few raised eyebrows. I reminded anyone who commented that we're all adults here. Give me a desk full of spreadsheets, and I'm happy.

With the apple-cinnamon scent urging me forward, I get into a groove and focus on the job I came here to do. It feels good to work. The player statistics fall into place, and I start making sense of all the data points I've been tracking.

"Morning, Tink." Hunter sounds sleepy, and I know without even looking that he probably doesn't have on a shirt. So I look.

There he is, rubbing his eyes, holding an e-reader with Bogie standing next to him, wagging his tail. "This one." I point at the dog. "I have a bone to pick with your dog."

"Uh-oh. Bogie, what did you do?" He looks at the dog, who, naturally, says nothing. His tongue lolls from his mouth, and his tail wags.

"He snuck up on me while I was sleeping. Put his face right next to mine and started doing this heavy breathing thing."

Hunter chuckles. "Yeah, he does that. But only to people he likes. It's how he wakes me up most days. He wanted you to invite him up to snuggle."

"Well, I thought it was an axe murderer coming for me."

"You should really watch the chocolate consumption before bed." He looks over my shoulder at what must look like an Excel nerd's dream. "What's all that?"

"First, tell me what you're reading." I point at the device in his hands.

He looks down. "Love this thing. I'm toggling between a Louise Penny mystery and that one you were reading about the duke."

I laugh. "You are not."

He holds it up to show me, and sure enough, he's queued up a Scottish period romance. "You never cease to surprise me, Reyes."

He shrugs. "What can I say? I'm complex," he deadpans.

"Now, your turn. What's all that? Can you...explain it to me?" The words sound like the usual grumpy grunt I've come to expect from Hunter, but there's something vulnerable in his voice, as though not liking when he doesn't understand something.

"The algorithms?"

He crosses his arms and nods. "I guess. What are you looking at that makes it clear that a player has potential?" The way his brow creases and his mouth edges down makes him look unhappy about the question. There's something else behind it besides mere curiosity.

"Are you questioning my methods?"

He takes a step backward. "No. Of course not. I want to understand them."

I tilt my head and study him. "You do?"

"Yes."

I'm not sure how I feel about letting him into my world. It's not that I don't think I can explain it well enough, but my coding abilities are my one superpower. What if he thinks it's not very interesting? I've spent most of my life as a woman in the STEM field, showing people I'm capable of doing the work while fending off the perception that what we do is nerdy, but I'm not in the mood for defending myself right now.

"I have to warn you, it might be boring."

"Try me." His tone is challenging, and the smirky sparkle in his gray eyes edges back.

Maybe I can teach him something. That gets me interested.

"Okay, pull up a chair, but first, go to the kitchen where you'll find eight muffins. Please pop one onto a plate and bring it as payment." I don't bother suggesting that he bring two so he can have one. I already know about his fitness foods, and I'm pretty sure today isn't a cheat day.

"Seven."

"Sorry?"

"There are seven muffins in the kitchen. And I'm the one who should be sorry. I ate one without asking."

My mouth opens, but I struggle to find words. "You—you did?"

"Guilty."

He smiles like a canary-nabbing cat, and it's hard to find fault with him. I nod. "Okay, then. Looks like you're getting the good end of the deal here."

"I'll make it even if you want. Anytime you're in the market for a soccer coaching session, I'm your guy."

I laugh at that ridiculous idea and turn back to the computer screen, waving him in the direction of the kitchen. I don't want him to see the smile on my face. I know he doesn't mean he's "my guy" in any way other than soccer coaching, like he said, but the words make my face heat regardless.

I tap out a few coding instructions and watch as the data populates the screen. While he's busy in the kitchen, I pull up his file and decide which data I want to share. It's like a patient asking to see a medical chart. Without a proper explanation, some of the levels and scores would look troubling.

Even though it's his data and his body I'm analyzing, I don't want to give him too much information all at once. Some of it may feel misleading if I don't present it correctly. I shake my head at myself. I don't even know what he wants to know. This will probably be a five-minute lesson, and his eyes will glaze over. I don't need to overthink it.

Kyler's storage area is a mess of skate wear, from helmets to elbow and knee pads. Several surfboards are propped against one wall, and a box of surf paraphernalia sits beneath them. I see jars of board wax, various rash guards that companies have sent him to sample, and supplements with sun-protective properties. I look forward to when he comes back from his trip because I want to learn more about his growing business, but for now, I do my best not to disturb anything.

"Crazy that Ky made a job from spending every available hour at the beach," Hunter says, approaching me with an outstretched arm holding a muffin on a plate. In his other hand, he has a coffee cup with a teabag hanging out.

"Could say the same about you, no? You play soccer for a living. That's pretty awesome."

He perches on the edge of the desk, his leg bouncing. His muscled thigh flexes with each motion, and he raises and lowers the tea bag in his cup.

"It is awesome. There isn't a day goes by that I don't know it." His voice is quieter than usual, almost reverent. I turn to get a better look at him, and he hops up from the table and drags over a chair covered in hoodie sweatshirts.

Shoving them aside, he settles into the chair and scoots it next to mine so he can see my computer screen. Without realizing it, I lean away and reposition my computer so I can sit farther from him while still allowing him to see the screen.

"What am I looking at?" he asks, pointing. Before he can touch my screen, I push the laptop out of reach. He jerks his hand back as though the computer hissed at him.

"Sorry. I have a thing about fingerprints on my screen." I feel sheepish about my neuroses, but obsessively wiping his prints off seems even worse. See, this is why I don't let people sit next to me while I'm working. It already feels like a bad idea.

He folds his arms and leans as far back as he can without his chair tipping over. "Understood. This is your domain. I'm an observer. Don't hesitate to put me in line."

"I wasn't—"

He stops me by putting a hand on my forearm. "Gracie, we're good. You do you. I'm happy to be here getting a tutorial." His voice is calm, and I don't feel judged, so I pull the computer closer to show the columns of numbers I isolated when he was in the kitchen.

The light in the room is dim, so the computer screen looks

especially white. The numbers are arranged into three columns, so I start with the basics. "These are power numbers that we take from the wearable devices that record your speed and effort. I'm sure you're familiar with those."

Hunter shrugs. "I know they're collecting information, but unless Coach tells me something specific, I don't keep track."

"Probably a good idea. For a player, the best thing you can do is go by instinct and know your body on the field in different conditions. It doesn't help if the device gives you information that you can't interpret by feel."

"Makes sense." He scoots his chair a little closer. I catch a whiff of that pine scent I noticed when he was barbecuing, but now the firepit smell has been replaced by a clean, soapy scent that I inhale deeply before I realize I've done it.

"Good. Now, we look at game data, which takes a lot longer to analyze because there are so many variables. It's also why different analysts can give you vastly different results. There's no one method."

I walk him through how I collect data, gathering everything from movements on the field during games. "I look at where, when, and what you're doing and analyze oxygen uptake, muscle fatigue, and bounce-back rate after a collision with another player. Still, those physical measures are pretty easy to look at objectively."

I can't help it. When I start talking about data and numbers and analysis, I fall down a rabbit hole. Even in the presence of the most distracting guy I've ever met, I can't keep from losing myself in the numbers, going on about things he can't possibly care about.

Hunter turns toward me and once again puts his hand on my arm, which stops my endless blather. His hand, so large, strong, and warm, sets off goose bumps in its wake. "Wait, are you serious? You're looking at all of this?"

"Oh yeah." I swallow hard as he removes his hand. "And wait, there's more." My voice comes out like the croak of a lovesick frog.

He leans in close, all restless energy and impatience, while I tee up how I create a model. I show him footage from the game against Houston. As soon as he watches the part where he slide tackles the Houston player, Hunter puts a hand over his mouth. The player doesn't get up. He lies writhing on the field while Hunter goes mental on the ref. He looks embarrassed.

"You probably think I'm an animal."

"No. I think it's an aggressive game."

"It is, but you have to know…I'm not out there trying to hurt people. Something takes over. All my inner demons, all the voices from the past form a chorus, and it's all I hear. I'm not the same person you see here when I'm playing."

I don't know him well enough to understand his past, but he frowns, looking wrecked over his behavior.

"It's gotta be hard when that thing that makes you successful is the same thing that tears you down."

He nods. I let him sit with it for a moment.

"But that's not what I see when I look at you on the field. I see a complex series of inputs that create a sort of chemistry and magic when they work together."

I pull up an animated image of Hunter that I've imbued with functions that allow it to move on the screen like a player.

"This is your avatar. It's basically like creating a virtual person that I imbue with your characteristics, and then I run it through every scenario I can think of with your skill set, which changes weekly. Then I add data from other players. It gives me a best guess at what someone on the field is likely to do and what the outcome will probably be when you interact."

"Holy shit," he says, brushing my shoulder with his arm as he points at the screen, all the while careful to keep his fingertip at a distance. "You're making a collection of virtual soccer matches and playing with us like a gamer." He sounds more accusatory than delighted. "I can't decide if that's the coolest thing ever or if it makes me feel like a robot who isn't in control of my own impulses."

His breath ghosts the skin of my neck, heating my skin and making me shudder. He needs to stop doing this.

No, he needs to do it more.

"You're not a robot, of course. You're sentient for one thing, and you're in control of your movements to a degree, minus some statistical variance, of course. And you can't be programmed, but you can be influenced. Or at least most people can, but with you, that's where it gets interesting, so I'd hate to have you think you're nothing but data—"

He holds up a hand and gently places a finger over my lips. "Tink. You can call me a robot all day long. I'm fascinated by this shit." He removes his finger, but not before staring at it and meeting my eyes. My breath catches, and he smirks like he knows all too well the effect he has on me. On all women, no doubt.

I take in a breath and steady my nerves. I'm the one with the information here. I'm in control.

"The interesting thing is that when I looked at the data and the expected outcomes on the field, you defied every single one. You did better than you should have. You beat every statistical prediction. That's what convinced me the team needs you, whether management's angry with you or not."

He looks surprised.

He should. My data often turns up contrary results. But it's almost never wrong.

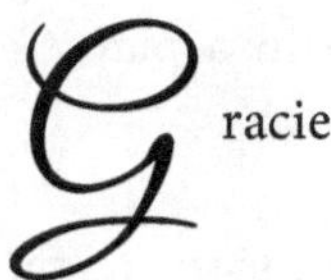

racie

WORK IS a little more interesting when I move the furniture around in my office, giving me a view out the window of the Devils practice field. If "interesting" means the same thing as "unproductive." I barely get through one set of data before my mind wanders to what Hunter is doing on the field.

And what he's doing is taking full command of the ball, bossing his teammates into position, and coming within inches of slide tackling anyone who gets in his way. He stops short of injuring himself or his teammates, and I wonder if he's thinking about the analytics lesson I gave him. Sometimes knowing a little bit is knowing too much, and I don't want him to be in his head when he's an instinct player.

I also don't want to spend too much time watching him practice.

Gerald Moder knocks on my door and walks into the middle of the room without waiting for me to respond. Wearing khaki pants and penny loafers with his zip-up Devils jacket, he looks one part preppy dad, one part diehard fan. Most of the C-suite dresses similarly, but I still haven't managed to incorporate any Devils gear into my plain pants and blouse look that feels safe if a little boring.

"Hey there," I say, glad I'm looking at my computer instead of at the practice field, even if watching players is related to my job. "I've been working on the rookie report. There are some good prospects on academy teams I think we should have on our radar, even if it takes a couple of years before they're viable."

He nods and rubs his hands together. "Good to hear. I'd like to compare lists once you're set on yours."

"Of course. I'm sure there's some crossover, but I'm looking for different skill sets than what might show up in a player's stats."

"That's what I'm counting on."

I nod, grateful he seems to value what I can do for the team. Every success I have here will pave the way to getting out of the doghouse among the handful of Silicon Valley bosses who think I'm too rigid and difficult. I need to kill it in such a resounding way that they'll be tripping over themselves to hire me back.

But first things first—I need to put all my energy into doing well for the team.

Gerald looks me over from head to toe. It's not at all lascivious, more like he's trying to figure out if my pants match my shirt. I look down to be sure. "Something's missing, and I've been trying to put my finger on it."

He wags a finger and backpedals out of my office. Leaning to where he's left something outside the door, he picks up a tote bag and brings it inside, plopping it on the chair opposite my desk. He nods toward it. "Have a look."

I come around my large oiled-wood desk and open the tote. Inside, I find a stack of yellow, red, black, and white clothing, all bearing some form of the Devils logo or branding. Gerald plucks a white baseball cap from the pile and pops it on my head. Backing up, he surveys his work. "That's more like it. You're a Devil now, might as well dress the part."

There are at least three hoodies, a stack of tees, socks, pajamas, and a scarf in the pile. It doesn't even include half the items of clothing I've seen people wearing around the office.

"Thanks. I'll try to show more team spirit." I adjust the ball cap so I can see a little better and salute him.

"You're fine. I'm not suggesting anything is wrong with your clothes. Just wanted to give you a team welcome, is all. You're a Devil now, and we take care of our own." He winks, every bit the genial boss I've never had in the half dozen years I've spent crunching numbers for some of the best in the business.

I'm surprised by the sudden welling of emotion I feel and swallow hard to tamp it down, lest he think I'm the type who goes to pieces over a kind gesture.

I'm absolutely the type who goes to pieces over a kind gesture. Or animal. Or a Hallmark movie.

"Well, thank you for the warm welcome. I'll wear my Devils gear proudly."

Gerald smiles like he's satisfied. "We feel lucky to have you, Gracie. Keep up the good work."

When he leaves, I move slowly back to my desk, pausing at the window to take in the field below, not at all worried this time about getting caught staring at the team. I'm part of the Devils now. Their well-being is part of my job. That includes the players on the field and the ones we'll one day recruit.

For the first time since I arrived in Los Angeles, I feel like it might be home.

CHAPTER 13

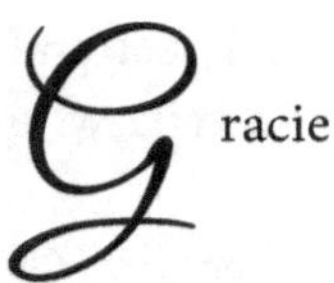racie

"I THOUGHT it never rains in LA." I stand in the lobby, staring out at sheets of rain pummeling the courtyard between me and the dry safety of my car. The clouds overhead aren't particularly dark, but the winds are blowing fiercely, sending the water sideways.

Even with my new Devils-branded umbrella in my hand, I'm no match for the rain.

"Yeah, global warming and all. Who knows?" Darby Green, one of the team's physical therapists, shakes his head but keeps his head down like a bull prepared to charge the red flag. "What's a little water? I'm going for it."

I watch him hold a magazine over his head and jog through the center of the courtyard, where he splashes through a puddle. "Goddammit." His words pierce the rain and the glass walls of the building, but he continues onward until I can barely see him in the distance.

"It can't last," I mutter, resigned to work another hour or so until this flash flood wears itself out, and I can leave without getting soaked.

Of all the days to skip lunch, I have to pick the one that has no foreseeable end. If I don't want to drive home sopping wet, I need to wait.

Back up to my office I go.

As I'm walking down the hallway, I'm surprised to find Hunter coming the other way. This floor is all corporate offices, and I've never seen him up here. I'm pretty sure Gerald Moder is content with his performance, so I don't think he was called here for a beatdown.

"Hey, you lost?" I ask, noticing that the assistant cubicles are empty. Rain or no rain, people like to leave on time. Maybe they have more to go home to than an empty house full of surf gear and a new muffin recipe. I'm not complaining. I like work, and sometimes I do my best thinking when the office is empty.

A few executives are still at work with their doors closed, their muffled voices audible on the phone.

Hunter stops in his tracks, whips his head from side to side and feigns confusion at his surroundings. "Wait, is this not the gym? I wondered what happened to the weight racks, but these barbells are kind of awesome." He lifts up a leafy plant from one of the assistant desks and starts pumping it.

I roll my eyes. "I'm sure the trainers will be impressed by how many reps you can do of a pothos."

"A what, now?"

I point at the plant. "That's a pothos. And you're right about them being awesome. They're almost impossible to kill, which is why I have three of them in my house."

He leans against the wall, and I notice that he's not wearing workout gear. In fact, his hair is damp and slicked back, and he's wearing jeans with one of the team hoodies. "You have a house? Then why do you live with Kyler?"

"Because my house is in San Francisco. Kind of a long commute."

"Oh, got it. You going to sell it so you can buy something here? Not a lot of inventory right now, but if you're buying and selling in the same market, you're always good. Interest rates are tricky, though, so are you considering keeping your house and renting something here?"

I cross my arms. "So many questions, soccer star. I had no idea you were so dialed in on real estate."

"I'm dialed in on you, Tink. I could give two shits about real estate."

I suck in a breath with such force I'm sure he hears it. The back of my neck prickles with heat, and tiny beads of sweat form on my forehead. He grins, aware of exactly what effect he has on me. This is his game. He plays with women, knows what heart-stopping things to say, and understands how to make us want him.

I don't *want* to want him.

"Well, it seems you know a lot about it." My words sound garbled in the sloshing seas in my brain. I start to move past him, aiming myself like a missile toward my office, my safe haven. I just need to get there, close the door, and take off half my clothes because he heats me up like a damn pizza oven.

But he blocks my way, stepping directly in my path so quickly that I can't stop moving before I run right into him. My hands come up to brace myself, landing on his chest, which feels like granite beneath the soft cotton fabric of his hoodie. I also catch a deep whiff of pine and fresh laundry. I inhale deeply.

He takes hold of my shoulders and walks a step backward, so I'm steady and my hands drop from his chest. They almost ache to touch him again, but I shove them behind my back preventatively. "Oops, sorry," I say.

"My fault. I wasn't done talking to you."

I swallow thickly and look up at him. At this proximity, I'm acutely aware of how much he towers over me. I brace myself to have a conversation without melting into a puddle. I can do this, I feel certain. "Okay."

"Have you eaten?" he asks.

I blink at him like he's begun speaking in a foreign tongue. "Um…"

He pantomimes picking up a sandwich, taking a bite, putting it down, and chewing. Then he tilts his head toward me and motions between us. "Food. You. Me. Yes?"

I should tell him I had a late lunch. Or a really big granola bar. Or any other excuse I can come up with to avoid sitting across the table from him and trying to make small talk about real estate prices when I want to lick him like a melting ice cream sandwich.

"Yes. Sure. I could eat." Apparently, my brain is on autopilot, only looking out for my basic needs.

"Great." He looks at me. I look at him. "Did you need something from your office? You were headed this way." He points behind him in the direction he was coming from, and for a millisecond, I wonder if he came up here to find me. To ask me to dinner.

But that makes no sense, especially since we live in the same place and hardly need to make plans to see each other.

I try to recall why I was going this way. "Oh, it's pouring rain out there. I was going to wait it out before going to my car."

He chuckles. "Has no one shown you the secret way to the parking lot?"

"There's a secret way? Like with yellow bricks and elves and gingerbread cookies?"

"I think you're conflating about sixteen different fairy tales, and as far as I know, no cookies."

"Deal's off, then."

He shrugs. "Suit yourself. Get ready for soak city, sister."

I look down the hallway at where I can still see sheets of rain pouring down outside the building's windows. I don't want to eat dinner with him, wet like a drowned dog.

"Tell me about the secret way," I whisper conspiratorially even though no one is around.

He hitches a thumb over his shoulder. "Follow me."

CHAPTER 14

$\mathcal{H}$unter

THERE IS NO SECRET PASSAGEWAY, but there is a warren of connecting hallways that avoids at least some of the outdoor passage to the parking lot.

Once we've made it from the main headquarters building to the training facility via a basement hallway, we pass the mailroom and the kitchen, where the staff prepares meals for us after training. "I can't believe I didn't know this was here," Gracie says, looking around like she's in Wonderland.

"Not much reason you'd know, unless you're picking up fan mail or looking to grub with the team."

I swipe a mini bag of chocolate chip cookies from a snack bin and open it for Gracie. "To tide you over."

If I'm being honest, I may not take her straight to dinner, and I don't want her to be hungry. She practically inhales them, smiling with each bite. "Not a lot of grubbing with the team since I started here."

"I noticed."

She casts a sidelong glance. "I'm sure you did." Her deadpan skepticism belies the reality that I look for her whenever I'm in the main building, but she doesn't need to know that. I like seeing her, and she seems to go out of her way to avoid me at Kyler's house.

"I'm very observant, Tink. I notice everything."

Right now, I'm noticing how she's biting down on that plush pink bottom lip, and it's making me want to reach my thumb out and pop it from between her teeth so I can run a finger over it. But that would get me thrown out on my ass for harassment and get me pummeled by my best friend, not to mention losing a place to live that's started to feel like home. So I shove my hands into the pocket of my hoodie and quicken my pace down the hallway.

When we reach the elevators, I take Gracie up to the roof, where we have a futsal facility. I should be escorting her to the parking garage, but I can't resist the opportunity to let her into my world. And to see her in my jersey.

"What's this?" she asks, taking in the series of smaller soccer pitches with their rubber floors and tiny goals.

"Futsal. It's a six v six game, faster, more technical. It's a good training supplement to what we do out there." I gesture over my shoulder with a thumb even though we can't see the practice field from here.

"That's kind of cool. I'd kind of like to see it in action sometime."

"I can do you one better." I walk over to where we keep the equipment. In a bin at one end, we have soccer balls and pinnies. In a big cardboard box behind the check-in desk sits another big cardboard box filled with shoes and shin guards.

"What size are you?" I ask.

"What size of what?"

"Shoe size. Seven?"

"Yes, but I'm already wearing shoes." She points at her two-inch kitten heels, which look great with the long skirt she's wearing, but I shake my head and hold up a pair of indoor soccer shoes from the box. "Youth teams sometimes use the facility, and you know kids, they're always leaving shit behind, so we've got pretty much every size."

"Is it like bowling? Am I not allowed to walk on the floor without those?"

I chuckle at the sweet innocence of her question.

"No, sweetheart, you're not allowed to play futsal without them."

Her eyes get round, and she looks from me to the empty court, shaking her head. "I'm not a soccer player."

"Good. Because this is futsal. Totally different game." I hadn't planned on bringing her up here to play, but now that we're here, it seems the best idea in the world. I'm already wearing indoor soccer shoes, but I'm not accustomed to playing in jeans. Maybe it'll give her an advantage as I run stiffly in denim.

Meanwhile, Gracie stands there with her arms crossed, still shaking her head. "I'm wearing a skirt."

Unwilling to indulge her excuses, I move to a glass display case near the check-in desk and slide it open. Inside, there are logo jerseys, sweats, and socks. In under ten seconds, I assemble an outfit for her of black track pants, a Devils tee under one of my jerseys, and a pair of socks that will fit the shin guards I pull from the box. "For when you defend a pass. I don't want you getting a shiner on your shin," I explain, handing her the gear.

"Are you kidding me?"

"You taught me about analytics. You showed me yours, I'll show you mine. And I promise to feed you when we're done."

She crosses her arms and side-eyes me like she doesn't understand. "You want me to play soccer? With you?"

"It's futsal. And yes."

~

TEN MINUTES LATER, Gracie emerges from the women's locker room. She looks fucking adorable in full Devils regalia, even as she looks down at her clothes and grimaces. "Not sure about this, soccer star. Something tells me you're looking to get some kind of roommate upper hand by slide tackling me. I can still recommend you for transfer."

I make the gesture of crossing my heart. "I would never. No slide tackling. I'll even play in socks if that makes you feel better."

She perks up at that suggestion. "Actually, now you're talking. Let's play in socks."

"Both of us?"

She shrugs. "I've never played before, so I won't know the difference, and it'll keep us both off the injured list."

I spin a ball on my index finger and drop it to my foot, where I start juggling it from knee to foot to knee. "It might be slippery," I warn.

She takes an exaggerated step onto the court and slides a few feet in her socks like a kid trying to skate across the kitchen floor. "Works for me. It'll give me some speed."

So I set us up on opposite sides of the court and put the ball into play, fully expecting to go easy while she gets her soccer legs under her. There's no need. Gracie charges at me and goes straight for the ball, kicking it away from me and windmilling past me like a tumbleweed in her slippery socks.

I turn and chase her, so within seconds I'm back in front, defending my goal as she tries to advance. I keep some distance between us and shift from side to side, making it hard for her to choose a direction and charge forward.

She goes left, but I'm there faster, blocking her again. Frustration builds in her eyes, and she squints at me like a truck about to hit the gas. Before she can move, I dive in and sweep the ball away from her feet, dribbling it easily in the other direction while she gives chase.

I want it to be a fair fight, so I don't go full speed toward the goal. She catches me in seconds. She runs alongside me and suddenly disappears outside my peripheral vision, so I turn to find her, right as she leaps up and clings to my back like a koala. "Hey! Ref! Player interference," I yell, and she giggles. The soft sound of her laughter right next to my ear is a kind of music I've never heard before. Light and carefree like tiny windchimes. It makes me lose sight of what game we're playing when all I want is to elicit more of that sound.

I spin around, but Gracie hangs on tight. I lose track of the ball for enough time that it rolls a few feet away. Never letting the ball out of her sight, she's off my back in an instant and running to retrieve it. "Didn't hear the ref blow a whistle, so game on!" she shrieks, taking the ball and all the speed she can muster straight to the goal.

Pausing to look over her shoulder, she smiles. I'm not even trying to catch her at this point. Watching her in action is too good.

She brings her foot back, boots the ball into the net, and raises both fists in victory. When she trots back to me, taking tiny steps to keep from sliding in her socks, she holds a hand up. "One-nil, and I think you let me have that one, but I'm a foot shorter than you, so I'll take it."

I give her a high five even though we're on opposing teams. "No, that was a legitimate goal. Of course, jumping on my back goes against just about every rule in soccer."

"Yeah?" She feigns innocence, batting her eyes. I like this lighter side of her and wonder why she hides it most of the time.

"Yeah." I jog to the goal and retrieve the ball. "Okay, loser buys dinner, so you better believe I'm gonna bring my A game now."

"Dinner? Who said anything about dinner?" she teases.

"Though if my winning streak continues, I could go for a steak, I suppose…"

I drop the ball between us at midcourt and let her dribble it for a few seconds before I swoop in on defense. The court isn't very big, and I'm tall, so it only takes me a few long strides to get from the midline to the goal. I need to rein in my tendency to go hard, especially since the last thing in the world I want to do is hurt her.

Gracie slips in her socks and whiffs the ball as she attempts to keep it away from me, but I cut to the side and intercept it before it can go out of bounds. Now I'm in control, and I take the opportunity to mess with her a little bit. I pass the ball from foot to foot, staying in one place and daring her to try to take it away from me.

Her brows drop in concentration, and she watches the ball with a determination that explains why she's so good at her job. I cut to the side, and she follows, but her socks make her slide. I start to laugh as her legs do the splits, but she quickly recovers and comes charging at me. I go the other way with her hot on my heels.

That's the great thing about the futsal court—it's small, so the game becomes much more technical and doesn't require much running. She's small but quick, and that gives her an advantage.

I take the ball toward the goal, and Gracie runs with me. As I'm about to take my shot, she comes in with a last-ditch attempt to stop me, her foot shooting out to meet the ball. It meets my foot instead, right after the ball has left it. I lose my balance and fall on my ass, and the ball sails into the net.

Gracie's hands shoot to her face, covering her mouth. "Oh my gosh, I'm so sorry." The muffled words and her horrified look make me laugh.

"All part of the game. Nice D," I tell her, enjoying her pink cheeks and guilty expression. "And if you didn't notice, it's one-all." I swivel around so I'm sitting facing her with my knees bent.

"You're not calling a foul? Do you get a PK or something?"

"You didn't foul me. That was great defense. Relax, Tink. It's all good."

She extends a hand to help me up, but I'm twice her weight. When she tries to pull me up, I end up pulling her down instead. She lands in my lap, looking surprised.

"That wasn't supposed to happen."

"My fault." I scramble up, pulling us both onto our feet. When she lets go of my hand, I'm struck by how empty I feel without it in my grasp.

I scramble toward the goal to retrieve the ball before I can overthink it. "Okay, game point."

"We're only playing to two?" she asks.

"You want to go for more? Depends on how hungry you are. I figured this could be the tie breaker."

She nods. "Good point. I'm hungry. Let's stop at two."

I put the ball in play again and kick it to the side so we can both go after it. Usually, there are five other players around, so I'm kind of pretending there's a teammate to our right. Gracie runs toward the ball, but her momentum is too much to stop herself, and she slides past it.

I go for the ball, laughing as I take control, but she comes at me with full force. Her socks send her sliding toward me, and I don't want her to fall, so I sweep her up in my arms to stop her from flying into the sidewall.

"Hey! Ref! Penalty!" She flails around in my arms, but I don't let her go. Holding her like my arms are a basket, I walk toward the ball and nudge it toward the center of the court. "Put me down! No fair using your height and muscle advantage!" She continues yelling, but she can't hide her grin.

As I look down at her face inches below mine, it would be so easy to take what I've wanted since I was in high school. It would be so easy to close the gap between our mouths and feel her lips against mine.

Who am I kidding? I don't want to feel them. I want to devour them.

I'm intensely aware of my hands, one on her hip, the other wrapped around her thigh. The side of her rib cage presses against my chest, and the top of her head grazes the bottom of my chin. At each point of contact, I feel wild heat and an intense fucking awareness of her.

How much I want my hands roaming over every inch of her skin. How much I crave this feeling of holding her close.

My heart thuds against my ribs, and I'm sure she can feel it. I think I feel her heartbeat as well, quieter but equally furious. It makes my dick twitch in my pants. I know I need to put her down before the last bit of restraint snaps, and I dive in, taking her mouth and every other part of her.

I allow myself one last moment of believing in *maybe*.

Maybe she feels the same way about me.

Maybe the last dozen years have been us finding our way back to each other.

Maybe I can kiss her without Kyler losing his shit or her losing her job.

That's where the bottom drops out. The thought that stops me from charging forward is the idea of Gracie losing something. Especially something she's worked hard at and deserves. I don't know if the Devils organization has a clause like the one at her former job, but what if it does? I already like her too much not to care about her future. I can't be responsible for risking her job, especially when I only know what I want. I have no idea what's in her head.

I'm thinking all of this while I loosen the grip on her in my arms. Her expression goes from an intensity that rivals my own to something different. The corners of her mouth sink. Her eyes dull. The look is a combination of disappointment and acceptance. And a second later, she blinks twice, and her expression returns to calm. She's already over it.

I'm not.

My head tips down another inch. I'm not teasing her so much as taunting myself. Look but don't touch. This is as close as you'll ever get to Gracie Albright.

I lower her to the ground slowly, watching her legs stretch out until she's on her feet. Without looking back at me, she walks to the centerline and prepares to resume play. And just like that, we're two opponents.

She gives me a ferocious stare, makes a V with her fingers, and points from her eyes to mine, telling me she's got my number. "Put me in Coach, I've got this."

Shifting from one foot to the other with her hands hanging down in a ready position, she waits until I nudge the ball into play. She dives for it without missing a beat, taking it from one socked foot to the other and sliding toward the goal. I turn, and two strides get me in front of her. She darts to the left, but I follow her.

Pretending to go right, she gets me off balance for long enough for a fake out. She turns her back on me, controls the ball, and shoots.

It hits the net like she's done it a thousand times.

Gracie looks at me like she can't believe it. "Did you let me have that one?"

I hold up my hands in protest. "Nope, you made that goal, fair and square. Nice fake. I bought right into it."

She nods and comes over for a high five. "I'd say best three out of five, but I'm hungry and I know to quit while I'm ahead," she teases, her eyes dancing with delight.

I don't dare tell her that I wasn't about to let her take me to dinner, so I may have slowed my roll for an extra few seconds. It doesn't matter. The point is that I'm getting what I came for, which is the right to take her to dinner, even if it's under the guise of losing a soccer bet.

I'll take any excuse to spend time with her, even if it tarnishes my soccer cred a tiny bit in the process.

"What do you feel like eating?" I ask, only slightly worried she'll pick some hideous fast food joint or ask for a dinner of donuts and Slurpees.

She rubs her hands together with a big grin. "I'm a meat-and-potatoes girl. Will it kill your austerity plan if we go for a steak?"

"Nope. It won't kill any plans at all." Except the plan to make her mine. That plan is dead in the water, and it's already killing me.

CHAPTER 15

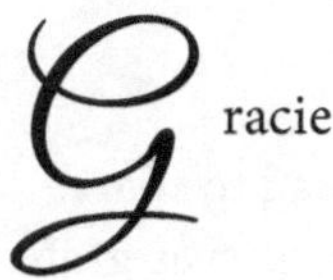racie

"Baked potato with the works?" Our tuxedoed server holds my leather-bound menu in his hands and waits for my decision. I bite my lip and debate.

"Just sour cream and chives. No butter, no bacon." I say the words before I can change my mind. I want the butter, no question, but I know it will probably make Hunter turn green with the amount of extra fat and cholesterol. I decide not to gross him out too much with the zillion calories I'd like to devour on a potato.

"Really?" Hunter cocks his head. "But you love all the butter. What gives?"

"Trying to be a tiny bit healthy. You and Ky are rubbing off, I guess." More like the guilt over watching them say no to baked goods and butter.

He chose a nice place, especially considering that we're both back in our non-futsal clothes after each taking a turn in the locker rooms for a quick shower. But LA people seem to wear jeans everywhere, even to a buttoned-up steak place, so Hunter in his hoodie fits right in, and I look like a regular working stiff.

The restaurant is dark, which works to my advantage because my hair is a hornet's nest after racing around the futsal court, and no amount of smoothing it with wet hands was going to tame it. The less Hunter can examine me in bright light, the better.

We're tucked into a booth in a dimly lit corner of the restaurant, where a three-sided bar divides the room and puts a physical barrier between us and most of the people in the restaurant. I'm not sure if Hunter gets recognized as a sports celebrity when he goes out, but there's little chance of anyone noticing him here. Only his profile is visible, and even then, someone would have to be looking hard to notice him in the dark space.

"And for you, sir?" the server asks.

"Same," he says. "And we'll start with a Caesar salad to share."

I cock my head at him in surprise as soon as the server grabs the wine list and leaves to put in our order. "Same? I thought you were a 'no sour cream, dry chicken breast' kind of guy."

"I told you, Tink. I get a cheat meal once a week. You're my cheat."

I try not to react to the idea that I'm his anything, but it's useless. My skin heats and a little zing in my chest reminds me how much I liked it when he swept me into his arms.

"Okay, works for me. As long as your coach doesn't yell at me when you're dragging because you have dairy in your veins."

He chuckles. "I'm not a monk. I know you think I eat only nuts and seeds, but that's more your brother than me. Besides, we're drinking water, not wine, so there's a little self-restraint."

"I know. I'm giving you a hard time. And I'm not quite the 'sugar cereal and Reddi Whip' gal I pretend to be. I have heard of vegetables." I tilt my head, mock-considering. "I mean, mashed potatoes are vegetables, right?"

"Hundred percent." He shakes his head as though he's giving

up the battle. "Would you rather eat mashed potatoes or french fries? Tough call."

"Both."

"Can't have both. Those are the rules of 'would you rather.'"

I lean back in my chair and do a slow survey of the restaurant before answering. Dark ceramic tiles cover the floors, and the ceiling has distressed beams and wrought-iron chandeliers. There's nothing to absorb the ambient noise, so the place bounces with the energy of every conversation around us. The place is a whirl of loud chatter, metal lids being placed on plates, glasses clinking, and a barely audible jazz soundtrack.

"I wasn't aware there were actual rules to this conversation." I cross my arms.

"Oh, Gracie, haven't you ever played 'would you rather?'"

I shake my head. "No, and now I'm worried it's like truth or dare, and I'll end up having to tell you my darkest secrets or run a lap around the restaurant flapping my arms like a chicken."

He laughs. "As much as I'd love to see that, you're safe. The rules are that I'll give you a choice between two things. You have to choose one or the other, and you need to do it fast."

"Okay, I think I can handle that."

"Great. *Star Wars* or *Star Trek*."

"*Star Wars*."

"Big dogs or small dogs."

"Big."

He smiles. "Good answer. Bogie approves."

I wag a finger. "Hey, no editorializing."

"Fine. Brush your teeth before morning coffee or after?"

"Both."

"Ah, interesting." He shakes his head at himself. "Sorry. Okay, morning person or night owl?"

"Night." I wait for some sort of commentary, but he only nods, observing me with his lips pressed together. "Okay, I know you're thinking something. Do we need to talk about it?"

Our server interrupts by wheeling over a cart with Caesar salad ingredients and proceeds to make the salad tableside. He tears the lettuce into pieces in a large wooden bowl and makes paste from anchovies and egg yolks before beginning to beat in oil, vinegar, and some Dijon mustard. I watch in rapt fascination, taking mental notes so I can do this myself sometime.

He adds croutons and tosses the salad before dividing it onto two plates. We toast each other with our water glasses before digging in.

"Oh my god, this is so, so good," I say with a mouthful of food.

Hunter nods. "Yup."

I take another bite, and we eat in silence for a moment. I feel Hunter's eyes on me and worry I must have dressing dripping down my chin. With the initial pangs of hunger satisfied by a few bites, I wipe my mouth and put my napkin back in my lap. Hunter cuts through a large piece of lettuce and uses his knife to fold the perfect-sized bite onto his fork.

"Okay, I think it's my turn," I say, putting down my fork. "Would you rather..." I realize I didn't think this through. I'm dying to get off the hot seat and ask Hunter a few probing questions, but I don't have a ready list. Brain racing, I come up with one. "Jane Austen or Harlen Coben?"

"Ooh, tough. I'm a mood reader. Today...Coben."

"Sleep in a tent or sleep in an RV?"

"Tent." That surprises me because he seems like he'd want a cushier bed, but I keep going.

"Ocean or lake?" I take a sip of water.

"Depends, am I skinny-dipping?"

The water sprays from my lips, and I'm sure I turn red as a beet. "Hunter!"

"Honest question."

"What does it matter?"

"Trust me, it *matters*." If I wasn't already fanning my hot face, this kicks it up another notch. It's all I can do not to picture him standing naked atop a rock, ready to jump into a lake. Okay, now I'm picturing it.

He's right. It matters.

And god, does he look amazing. All broad shoulders, trim waist, muscled soccer thighs, ripped abs. My hand shoots to my mouth because I may have drooled. I don't even need to picture him naked on the beach, sun streaming down, ready to race into the ocean, but I can't help myself.

I lean back in my chair, skin damp, feeling utter defeat. "You win."

"What do you mean, I win?"

"If the object of this game was to evoke utter mortification from me, you definitely win."

He steadies his eyes on me, watching quietly as I attempt to tame my hair into a ponytail to get it off my two-hundred-degree neck. I fish in my purse for a rubber band and tie it out of my face, but a few strands break free and fall in front of my eyes. Better, so he can't see the embarrassment.

Hunter leans toward me until his face is inches from mine. When he speaks, I can feel his breath on my skin, but I'm not about to back away. "The object of the game was to get to know you better." His voice is a low growl, and it feels like flames licking my neck. I resist the urge to fan my skin even though I might spontaneously combust.

He nods slowly. "Mission accomplished."

CHAPTER 16

unter

IF I HAD a photo of the look on Gracie's face, I'd tuck it away in my wallet for those times when I need reminding that sometimes life gives you everything you ever wanted.

In this case, it takes them away just as quickly. Our dinner was only supposed to be two people with hunger pangs satisfying a bet over a futsal game. But I'm such a horny asshole that I had to turn it into a game, a test of wills, an opportunity to see how far Gracie would let me go before putting on the brakes.

Every time I embarrass her, it brings out that berry glow in her cheeks, and I feel like I've won every damn lottery.

The guy with the monster ego wants to think it's because she feels some fraction of the heat that thrums in my veins the closer I move to her. It was all I could do during dinner not to yank her chair next to mine, take her chin in the palm of my hand, and find out if her lips taste as good as they look.

I'm not an animal, and I don't fucking dare push her to where she doesn't want to go. But what if she wants to go there? As each day passes, the more I need to know.

As I drive her back to the Devils headquarters so that she can get her car, I feel a tension between us that didn't exist before. It's the crackle of electricity in the damp night air before a lightning storm that threatens every tree and bit of dry brush for miles. And I want to fucking burn everything around us to the ground.

I know I can't. And I know it's not even for my benefit that I need to keep my hands to myself. She took the job with the Devils as an important career move. She needs it to go well so she can stay on track and find her way back to a better job in Silicon Valley. I can't be the jerk who jeopardizes that because I can't keep my dick in my pants.

Kyler warned me, and now I'm warning myself.

Hands. Fucking. Off.

"You okay?" Gracie's quiet voice snaps me out of the conversation in my head and makes me realize I haven't spoken to her for nearly ten minutes.

"Sorry. Yeah, I'm good. Thinking about the exhibition game next week."

"Oh. D'you get nervous about those even though they don't count in the team record?"

"Yeah, it almost doesn't matter if it's a league game or not. Everything counts. Coaches watch everything we do, and the biggest thing is to play hard and not get injured." I laugh, realizing she probably knows things from analyzing my performance numbers that I don't even know. "I'm sure that's hard to believe, from someone like me who is a little lamb on the field."

Now it's her turn to laugh. "You do your job, that's for sure."

I wait, hoping she'll elaborate. It's not for the ego massage that I want her to say something positive about my game. I want to know that she thinks I'm talented. I want her to see me as more than another body with stats and probability. I want her to see that I have something to offer her, even though I can't offer her anything.

"Anyhow, I get in my head sometimes," I mutter.

"Don't we all. I just figured out a way to make it my job."

"Never thought of it that way."

She's silent for so long afterward that I glance at her face, which is lined in concentration. Before I can ask what's wrong, she blurts, "By the way, there's similar language in the code of conduct here. About relationships within the company. I checked."

"Oh. Yeah? What made you check?" I ask as casually as I can, but I'm dying to know if she's considering a relationship with someone at the Devils organization.

"Being thorough. Figured it was good to know."

"Data is good. Someone taught me that."

That gets me a hollow laugh, and I wait to see if she'll elaborate. She turns her head to look out the window and says nothing more. I pull into the parking lot, which is mostly empty. It's easy to spot her little electric car lined up precisely between the white lines delineating the parking space.

Rain still lightly pelts the windshield, so I lean over and fish an umbrella from my back seat, then carry it over to her side of the car. Holding it over her head, I walk her the few paces to her car and wait for her to unlock her door.

This is where I have to stop myself from following my instinct, which says to lower the umbrella and let the tiny rain-drops fall on us. To pull her in close and kiss her the way I've wanted to all night long. To press her against the side of her car and let her know how much I want her.

But this is Gracie, and I fight every instinct that tells me to get closer to her. I need to step away even though it fucking hurts.

"Good night, Tink." I give her a kiss on the cheek like the

gentleman I most certainly am not, not when all my thoughts are about how good it would feel to be inside her.

"Good night. Thanks again for dinner." She offers me a smile, slides into her car, and closes the door like it's the easiest thing in the world to say goodbye. And I stand there, wishing I had something sharper and wittier to say. Then I might have a chance at making her stay.

CHAPTER 17

*H*unter

OKAY, she may actually be trying to kill me.

It's the only explanation for why Gracie stands in the kitchen wearing only a flimsy tank top and tiny shorts. Why is this what she sleeps in?

Sunlight streams through the window at that early morning angle, looking even brighter than the pale yellow should be. It's almost blinding, bouncing off the gleaming stainless steel appliances in Kyler's kitchen. But that's not what has my focus.

The light has the effect of making Gracie's outfit almost translucent, and I swear I can see every outline of her body in stark relief. The perky roundness of her ass. A narrow strip of pale skin peeking over the waistband. The generous curve of her breasts, which she hides under those baggy shirts... I'll never be able to unsee what I'm staring at with my mouth agape right now.

And she's swaying from side to side as she stirs her coffee, grooving to music on her headphones, I imagine, though I can't see them through her mane of uncombed hair.

She turns, startled to find me there. Her arms instantly cross over her chest, and she takes a step backward, which traps her against the kitchen counter. Holding up a teaspoon in defense, she blinks at me like a cornered animal and pulls out one of her earbuds.

"You gonna murder me with that?" I ask, mirroring her stance with a smirk.

She looks at the spoon as though noticing it for the first time, and her hand falls. "Don't think I couldn't."

"Death by stirring?"

Her features relax, but she doesn't quite smile. "Exactly."

"Sorry I startled you."

"It's okay. I didn't hear you." She points at the remaining earbud. "I like a little Taylor Swift in the morning."

"Who doesn't?"

I should leave and give her some space for her morning ritual. It certainly won't kill me to wait ten minutes before making my protein smoothie, but I can't make myself walk away.

Gracie solves the problem for me, grabbing her coffee cup and slipping past me. "Have a great day," she says as I turn for one more glimpse of her tight ass under those shorts. But without the sunlight, all I get is a look at baggy gray shorts and the swish of hair trailing down her back.

I am a goddamn pervert, and I should be ashamed of myself for ogling her this way. Yet I feel oddly satisfied to have one more tiny shred of information she probably didn't mean to give me.

But except for the few "would you rather" answers I managed to glean the other night, everything else about her is still a mystery.

It's why I do the smart thing and head off to practice an hour early and take my frustrations out on some barbells.

~

A COUPLE OF HOURS LATER, the sun is hot and bright, and I should be focused on Dario Conner, our striker, who's dribbling toward me with fire in his eyes. He's as determined to get past me and take a shot as I am to take the ball away from him, preferably leaving him on his ass.

He and I work hardest in practice when our emotions run high. He gives me the best workouts and training to take on any striker in the league, so we spend a lot of time together. Off the field, less so, because he's a single dad and focused on raising his five-year-old son. But he shows up ready to play, with his head in the game, every damn time.

It's more than I can say for myself right now. He gets past me easily and sends our keeper diving at a shot straight into the corner.

Coach blows his whistle, and I know what he'll say before he's uttered a syllable. "Reyes, you lost focus."

I nod, jogging back to the line of my teammates, warming up with the same drill. Defender pitted against offense, each of us matched in a one-on-one that shows exactly who's bringing their A game. If this were closer to the regular season, my lack of focus, even for a few minutes, would be a big problem.

I raise a hand, signaling to my coach that I'm back on track. I have to be. Thinking about my roommate in a flimsy tank top is not going to get me there.

Our exhibition game against the San Francisco Strikers is coming up in a couple weeks, and it's the team's first matchup with them since the playoffs. The Devils social media feed has ramped up its postings, getting fans ready for the new season. There will be jersey giveaways and free donuts if we score a certain number of goals—all manner of incentives to get fans into the stadium.

And we need to do our jobs on the field.

It's not lost on me that some of the fans will be happier to see me back than my own teammates seem to be. It makes me yearn to get back to the regular season, where I can prove that I'm more valuable than some of my teammates think I am.

My body feels overworked from the extra sessions after our regular training. Jimmy keeps warning me to take it easy, telling me my muscles need recovery time after being torn down by extra weight and reps. I keep telling him I'm fine.

The reality is that I need the energy release these days. It feels like the only way to keep my aggression at bay so I can show at least a tiny bit of restraint on the field.

"Or get laid, man." Jimmy's advice last night might normally have been a good fix. There's a reason I've always had a healthy sex life, and the women who've come and gone have seemed more than willing to help in that regard.

But now, the idea of meaningless sex to get my rocks off leaves me cold. I don't want to think that my reasons have anything to do with a certain brunette roommate working in the corporate offices, but who am I kidding?

My eyes travel upward to the floor where she works. The sun hits the glass hard, and there wouldn't be any way to see inside the offices. Still, I can't help sneaking one more glance in that direction. Wondering whether she's thinking about me.

racie

THE CONVERSATION with my work friend Ashley goes something like this:

"Hey, you're still new in town. Let's hang out, and then I'll introduce you to some people."

"Oh, you're sweet," I say. "But I don't want to be a burden during your free time." In other words, I'm a homebody, and I don't want to disappoint her if she thinks I'm fun.

"Nonsense," Ashley says, which is how I find myself at lunch, trying to come up with something to talk about. I settle on our common element, work, and try to glean some information about corporate communications, which I know nothing about.

"What are you working on this week?" I want to roll my eyes at myself for asking the worst question ever.

We're sitting in the cafeteria, where tables for four break up the cavernous space and a large hot food counter takes up one wall. The choices are pretty standard work lunch fare—sandwiches, salads, burritos, chips, drinks.

My burrito is getting cold while I decide whether to pick it up or cut into it. It's covered in red sauce, so I opt to cut it down the middle. Melted cheese oozes out, and I scoop up a forkful on a tortilla chip.

Ashley munches through a Greek salad, avoiding the olives.

"I handle all media requests for interviews with players, and I head up our social media team, which is a major way we stay in touch with fans. You know, behind-the-scenes videos, player spotlights, days when we mic them and hear their commentary while they run drills."

She seems a little bored answering my question about what she does for the team. Like she's said these words a hundred times and doesn't have to think about them.

"Have you been doing this a long time?" I'm fully prepared with questions and small talk to get us through our first lunch, but she stops me with a raised hand.

"Eh, no more work talk. We both do that all day long. Let's talk about something fun. Are you dating anyone?"

Her directness startles me, and I almost choke on a bite of burrito. I manage to save myself with a sip of water, but not before I feel like the room gets about ten degrees warmer.

I look around to see if anyone is within earshot before answering. The room is about half empty, and the people eating in here are mostly corporate types who work in the building. Not a player in sight.

"Um, no. Not really."

"So sort of?" she presses, eyes wide and interested for the first time since we got our food.

"No, not at all, actually."

Ashley snaps her fingers. "Well, we're going to have to change that, aren't we?"

Unsure what to say, I give her a guilty shrug. Does she know me well enough to set me up on a date, or is the only necessary criteria that I'm single?

"It was rhetorical. Of course the answer is yes. You're so eligible. And you probably don't know anyone except people in our offices. And the players." Her voice takes a conspiratorial tone. "Don't date a player. That never ends well."

"You're sweet, but I'm good. Really. I'm still figuring out the city. I'll get to dating eventually."

"Nonsense. I know so many good people." She starts scrolling her social media and showing me pictures of various men. They're all versions of the same guy—professional, thirtyish, clean cut. Normally, if I had a type, that would be it.

So why am I suddenly examining the photos to see if they have tattoos? That was never my thing. I try to push away the thought that it might be my thing now that I've seen the magnificent arms of Hunter Reyes. Maybe he's the source of my sudden boredom with average-looking men.

"Thanks." I realize Ashley is staring at me, and apparently, I haven't responded to the photos on her feed. "They all look nice."

"They are. Totally. This one is Steve, my boyfriend." She zooms in on an image of her with her arms around a tall, smiling guy who looks like her other friends. "We met on a dating app about a year ago. Still going strong."

I take a closer look at Steve sitting on a sailboat with a group of his friends. Each holds a drink in his hand and smiles broadly at the camera, wearing sunglasses or a baseball hat. They all look wholesome. If you'd asked me two months ago what kind of guy I'd end up with, I'd have pointed at any one of them and felt like he was a good bet.

The only thing that's changed now is the amount of time I've spent with Hunter, and that has no business changing my outlook on dating.

"Aw, that's awesome."

She nods. "He's a sweetie. And he has lots of single friends." I start to wonder if her mission to find me a date is a way to find common ground. If I date one of Steve's friends, we can hang out as a couple. It doesn't sound like a terrible idea, especially since I need something to distract me from thinking about Hunter all the time.

The bet he and I made drifts into my mind, but I dismiss all concern. One date with the friend of a "sweetie" is not going to lead to a hookup. That's not me. Hunter is all but certain to lose that bet, although he's trying pretty hard to hold up his end. I've come and gone at some early and late hours, and there's been no sign of a woman at Ky's house.

For the first time, I consider whether I've made a sucker's bet, based on rumors that have no bearing on the guy I've gotten to know a little bit since he moved in. It makes me think about Hunter more than I should.

Mixing work and dating did not end well for me before, so I'm the last person who should be entertaining the thought. Besides, even if Hunter isn't dating a string of women, it doesn't mean he wants to date me. We couldn't be more opposite, and if he does have a type, it's certainly not a curvy nerd girl who bakes.

He and I are a non-starter, so maybe the best thing I can do is go on a date with someone else. Someone who has nothing to do with soccer or data. A pharmacist, perhaps. Or a drummer. He doesn't need to have tattoos. He doesn't need carved muscles. He needs to be nice. And maybe even a little bit nerdy so I don't feel nervous around him.

"Okay," I agree. "Set me up."

CHAPTER 19

unter

GRACIE HAS BEEN LINGERING in the living room for the last hour wearing a blazer and the kind of dress I've never seen her wear to work. It's a black slip of a dress that hugs every curve, and I can't make myself look away.

It's short, leaving a few inches of skin visible above her knees, which is the view I've become accustomed to whenever I catch her in that little outfit she wears to sleep. And while I'm grateful to see her legs on display, I'm wondering why they're on display. And who they're on display for...because I'm pretty certain it's not me.

I've been watching her from the kitchen, where I'm sipping a berry smoothie and leaning my elbows on the counter, staring at my phone. But really, I'm staring at her.

Every so often, she looks toward the front door, which hasn't moved or made a sound, so I'm not sure why she's so jittery. I do have my theories, however.

"You waiting for someone?" I ask, finally. Her nervous energy is making me nervous, and at least talking to her gives me an excuse to walk over to where she's sitting. That's when I notice the low cut of the dress. It's different from the crew neck sweaters she wears to work. Even when she throws on some piece of team gear, it's usually the zippered jacket over a crew neck shirt. She doesn't show skin, which is only appropriate for the workplace.

I've taken to feeling kind of special being the only one at the Devils franchise who sees her in less, not that I run around telling people our head of data operations has knockout legs and great tits. It's my secret.

"Um, yeah, I am." She adjusts her dress, giving me a glimpse of a black bra cup beneath it. Her cleavage makes a seductive V that has me following the curve of her breasts as low as I can see.

When I look up, I catch her surprised look at me ogling her. "You look good, Tink. Are you getting ready to lose our bet?"

She looks down as the flush invades her cheeks and starts to adjust the dress.

"Hey, wait. No. I didn't mean to imply you're out for a hookup, only that no guy would be able to resist you. If you're going out with a guy, he's lucky to be with you. That's all. Not because you have a gorgeous rack."

"Hunter!"

"Sorry! Just being honest."

"Well, stop!"

"Sorry," I say again. But I'm not sorry. Riling her up and earning that blush has become my new favorite hobby. As I return us to the bantering I'm used to, I forget for a moment that she's dressed like that for another guy. The thought comes barreling back, and I frown.

"So who's the guy, anyway?" I ask.

She looks away. "Blind date. Ashley set me up," she mumbles.

I feel both relieved and depressed by the idea. Relieved

because she doesn't even know him, which means there's a decent chance she won't like him enough for a second date. But what if she does? His liking her isn't even a discussion. The second he realizes her fierce brainpower resides in a package that beautiful, he'll be picking out engagement rings.

So why aren't you working harder to win her over?

The thought comes unbidden, but I have an easy answer. Because I'm a hotheaded athlete who didn't finish college. I'm not fucking good enough for Gracie Albright, and she'll prove that by kicking ass at her job and moving back to Silicon Valley, where she belongs with the other geniuses.

The thought makes my already dismal mood sink a little further into the abyss.

"Good. Great. Glad to hear it." I don't mean any of those words.

I nod. She nods.

"Um, do I look okay?" she asks.

I stare at her in disbelief. I can't believe she doesn't know the answer, but this woman doesn't fish for compliments. Eyes squinting and lower lip trembling, she looks beautiful in a way I've never seen in any of the women I've dated.

Her round eyes make her look innocent, even though I know she's smart as a whip. The delicate curve of her nose and rounded cheeks are soft, but there's toughness in the line of her mouth, which can snap out sassy one-liners and unleash monologues about science and data.

That's saying nothing about her curves and milky skin that has me jerking off in the shower most nights, thinking about how good it would feel to touch her.

And this woman…is asking me if she looks okay.

"You look fucking great."

Her eyes go a little glassy, and her throat works as she swallows. The words seem to calm her. "Thank you."

The rasp of her voice gives me the slightest inkling that the compliment affects her, which means maybe I affect her. It's the only sign I need. For now.

A second later, the doorbell rings, and she jumps up, suddenly nervous again like a hummingbird on crack, smoothing her outfit and her hair instead of opening the door.

I wait for her to walk toward the door, but she stands frozen, looking at the entryway like it might swallow her whole. "Want me to get it?" I ask.

She bites down on her bottom lip, and it's all I can do not to close the distance between us and replace her teeth with my own. It's all I can do not to pull her against my body so I can feel her soft curves against me and tell her to forget all about her date.

But reason takes over, and I retreat to the kitchen, far enough away that I can offer moral support if she needs it, but out of view of the front door. "You've got this, Tink. Go get 'em." I try to give her my most convincing vote of confidence, but I'm hardly rooting for this guy. I'm doing what seems like the right thing to do even if I hate it.

Gracie smooths the skirt of her dress and takes a deep breath before yanking the door open. Leaning against the kitchen counter, where I wish Gracie was next to me on a barstool, I see a blond guy who looks like he stepped out of a J Crew catalog in a navy blazer and khaki pants. With his boat shoes, he's a walking ad for a yacht club. All he needs is a captain's hat.

He smiles at Gracie like he's won the lottery because he fucking has. At least the guy is smart enough to realize it. He introduces himself as Bart, and I want to throttle Ashley. I make a mental note to say something controversial at our next press conference and give Ashley an extra mess to clean up.

"I was thinking we'd go to R&D Grill, get some drinks, then head to Mama's to watch the Dodgers, more drinks, then, you know, we'll see."

Alarm bells start ringing in my head because this guy already seems like a douche. First of all, R&D, known colloquially as "rich and divorced," is a notorious hookup scene. Why would he take her there on a date? If he's a regular there and wants to show his swagger, that's a red flag right there. Or maybe he's clueless, which isn't much better.

"Oh, um, sure. Sounds good," Gracie says, shifting from one foot to the other.

"Great." Captain Bart trails a hand down her arm in a way that's far too familiar for someone she's just met, and Gracie flinches. I flinch too, half primed to launch from my spot in the kitchen and whisk her out of his reach.

"Shall we?" he asks, tipping his head toward the open door.

"Um, sure?" Gracie sounds unconvinced, which raises my dude antenna. If she's having second thoughts, should I do something? I'm not above faking an aneurysm here in the kitchen to give her a reason to abort mission.

Before I can say or do anything to stop this date from happening, Bart escorts her out the door with a hand on her ass. If this is what she wants, I need to let her go.

But, I tell myself, if she gives me a sign that she's having second thoughts, all bets are off.

Before she's out of sight, Gracie turns and gives me a plaintive look, squeezing her eyes shut like she's being taken against her will. Is that the sign I need? Maybe.

Moving to the kitchen window, I will Bart to take his hand off her ass, but he doesn't. I suppose it should give me a minor sense of relief that he's otherwise acting like a gentleman, opening the passenger car door for her and helping her inside, but the cynical side of me thinks he's using the gesture as another excuse to touch her.

He's not exactly pushing the boundaries of consent, but I can see her stiffen each time he puts his hands on her. The idea of her not consenting causes a surge of rage to slice through my gut.

Gracie is a grown woman, and I'm sure she can take care of herself. She's gotten by for years before I showed up in her life, so I shouldn't overinflate my importance or act like she needs me to rescue her.

Then again, I have no plans tonight.

racie

THE FIRST THING Bart tells me on our drive over to R&D is that he was there last night and he's still recovering from the hangover.

"Normally, I know the drill. A full glass of water and two aspirins by the bedside at all times, right? Only last night, I think I passed out before I could do the right thing." He laughs and guns the engine of his Mustang. I look out the window and wonder what the appropriate torture for Ashley is going to be for sticking me with Bart.

I should give her the benefit of the doubt, I suppose. How could she know that a hard-partying guy like Bart wouldn't be my soulmate? And hey, maybe he can be. I need to get past what he's saying about the past three nights of drinking at different bars and find out.

"What do you do for fun?" I ask.

"This," he says, eyebrows bouncing. "Spending time with a

beautiful lady. Touch is my love language." I feel an actual lurch of bile that I need to suppress at his cheesy response. I may not be the most social being out there, but I've been on plenty of dates and had a couple of boyfriends. I know sometimes we all get nervous and say silly things we wish we could take back. Bart doesn't seem to have that self-reflective gene.

"I was thinking more like pickleball," I mutter, wishing I'd asked Ashley more questions before letting her set me up.

He rests a hand on my knee. It feels far too personal to have his thumb rubbing my bare skin, so I shift so his hand falls to the seat and try to make it seem like I'm fascinated by something outside. "I didn't know there was a Sweet Cream place so close to West Hollywood."

"Yeah, right there." He drapes his arm over the back of my seat instead, and I decide I can live with that. As we drive, my mind drifts back to Hunter standing in the kitchen, his muscled, tattooed forearms on full display, the sinewy bulk of his shoulders straining against the thin fabric of his shirt.

His face was a complicated maze of emotions, and I can't help thinking maybe some of them had to do with not liking the idea of me going on a date. I push those thoughts from my head because I need to deal with the present, where Bart is honking at the car in front of us for slowing down.

"Dude, figure it out!" he yells out his window. The guy in front of us gives him the finger out the window and stops the car at the valet stand at R&D Grill. Great, now we get to dine at the same place. But Bart's car shoots into traffic to go around the other car, earning him some honks as he cuts people off. "I'm not paying seventeen dollars for valet," he says, zooming down the block and taking a hard right at the next street.

Slowly, we creep up the road as he checks each available break between cars to see if it's a driveway. Finally, when we're about four blocks up, someone pulls out of a spot. Bart parallel parks and hops out of the car.

I open my own door, and we walk the four blocks to the bar. "I get it. Seventeen dollars to park is insane," I say.

"Right? I'd rather spend that on another drink." Bart walks at a quick clip, as though he can't get that drink soon enough. Funny, I feel the same way.

The bar is packed. It's only a small, eight-seat bar with a couple of high-top tables against a window that looks out onto the sidewalk, where more than a dozen people are waiting to squeeze inside. Bart waves at the host, who ushers us past the crowd and over to a tight corner of the bar near the kitchen.

From our vantage point, I see that half of the place is a restaurant, hence the "grill" in the name. It seems less loud and crowded at those tables, but I try not to look too longingly in that direction. I want to be a good date, even if I can already tell this will be a one-and-done. It's the people-pleasing part of me.

Bart flags down the bartender and asks me what I'd like. "Glass of white wine. Thanks." He orders himself an old-fashioned, leans his back against the bar, and smiles at me. His eyes dart around, surveying the crowd as though he's checking to see if he recognizes anyone.

"Are you a regular here?" I ask.

He nods. "Yeah, I get here about once a week. Sometimes twice. It's kind of a scene, but you know how it is when you're single. You go from here to Bud's to L&O." He laughs, and I don't bother telling him that I've never been to any of those places.

The bartender pours my wine into an oversized glass, which Bart hands to me. Our hands brush as he transfers it, and I'm hyperaware of the contact. Hyperaware that there's zero feeling when his hand touches mine, except the slightly clammy feel of his skin. It's nothing like the crazy zing I feel at the barest hairline graze from Hunter.

A barstool opens up, and Bart slides onto it, moving me with both hands on my waist so I'm standing between his knees. I'm still close enough to the standing room only crowd that I get jostled when people move past me to and from the bar, but I don't want to stand even closer to the bulge in his pants. It doesn't feel good that he keeps touching me. I'm not flattered, and I don't feel the least bit of chemistry.

Does he? Could he possibly feel anything when I'm about as turned on as a mildewed towel?

Maybe this is dating in LA. Perhaps it's different from what I'm used to after so many dinners with techies who were happy to get out of their cubicles and take off their headphones. And I'm including myself in that lot. If this is what I'm in for by saying yes to blind dates, I think I'd rather stay at home and sneak glances at my hot roommate. At least that makes me feel something.

The bartender finishes making Bart's drink and winks as he hands him a shot to go with it. Bart downs the shot and takes a healthy gulp of his drink before holding his glass out to mine. "Cheers. To Ashley, the matchmaker."

We clink glasses, and I take a sip of wine. Bart locks me between his knees, and through the thin silk of my dress, I feel his hand on the back of my thigh. If I step forward, it forces me closer to him. If I move back, I'm pressing my flesh into his hand.

"Take your goddamn hands off her." The rumble of that deep voice sets chills along my skin.

Bart's brows furrow in confusion, and he looks from me to the hulking figure of Hunter standing next to us. "You heard me," Hunter says with clear menace in his voice.

"She's my date. You can go pound sand," Bart says. He slugs down the last of his drink and raises the glass toward the bartender to ask for another.

"Doesn't give you the right to manhandle her."

Bart's hand leaves my thigh, and he raises them where Hunter can see them. "Happy now? Not that it's any of your fucking business."

"That depends," Hunter says, his breath ghosting my cheek

and making me feel things that Bart's sloppy hands never could. "Are you happy, Gracie?"

Bart's lips spread into a smile. "Oh, so you two know each other? Is this part of a game or something?" His legs tighten around my hips, and he scoots forward on his stool as though he's been invited to a threesome.

"It's. Not. A. Game." Every word that falls from Hunter's mouth hits my ears like champagne bubbles, lulling me into a fizzy sort of dream that starts and ends with him. "Back the fuck away from her. Give her some goddamn personal space."

Bart's knees drop open, and I take a step back. "Better," Hunter says. Before I can gather my wits, he nods at me and pushes through the crowd, leaving me on my date. I can see him heading toward the back of the restaurant, and before I think too long about it, I tell Bart to give me a minute and chase him.

"Sure, I'll be here," Bart says, looking over my head as though there might be someone better he can talk to. I hope there is.

When I get to the back of the restaurant, I see Hunter in the alcove past the open kitchen. There's a hallway with vintage photos of Los Angeles and candles burning on a narrow table against the wall. Hunter is sitting on a toile-covered bench situated opposite the restroom doors.

"How are you here?" I ask.

He laughs and pantomimes driving, then makes a walking gesture with two fingers. I cross my arms and shake my head, unimpressed by the explanation.

"Okay, fine. *Why* are you here?"

"I came to check on you."

"You what?" I can't process the information, unsure if I'm flattered that he cares enough to check on me or annoyed that he came to spy on my date. Like I'm such a social basket case that I need him to check on me. If I wasn't constantly reminded that he's Kyler's best friend, it hits me squarely now. He sees me as his responsibility, like a kid sister you watch out for on the playground when she tries the monkey bars for the first time.

I want to remind him that I'm thirty-three and this isn't my first date, but there's a small part of me that likes that he came here to look out for me. I have no idea what to make of that. Or him.

He hikes a thumb over his shoulder in the direction of Bart. "Back at the house, he seemed a little overly invested in touching you. Just wanted to make sure you were okay."

"Overly invested?"

"Handsy. Are you into that? Should I leave you alone?"

My temper flares. I need to set him straight. "I'm not some newbie dater who can't handle herself, if that's what you're thinking. I carry pepper spray, FYI."

He smirks, nodding. "I don't doubt it for a minute. Look, I'm not trying to offend you. If you tell me you're into him or whatever, I'll head home. No harm, no foul."

I should tell him to go. But I don't want that.

Reaching slowly toward me, he pulls at my forearm, gently uncrossing it from the other one. Then he takes both of my hands and tugs them down to my sides, urging me to relax. My shoulders fall, and I take a deeper breath. Standing in front of him, I puzzle through the complexities that are this man.

One minute, he seems more than happy to shove me out the door on a date. The next, he steps in because his radar correctly tells him I'm not into Bart.

Letting go of one hand, he releases his grip on the other one and lets his slide away almost entirely. But then he wraps one finger around mine and hangs on, keeping the vaguest connection but not letting go. He looks at me, but his dark gray eyes are unreadable in the dim light of the hallway.

I don't need to see him. I go by feel, my body quivering at the merest touch of his hand.

"Take me with you," I whisper. I don't know what I want from him yet, but I know that I want something. I also know that I'll follow him out the door in a heartbeat if that's what he's asking.

Even in the dim light, I see his eyes darken to a molten charcoal. The hungry way he's looking at me makes me want to slide onto his lap and feel him between my legs.

"I'll take you anywhere you want to go, Tink." I shudder as the images rush through my mind of all the places I want him to take me and the way it will feel. Slowly in the back seat of his car. Hard against the kitchen counter from behind. Languidly on the sofa bed in his room with his clean scent wrapped in the sheets and our sweat-slicked bodies moving in perfect sync.

My eyes drift shut as my imagination runs to a place I've never allowed it to go.

I'm a woman who fantasizes about solving complex algorithmic problems. I don't fantasize about men like this.

Until now. Until this man blows everything I knew about myself to bits.

A small moan escapes my lips, and my eyes pop open to see if he heard, but the noisy restaurant saves me from embarrassment.

A slim warning about the danger to my job wriggles into my brain, but I banish it.

"I want to go to a hotel." The words are as surprising as if someone else said them.

"Done."

Hunter stands and takes a firmer hold of my hand. It's the only place he's touching me, but my skin flames like he's holding a match. It's a world away from the clammy, uncomfortable response I had to Bart's unwelcome touch.

I want to follow my instinct, to be whisked away without considering any consequences except deep sexual satisfaction, but the good girl in me doesn't want to leave my date in the lurch. I stop.

"Do I need to say goodbye to Bart, tell him I'm leaving?" I look in the direction of the bar.

In two strides, Hunter is back in the restaurant, never letting go of my hand, and peering over the crowd. He turns back toward me and shakes his head. "He seems to have occupied himself." He frowns and rolls his eyes. "Send him a text."

He takes out his phone and fires off his own text. When he gets a reply, he nods. "Bogie's dog sitter. All set."

For the first time since we bumped into each other at the airport, I feel free to look at him without being sneaky about it. Turning my face up to his, I take in all the features I've pictured as I drifted off to sleep each night, idly wishing I could touch them.

I reach for the side of his face and run a finger from his sculpted cheekbone down to his chin, letting the tip rest on his skin before pulling away. His eyelids droop as he lets in a long, slow breath. I know exactly how he feels.

He reaches for my hand and places my thumb against his lower lip, and I slowly rub it back and forth, feeling the contours until his lips part and he gently sucks my thumb into his mouth. His tongue rolls over it enough to fire up every nerve ending in my body. I feel hot, breathless, dizzy.

Letting my thumb go, he brings my hand between us, holding it in a firm grip. I'm vaguely aware of the restaurant sounds behind me, and I know it's my last chance to turn around and resume my date like the good girl I've always been.

But I don't want to be that girl right now. I don't want to think about mixing work and romance. I just want this man.

Hunter guides me toward the back door of the restaurant, and he kicks it open. The damp night air hits my face as we walk outside, and for the moment, I'm not looking back.

CHAPTER 21

$\mathcal{H}$unter

WE BARELY TALK on the drive to the hotel. My mind is dancing with a minefield of thoughts, each one more frantic than the next. *I want her. God, do I want her.*

But as we roll through town, a newer, more calming realization takes hold—she wants me, maybe as much as I want her. All of those stolen looks and small moments around the house weren't a product of my wishful thinking.

In the time we've shared Kyler's house, I've learned enough to know her choices are deliberate, and my chest tightens at the idea that she's choosing me.

I don't want to piss off Kyler, but fuck him. He's a grown-up, and if he's my closest friend, he should be happy that I want to do right by his sister. I'm sure there are plenty of vacancies at half the hotels in town, but I want to take her someplace special. I also don't want to drive very far to get there.

The first place that comes to mind, since we're in West Holly-

124

wood, is Château Marmont. The team has been hosted at some meet and greets there, and there's enough celebrity clientele that the front desk staff can usher us to a room without a lot of eyes headed our way.

That's good for me, given that I don't need any more controversies surrounding my career, and going into a hotel room with a woman definitely would get some media attention. Not to mention that Gracie's bosses would not like it one bit.

Gracie looks out the passenger window, and I worry she's losing her nerve. The way her eyes bored into me in the back of the restaurant and her clear instructions left no question about what she wanted, but maybe she's getting cold feet. I can't see enough of her face to tell.

I squeeze her knee and leave my hand there. "Hey." She turns from the window, and I see her bottom lip between her teeth. As I suspected, she's nervous. "We don't have to do anything you don't want to do. I was trying to get you out of an awkward date, that's all. If you want to hang out and order room service, that's great with me."

She nods, but her expression is complicated—neither a smile nor a frown, eyes narrowed in concentration. "Okay, sounds good."

I want to ask her to elaborate, but it's enough to know she wants to be here with me. However it unfolds is okay. The last thing Gracie needs is another caveman making her feel uncomfortable. I want to get her to the hotel so badly that I'm cursing every red light under my breath.

When I pull into the valet area and an attendant opens our doors, all of the frenzied haste I felt moments before fades into the distant buzz of the city below us. It's so quiet up here in the Sunset hills, and for the first time since my house burned down, I feel grounded. Sure, it's the warm evening air and the starry black skies, but it's something else that has nothing to do with my surroundings.

Walking around to Gracie's side of the car, I hold out my hand, an offer I hope she'll take. I'm not about to force it. If she's had enough of handsy men for one night, I'll follow her inside and make good on my room service offer. I haven't eaten since lunch, and I wouldn't mind some comfort food on a tray delivered to an upper floor of the hotel.

The softness of her skin lights up a deep part of my heart, and the feelings I've worked to repress spring free and hit me hard. I don't just want room service with her. I don't think I only want one night with her.

Easy, Sport.

I pull open the door of the lobby and place my hand on the small of her back to escort her inside. Maybe it's my imagination, but every time I touch her, it feels like she sinks deeper into my hand, supple and willing.

At the reception desk, I ask for a room for tonight, and the clerk starts typing on her computer, offering me different options. "A suite," I confirm. "That's perfect. And how late can we get room service?"

The clerk barely looks up, still typing. "You can get anything from our restaurant menu until eleven, and then the late-night menu until six-thirty in the morning."

I try to catch Gracie's eye to confirm my willingness to hang out and eat, no strings attached, but I find her looking at the floor. She takes a step to the side, putting some space between us.

I hate it.

I reach for her and gently put my arm over her shoulders before pulling her back toward me. With her blazer folded neatly over one arm, she takes a step closer, but she's stiff beneath my arm, so I let it fall from her shoulders.

Bending my head to hers, I tip her chin up so she'll look at me. "Hey, are you okay? We don't have to do this," I whisper. "You tell me what you're comfortable with."

She chews on her lip. "I'm a little nervous."

A loud crush of people comes in suddenly from the bar, and we turn to see a bride-to-be wearing a tight black dress and a veil and holding a martini glass. Her entourage wobbles along next to her in stiletto heels, each woman holding a similar glass, some with olives, others with lemon peels. "Excuse us, we have to get upstairs for our penis cake. It's an ice cream cake, so, you know…" One of the women makes a wide-armed gesture like she's parting the Red Sea. "Come, ladies, penis ice cream awaits. When will I ever say that sentence again?"

They all erupt in laughter and totter over to the elevators. Their glee and silliness seem to melt some of Gracie's nerves. Her delicate fingers grasp mine in a fist and hold them tight.

"I'm good. Really."

"You sure?"

She nods and meets my eyes. The hesitance in her eyes is gone. "I want this."

That's all I need to hear.

CHAPTER 22

racie

MY HEART POUNDS the whole way up in the elevator and doesn't stop when Hunter waves the key in front of the lock and the door clicks open. He hasn't let go of my hand, but that's the only place he's touching me.

His body feels like a magnet with an unavoidable pull. I want him closer, touching me everywhere.

For all the wildness of my racing heart and the almost painful desire deep in my belly, I also feel a weird sense of calm. Hunter must feel it too because he pauses inside the room as soon as the door shuts.

It's probably a well-appointed room, and I'm sure it has a bed, but Hunter is the only thing I see. He turns me so my back is pressed against the door, and his eyes roam over me from my face downward and back up again. There's hunger there that I haven't seen before. Raw, feral, and hot.

Cupping my cheek in his hand, he bends his head forward until our lips barely graze. He holds my face there and moves closer to me, pressing against my hips. My body responds without hesitation, my hips tilting against him to create the smallest bit of friction.

Hunter's mouth moves against mine, drawing me in with a kiss that gets deeper and hotter with every touch of his lips. My hesitation and nervousness turn into desire, as my heartbeat thrums beneath my rib cage, and I feel short of breath.

And then I'm not breathing at all, so lost in the feeling of Hunter's body pressed against me in all the right places. Every nerve ending sizzles, and every place our bodies touch lights up with awareness.

I can't even remember why I was resisting, not when it feels this good to have Hunter's hands on me. One palm roams over my shoulder, brushing over my waist and settling on my hip. His other hand moves from my cheek into my hair and behind my neck. From there, he guides my face to exactly where he wants it, tilting my lips against his and diving in again.

His tongue finds mine, swirling, sucking, tasting. It's so good. Too good. My body goes limp against his, but he holds me up with his firm grip on my hip. My head would fall back against the door, but he's holding that too.

Owning the kiss. Owning me.

The kiss feels like it lasts for hours, and I still need more.

I wanted to know how Hunter Reyes kisses a woman, and he leaves no question unanswered. If this is how he kisses, I can't understand why any woman who's experienced it has walked away. I guess it explains his reputation for being a heartbreaker. But I push that thought from my mind for now. He can break my heart all he wants later, as long as he keeps giving me this. All of it. Now.

Hunter breaks the kiss and stares into my eyes. Searching for something. Permission? I already know I'll give him whatever he asks for. Finally, he shakes his head in a slow, dreamy way. "Holy fuck, Tink."

I reach up and move the shock of hair off his forehead, the way he normally does, so I can see his face better. I don't want him letting go of any part of me to do it.

He continues to gaze at me with dreamy eyes.

"I know." My voice is soft, breathy. It sounds sexy, but I'm not in control of anything. I feel dizzy and elated and so damn turned on that I let everything go. I give in and let myself feel the sizzling electricity between us.

It's new. I've been attracted to a handful of men in the past, but this is a different level. My whole body craves his in a way I've never experienced. A voice deep in my core is begging me for more.

Hunter's thumb lightly rubs the back of my neck while he continues cradling my head in his large palm. He's looking at me like he can't believe I'm real. I feel the same.

"I want to keep kissing you, but I need you to know. This, you…" He takes his hand from behind my head and trails his index finger down my cheek the way I did earlier. "I didn't expect it. Didn't even know how much I needed it. Gracie, I didn't see you coming. Not at all."

I nod.

"But now that I have you, all bets are off."

Hunter's hand continues moving, his finger tracing the shape of my jaw and moving slowly down my throat. I go completely still, unable to pull in a breath. I watch him watching me as his finger trails lower over my dress, tracing the contour of one breast. My eyes flutter. It's hard not to melt into a puddle because he's leaving a burning trail on my skin as his hand moves down.

When his hand reaches my stomach, I brace for him to touch me lower, my panties wet and my core aching for his touch. But he stops abruptly and reaches for my hand.

"Not yet." He growls the words as though it hurts him as much to slow down as it hurts me to wait for what I want.

I follow him into the hotel room, noticing for the first time that there's music coming from somewhere. It's an easy jazz track that makes the whole scene of a wild fling in a hotel room even sexier.

The bed is gigantic, covered in a crisp white sheet over a perfectly fluffed down comforter, and I try to convince myself that I belong here, with my head on those large, white pillow shams, with my hair splayed out, and this man taking his time, doing things to my naked body that I've only read about in saucy novels.

And I panic.

"Hang on. This isn't me. I'm not that girl."

He turns, still holding my hand. Since I've stopped moving, we're a few paces apart. He takes a breath and lets go of my hand. It makes me sad that I've ruined the moment, but I need him to know who I am.

"You're not what girl?" he asks calmly.

"The kind who goes to hotel rooms with every guy I date. And I know we're not dating. I just felt the need to be clear. I was trying to be all flirty and bold, but I don't know what I'm doing here, and I wanted to warn you. In case you thought I was, you know, a pro at hookups, I wanted you to know that's not me. It's not what I do."

His chuckle unleashes a new wave of goose bumps over my skin, and I can't tell if he's laughing at my confession or at the situation. "Gracie, I didn't come here because I thought you were a pro at hookups." He comes close enough to put his arm around my shoulders and pulls me toward him. "Do you want to go home? You're not obligated to stay in this hotel tonight, or even for the next ten minutes, if you're uncomfortable."

I take a long inhale and let it out slowly. My shoulders drop an inch, and I feel a tiny bit calmer. "I don't want to be a tease."

Hunter rubs a hand over his forehead and runs his fingers through his hair a few times. It isn't lost on me that he's gorgeous even with an anguished look on his face. He walks farther into the room and sits on the bed, patting the space next to him.

"C'mere, Tink."

I do as instructed, sitting far enough away that our bodies aren't touching. I put my blazer down next to me.

Hunter drapes his arm around me again and pulls me next to him. "You're not a tease." He cups a hand beneath my chin and turns my face to see his. The molten gaze is gone, and he looks like the guy I've gotten used to living in Kyler's office. Less intimidating but no less scorching hot.

"It's me. You and me. We can do whatever you want tonight, and if you tell me to take you home, that's what we're doing."

"Thank you."

Neither of us speaks for a minute. Eventually, I tip my head against his shoulder, which feels no less rock hard than any other part of him. "I'm sorry I'm freaking out."

"Nothing to be sorry about." He smooths my hair, running his fingers through it. I want to fold into him like a cat because it feels so good. "Can you tell me why, though? I mean, other than the obvious—the fact that we work for the same soccer club and Kyler would lose his shit."

I shake my head. "It's not about any of that. This is exactly where I want to be."

"O-kay…" He blinks at me, looking like a lost puppy. "Sorry, I'm not getting the issue, then."

Is he really going to make me say it out loud?

"You're *you*, and I'm me. I'm overthinking every kiss, every part of you I touch. Wondering how I'll stack up next to the women you've been with. That's…the issue."

I don't know what I'm expecting. Maybe I figure that after this moment of vulnerability, Hunter will realize that I sold him a false bill of goods by flirting with him in a restaurant hallway and suggesting we hole up here. But his face breaks open into a wicked smile that would be alarming if it didn't look so good on him.

"Well, then, we have no issue."

"No. Really."

He moves so he's kneeling in front of me. "Tink, I'm not here because I have some laundry list of moves or things I expect women to do to please me. I definitely only have one thing on my mind right now, and that's how I can make you feel good."

"Okay." I look down, embarrassed, but I'm still glad I said something.

"So here's what we're gonna do, if it's alright with you." He tilts my face to look at him with one finger beneath my chin. This tiny touch calms me.

His gruff whisper drags my breath away on each languid syllable. "I'm going to slowly, very thoroughly, find every pleasure center on your body until you are so…completely… desperate for me, so wet and swollen…that you're begging me to lick and kiss and…fucking consume you. I want you so goddamn turned on that all other thoughts leave your brain. So the over-thinking…" He snaps his fingers. "No longer a thing."

My skin ripples with heat so fierce that I have to swallow the sudden rush of saliva so I don't drool. "I want that," I practically pant.

"Okay." His eyes roam over me like a leopard deciding which part of me would make the best appetizer. "Good."

Hunter tips me back onto the bed, leaving my legs dangling. He doesn't give me any more time to negotiate whether this is a good or bad idea. I'm too focused on the seductive feeling of his breath against my ankles as he slides the shoes off my feet. Watching the care he takes is its own turn-on.

He kisses his way up my legs, taking his time at the area behind my knees. My head falls back on the bed, and I let out a moan. He's right. I'm barely aware of any of the worries and fears

I had moments earlier. I'm barely able to remember the hotel's name. Or my own.

"Gorgeous," Hunter says, staring at my legs. It almost stops me because I want to protest. I don't think any part of me qualifies as gorgeous, but the way he's looking at me makes me believe maybe I am. At least, maybe to him.

Moving me up the bed, he climbs up as well, straddling my hips but barely touching me. He gently reaches for the straps of my dress and slides them over my shoulders and down my arms. When I lean back on my elbows, it gives me a chance to look at him the same way he's been looking at me. He's so beautiful, with his hair raked back from his forehead, his angular cheekbones and straight nose, and the dimple in his cheek when he smiles. He's smiling now, and it makes me do the same.

Feeling more confident, I lift the hem of his shirt, exposing a tapered waist and a checkerboard of taut abs that I've been wanting to touch since the first moment he walked into the kitchen shirtless.

Hunter reaches behind him and yanks the shirt over his head by the collar. He flings it to the floor and does the same with the blazer I was holding.

"I'll fold it later," he says.

"Please do."

He smiles. "What am I going to do with you, Gracie?"

I give him my best deep, sultry voice. "What do you want to do with me?"

"So many things." His gaze moves from my eyes to my mouth to my breasts, and he sucks in a breath. "So fucking gorgeous. And way too many useless clothes."

Hunter's lips drop to mine, but with more urgency this time. He bites my bottom lip, holding it between his teeth before letting it go. "Every time I see that lip between your teeth, I've wanted to do this," he breathes against my mouth.

With my arms wrapped around his neck, I tug him closer so

he's lying on top of me. I can tell he's holding back some of his weight, but I love the feel of his strong body overwhelming mine.

The kiss gets hotter, deeper. Tongues moving and fighting for dominance. I can't get enough of him. I want to drink him in, but no matter how long we kiss, I want more.

His hands cup my cheeks, and he plants a long, soft kiss on my lips. "Relax, Tink."

"I think I'm relaxed." I sigh.

"You're getting there, but we can do better." I love how he says "we" as though he and I are on this mission together to make me comfortable and content. It's a side of him I keep glimpsing in all the sweet gestures he makes without comment, but before now, I convinced myself they were one-off outliers. The image of him as an aggressive, ruthless player on the field and a ladies' man off the field was glued in my mind, all from hearsay and evidence I hadn't collected myself.

I chastise myself for letting false impressions implicate him in a narrative he's done everything to fight from the time he walked into Kyler's house. I need to let those wrong ideas slide away in favor of the man who's here with me now, doing his level best to allay my insecurities and make me feel good.

"I'm sorry I had the wrong impression of you."

He backs away enough to look me in the eye. "I think I earned all those wrong impressions. I'm glad you don't hold them against me."

"Not anymore."

Hunter nips at my chin before working his way down my throat with a trail of kisses. His tongue sweeps against my skin, and my eyes fall shut. The pragmatist in me wants to memorize every sensation so I can remember this later.

But as Hunter works down the center of my chest, those thoughts drift from my head like they're caught in a river current that's too strong. His lips on my skin make me feel so good that my brain is no match. I'm forced to stay in the present and lean into every sensation.

So I let go.

Tracing the seams of my strapless bra, Hunter cups my breasts over the fabric. He kisses my skin over the tops of each cup before undoing the front clasp and letting the bra fall open.

I'd normally feel exposed, lying here with my dress pushed up to my hips with my breasts bare, but I don't. Not with the reverent way Hunter looks at me, like he can't believe his good fortune. Like he's rock hard and hungry for me. I don't feel like a shy data analyst. I feel like a strong, sexy goddess.

"Fuck, Tink. You are everything." Hunter bites out the words before lavishing more attention on each breast with his tongue. Circling one nipple, he groans. I groan louder.

My nipple goes hard beneath his tongue, and when he bites down, I feel an ache so deep inside that I arch beneath him, wanting more contact.

My reaction fuels him, and he presses his hips against mine. I moan and grind against him, shamelessly chasing more of that blissful feeling. I've never wanted a man inside me like I do right now. Reaching down, I cup his erection through his pants, swallowing hard when its sheer girth fills my hand.

Hunter sits back on his heels and pulls me to a sitting position. He slides the dress down over my waist, carefully exposing me until I'm only wearing panties. He tosses the dress on top of his shirt. I undo his belt, feeling the heat of his stare.

I'm torn between wanting to run my hands over his abs and wanting his pants off as soon as humanly possible. Haste wins.

I unbutton his jeans and pull down the zipper. Still on his knees, he slides the denim down his legs and leans to the side to get the pants off. I take in the sight of him, all hard planes of muscle and lightly tanned skin. He's perfection, and I unconsciously suck in my stomach a tiny bit.

Almost like he knows, Hunter grips my waist and bends to

kiss my stomach. His tongue makes circles around my belly button before kissing me there.

He slides down on the bed and kisses my inner thigh, running his hand higher. "So wet for me. I love that." His voice is so low and deep that I shiver. I don't care if it's obvious that I want him. In fact, I want him to know.

Continuing to kiss the delicate skin of my inner thighs, he hooks his fingers into the elastic of my useless panties and slides them down my legs, letting the fabric skim over my desperately aroused skin.

"Do you like this, Tink?" His smirk is all the hotter because he knows the answer. Because he's doing everything he can to make sure I am enjoying this even though he's going so slowly it's almost painful.

"I do," I breathe. I start to reach for him, but he intercepts my hands and pins them to the bed. He ducks down and continues kissing my inner thighs, moving higher until he reaches my throbbing center.

When his tongue flicks my clit, I almost come undone. It's such an intense, incredible shock of pleasure that I actually see stars.

"Oh god, Hunter."

He groans and gives me even more, his tongue working over the aching bundle of nerves until I'm arching and moaning and begging for more.

Soon I'm cresting the top of an orgasm, too breathless and brainless to do anything except ride it out. A wave of chills racks my body, and I start to go numb and hyperaware at the same time. It feels like I'm melting as the room shakes. Or maybe it's my body. I shudder and moan and try to wordlessly let Hunter know exactly how good I feel.

"Come on, baby. Give me everything," he urges. And I let myself go.

CHAPTER 23

*H*unter

I'M NOT DONE FINDING ways to give Gracie pleasure, not even close. But feeling her come on my tongue unleashes an incentive I need to get creative.

Gracie is lying on the bed with her arm over her eyes. She hasn't moved since the first orgasm knocked her sideways, and I have no problem gearing up for number two. I just want to make sure she's still with me.

"You okay there?" I can't keep the chuckle out of my voice because she looks so utterly satisfied, her cheeks blooming hot pink, her lips parted, her limbs splayed out, totally relaxed.

Gracie lowers her arm from her face and blinks her eyes open, looking at me like she's a little unsure. "This is real? That just happened?"

Now, I don't even try to stifle my laughter. "If by 'this,' you mean that you came so hard the people in the bar six floors down spilled their drinks, then yeah, it fucking happened."

She shakes her head, and her face gets even brighter, if that's possible. "Good god."

"I'm not even close to done with you, Gracie. So if you need a Gatorade or something, lemme know."

She rolls her eyes. "So smug, soccer star. How about you give me a chance to bring you to your knees. Fair's fair."

I like her sass. But more than that, I like *her*. Nothing about tonight feels like a hookup, and it surprises me. Making Gracie moan my name doesn't feel like the endpoint; it feels like the beginning of a life I never fathomed.

It's too much to process in the moment, especially when she props herself on her elbows and grins up at me, beckoning me closer with a curled finger.

"Yeah?" I tease back. "Bring it."

When I lean in, she pushes me sideways, so I roll onto my back. She positions herself over my legs and dips a finger beneath the waistband of my boxer briefs, making me shiver.

Nodding, she swipes her finger lower, grazing the tip of my cock with her finger but leaving me wanting so goddamn much more. "If you're going to torture me, just remember I can easily roll you back over and return the favor."

"Counting on it." I get one last look at her sexy smirk before she dips her head down and her hair splays out over my abs. I reach down and play with a strand of her hair, twisting it around my fist.

She works my boxers down my legs, going just as slowly as I did with her. She's making me crazy with anticipation, and her lips haven't even touched me yet.

I watch her assess my cock, which is standing at attention for her, saluting her as its warrior queen. "I'll go wherever you want to take me."

She smiles and wraps her hand around me, taking a long stroke down the shaft that nearly makes me jump out of my skin with a groan. A few more strokes and I have to tell myself ghost stories about rotten potatoes coming to life in order to keep from coming. I normally have much more self-control than this, but it's been a while since I've been with a woman, and she has me feeling something I haven't experienced in a long time—the idea that tonight is something other than a flirtation leading to a hookup.

It's new and I like it.

Gracie lowers her lips and gives my cock a teasing suck, eliciting a deeper groan that I hope reassures her how grateful I am to be here with her and only her tonight. She's more than enough, and it's my goal in this room to show her that.

As she takes me into her mouth, my hands tangle in her hair. Her breath and her lips nearly send me over the edge, and I look down and marvel at this woman who told me she was nervous an hour earlier.

She's not here to fuck a sports star. She's real and smart and unpretentious and good. She's everything I can imagine wanting. And not just tonight. Or maybe that's my aching cock talking. I can't imagine ever getting enough of her.

"Tink," I gasp. "C'mere."

She looks up and delicately wipes her lips. "Yes?"

"I want to come inside you. If you'll let me."

"Condom?" The breathless way she asks turns me on even more. I reach for my discarded pants and pray there's a condom in my wallet. I'm in luck. There are two.

She nods and takes one of them, kissing her way up my torso until she's straddling my waist. I pull her face down and tangle our tongues together, loving the taste of her mouth, loving everything about having her on top of me.

She circles her hips over mine, teasing me at her entrance until I can't take it any longer. Then she rolls the condom on.

I grab her ass in my hand to still her and slowly push inside, making sure she's ready to handle my size before I give her more. Her soft moans and deep kisses guide me and urge me on.

"Yes, soccer star…there," she pants.

When I finally get fully inside her, I have barely a shred of restraint left.

"Fuck, Tink," I grit out, needing her to know. "You. Are. Fucking. Everything."

I think about baseball, my grandmother's tulip garden, the unsexist pile of laundry in the Devils locker room. That buys me a couple of minutes to enjoy her tight, wet heat. But when she moans and tells me she's already ready to come, my resistance shatters to dust.

I lose control inside her and we rock together, my hips pistoning faster and harder until I can't stop. I curse, she screams my name. We probably register on an earthquake meter somewhere. It's too fucking good.

And when I've given her every last drop, I lower my face to her lips and try to wordlessly tell her how I feel. I desperately hope she feels it too.

racie

THIS SHOULD FEEL MORE awkward than it does.

That's my first thought when my eyes pop open to Saturday morning sunlight streaming in through the window, because we forgot to cover it with the velvet curtains, which hang uselessly on either side. The second thought is that I feel awfully good for someone who only slept about two hours.

Waking up naked in Hunter Reyes's arms should feel weird, wrong, or awkward at the very least. Instead, when I focus enough to take in his beautiful face sleeping peacefully on the pillow next to mine, I feel good. Happy. Satisfied.

So this is what it feels like to have great sex with a hot guy and not let my inhibitions get in the way.

Huh. Good to know.

I only have a minute or so to gaze at Hunter's relaxed face before he begins to wake up. I see the crease deepen between his eyes, the set of his jaw harden, the haze in his eyes return to sharp focus. It's comforting because this is the guy I've come to know over the past month. It's also a little sad because it means our fantasy evening is quickly being replaced by reality.

And the reality is that we need to keep last night under lock and key. There's too much at stake for both of us to risk word getting out. I'm preparing a speech to that effect in my mind when Hunter rolls toward me until his hips connect with mine. He has a wicked smile, some morning wood, and when his hands cup my face, I decide that my speech can wait.

AN HOUR LATER, once we've made use of the steam shower and some very plush towels, there's a knock on the hotel room door. I panic, wrapping the white towel tighter around myself and backing against the wall like a caught animal.

"Concierge," a voice calls from the other side of the door.

Hunter laughs. "Relax." I back into the bedroom, which is out of view of the smaller sitting room of the suite.

Hunter joins me a second later, holding out a shopping bag. "For you."

I don't make any move to take it. "That's not mine."

Hunter puts it on the bed beside me. "It is now. I wasn't sure of your size, so I asked for a couple. We can return the ones that don't fit later."

"You…bought me clothes?" I venture a finger into the bag, moving the tissue paper aside like it might bite. I see folded jeans, a few shirts, a baseball cap, and flip-flops.

"I figured if I wanted you to have breakfast with me, it was the least I could do. So you don't have to wear your clothes from last night."

"You're saving me from the walk of shame?" I'm so dumbfounded that any man would do this, let alone do it for me, that I need him to say it again. So he does, emphasizing that there's no shame as far as he's concerned.

I blink in disbelief. "You are…you're very surprising, soccer star. I like it."

He smiles. "Good. Because I like you."

It takes another hour for me to get dressed because Hunter pulls the towel off my body, and we get highly distracted, but eventually, we make it to a small greasy spoon pancake place that is dark enough inside that there's little chance of Hunter being noticed, especially at our table in the back.

He has on the baseball cap he was wearing when he walked into R&D Grill last night, and each time I look up at him, my mind goes straight back to the night we just spent. There's a permanent flush on my cheeks and a trail of sweat between my boobs just thinking about Hunter's naked body and all the things he did to mine.

House music plays through surround-sound speakers, but it's not so loud that it drowns out conversation. On a late Saturday morning in Hollywood, the place is packed: tables for two jammed with foursomes, stacks of pancakes coming off the grill at a breakneck pace, and plates under a warmer.

The servers move quickly between tables, refilling coffee and taking orders, all of which involve pancakes. The only question is what to eat *with* the pancakes, and most of the options involve meat. It seems like the polar opposite of the kind of place an athlete would find sustenance, but the pancakes smelled so good from the sidewalk that I wasn't about to argue.

I run a hand over Hunter's forearm, examining his tattoos in more detail. "How did you choose these?"

He looks down at the assortment of inked images—a yin and yang symbol, a lion and a dove. "A lot of them are reminders to seek balance. Find the Zen moments. I'm not always successful, as you can see."

"You should give yourself more credit."

He shrugs. "Maybe."

A fifty-something couple in all black workout clothes sits across the aisle with a big golden retriever wearing a service dog vest. I want to pet the dog so badly, but I know better. Noticing me smiling at their dog, the woman offers me a tiny piece of her bacon. "You want to give Lacy a treat? Go on."

"Oh yes. Please." I gratefully accept the bacon, and Lacy already knows the drill. She pads over and sits in front of me, assuming her best obedient-dog posture.

"Good girl," I tell her, rubbing her neck and patting her flank. I give her the bacon and the dog goes back beneath the table like she's done this a hundred times.

I catch Hunter smiling at me. "What?"

"Look at you, a dog lover. I never thought I'd see the day."

"Oh, come on. You know I love Bogie. He and I are buds. He's responsible for me being able to sort of throw a tennis ball now."

"I know you love him. I'm just saying you've come a long way from the wary girl who thought Bogie was plotting to kill you in your sleep."

I take a sip of coffee from a large yellow mug with a daisy painted on the side. "Wow, that's good." I've said the same thing the past three times I've taken a sip, and Hunter seems more amused every time. "Fine. I'll admit I had my doubts about Bogie, but he's pretty easy to love."

"Like father, like son."

"Yeah? Is that true for you and your dad too?"

The temperature in the room shifts as soon as I ask the question and realize I may have overstepped. Hunter goes pale, and I sit up straight, immediately backpedaling. "Gosh, I'm sorry. I don't mean to be nosy."

He holds up a hand. "It's okay. My dad died a handful of years ago, and he was...tough. Turned me into a force on the field, though. I gotta give him credit for that."

"I'm sorry you lost him." She presses her lips together, as

though debating whether to say more. Curiosity wins. "Was he your coach?"

"Unofficially. He encouraged me to play into my strengths, acting like a brute asshole, starting fights, pushing people away, using my muscles instead of my brain. He was right, I guess. I made a career of it."

I hate hearing him describe himself this way, and without thinking, I reach for his hand. He starts to pull away, as though to protect himself from emotion, but then he seems to give in. I like that he trusts me enough to do it.

The stiffness in his fingers gives way to my grip. "You do see that the player on the field is only a small part of who you are, right? I certainly don't see you that way."

Swallowing hard, he chokes out his words. "Sure you do. It's why you told Coach to keep me on the team."

I shake my head. "Because it's how you play. Not because it's who you are." I lock eyes with him, willing him to believe me. After a silent moment, he nods, letting go of my hand. Then he changes the subject, and I leave it alone.

It's a reminder that I have no business treating him like he's my new boyfriend and trying to learn about his family. He came to my rescue on a bad blind date, and I had an unforgettable night, but I don't want to pretend it's more than it is.

I tell myself to keep things light and superficial, but the idea of that makes me lose my appetite.

I should be starving since I skipped dinner last night, but I can't make a dent in the pancakes. Hunter has declared today his cheat day, so he's already chewed through half of his stack.

"Something tells me you're back to overthinking." He gestures to the uneaten pancakes. I make a meager effort to move the top pancake off the stack and cut it into bites, but I only put a tiny piece in my mouth. Looking down as I chew, I try to convince myself that I'm good with our hookup. Trying to talk about it will only make things feel weird.

"I'm okay," I say.

He points an accusing finger. "Liar."

"Fine. I'm thinking a little. I want you to know we're good. I mean, last night was something I'll probably remember until the end of days, but I'm not delusional. I can't put my job at risk, and I know we were a 'right time and place' situation. I'm not expecting anything."

Hunter puts down his fork and finishes chewing the bite in his mouth. The creases deepen on his forehead. "I wouldn't exactly refer to us as a 'situation.' That sounds like one step away from a problem."

I take a moment to assess the man sitting across the tiny stained wood table from me.

"I didn't mean to sound dismissive. I mean, I'm so grateful to you for rescuing me from my awful date and for showing me such a good time last night. I don't want to sound unappreciative for you doing me that favor, and like I said, I had an amazing time—"

Hunter reaches for my hand, which is flailing wildly holding a fork. It surprises me enough that I stop my monologue. The creases don't disappear from his forehead, but Hunter puffs out a breath. "Okay." It sounds like he's agreeing, but I'm not sure what he's agreeing to do.

"O-kay...?"

"Yes. If you think that last night was just me doing you a favor to keep you out of the mitts of Captain Blake, then go ahead and delude yourself."

"Well...wasn't it?"

Hunter drops my hand, and my skin goes cold. His tone stings.

He picks up his fork and stabs at his pancakes. Then, he puts a large bite into his mouth and chews slowly. I wait, hoping he'll say more after he swallows, but instead, he reaches for his water glass and drinks it down.

I realize that for as intimate as the night with him felt, I don't know Hunter that well. I understand what I've studied in order to evaluate his player prospects, and I've seen him go from zero to full-on rage on the field in seconds, but that's athletic instinct. Testosterone. Fierce competitiveness. I don't know if any of that applies to how he processes stuff off the field.

He signals for our server to bring the check. He gives her a nice smile and throws down some bills without even looking at it. "Thanks." Then he looks at me. "D'you want to take that to go or should we sit a while?"

From the antsy thump of his thigh, I don't get the impression he wants to do anything "for a while," and my mind races trying to figure out why his mood just changed so much. I replay the last two minutes of our conversation and try to see what I said that seems to have bothered him so much.

"I guess I can take it home."

He signals to the server to bring a box by pointing at my pancakes and pantomiming a square. She smiles at him. Her dark ponytail swishes and her hips sway as she shuttles to the kitchen. Why can't I be so free and easy? Why does everything I say and do feel impossibly uncool?

I reach across the table and put my hand on top of his, half expecting him to pull his away. But he doesn't. If anything, my hand seems to calm him a tiny bit, but he doesn't look at me.

"What just happened?" I try to get a view of his eyes, but with his head tipped down beneath the baseball cap brim, I can't get a glimpse. "I'm sorry if I said the wrong thing. Sometimes my mouth gets ahead of my brain."

The corner of his mouth twitches. It's not a smile, but it's a step in that direction. He blows a long breath between his lips like maybe he's trying to take a beat before saying the wrong thing. Like I should have done, apparently.

There's determination in his gray eyes when he looks up. "You said you don't go to hotels for hookups. Well, neither do I."

"I, um…" My brain sputters because, even though Hunter has treated me well, he and I don't have a future together. I'm only here in LA temporarily, and he's still a player.

The server returns with a to-go box, and I load in my pancakes, feeling defeated.

"I-I'm sorry. I guess I had the wrong impression."

"I guess you did."

He doesn't seem angry. More disappointed. Resigned. Like this is the world he lives in, where the truth gets blurred by surface impressions, and he deserves what he gets.

"Hunter, I—"

He cuts me off with the scrape of his chair on the floor when he stands. He points at my pancakes. "Should we go?"

We drive home in silence. I want to apologize, but I don't know where to begin. I'm still so confused because I really thought he was just doing me a favor last night, getting me out of a jam. Is he saying it meant more than that?

The urban sprawl of Hollywood Boulevard sweeps past with its mixture of trendy new restaurants, office buildings, and hole-in-the-wall nail salons until we turn up the hill. I've begun to understand what Kyler likes about living in the hills up above the city. As soon as we leave the busy boulevard, the air seems to change. The streets get greener. Trees offer dappled shade over streets with fewer cars, and the Hollywood sign peeks through intermittently on the peak ahead.

I roll my window down and try to inhale some bit of calm from the surroundings, still unsure how I managed to offend Hunter when all I was doing was attempting to thank him.

I know I need to fix this before either one of us goes into the house and we proceed with our lives. "Hunter, can we roll this conversation back so I can apologize properly and explain what I was thinking?"

Even from the side, I see the hard line of his jaw go slack. His cheek muscles unclench. His lips soften. "Sure. Maybe I jumped to some conclusions too."

We turn up the driveway to Kyler's house, and I swivel in my seat to get a better look at him. A new fleet of butterflies takes flight under my skin at the reality of how we spent last night and that we're here together now.

I feel the same magnetic pull, the sense of needing to touch him and have him touch me. I put a hand on his thigh, which is larger than my palm and taut with muscle.

"Last night was incredible and I—"

I stop midsentence because Kyler is standing on his porch, phone in hand. He cups a hand over his eyes to see through the windshield glare and gazes at us quizzically.

Hunter pulls the car to a short stop in front of the house and yanks on the parking brake. The spell between us dissipates with the abrupt halt of the motor. I hurriedly open the passenger door with an overly excited greeting.

"Welcome back!" I rush over and give my brother a hug, all but ignoring Hunter in hopes that Kyler won't pick up on the tension between us or the spark I can't drown.

Hunter slams the car door and comes over for a stiff bro hug. "How was the trip?"

"Good. Great, actually. I met some nice people," Kyler says. He holds a mug of coffee that wafts steam into the morning air. I check the time. It's close to noon. "I was just about to send out a search party when neither of you answered your phones. Where are you two coming from?"

"Breakfast," I blurt out just as Hunter says, "Errands."

Kyler laughs, looking from one of us to the other. "Which is it?"

"Both," I say, pulling my box of pancakes and my shopping bag from the car. "I asked Hunter for some shopping information, and he was hungry, so he offered to show me in person if I bought him breakfast."

"What a sport," Kyler says, eyeing his friend. "You managed to point her toward a mall in exchange for a free breakfast?"

I realize I'm making things worse. "That's not—"

Hunter interrupts. "She tried to pay, but that's not how I roll. Don't worry, man."

Kyler looks me up and down, and I wonder if he can sense anything different about me. I wonder if having a night of the best sex of my life shows on my face. Or my just-fucked hair. Putting a hand to my head, I try to smooth my hair and gather it into a ponytail. I pull the band from my wrist and secure it.

"Okay, good. So what's on the agenda today?" Kyler is already walking back into the house, moving on.

"Tatum is flying down from San Francisco. I'm spending the afternoon with her."

"Nice. Say hi for me."

I look at Hunter and mouth, "Sorry."

His answer is a hand on the small of my back as we walk into the house. It's reassuring, but I want more. Thanks to my big mouth and my brother's timing, it's the only thing I'll get for now.

 unter

IT'S all I can do to suffer through an hour in the kitchen listening to Kyler recount the highlights of his business trip and all the "epic surf" destinations he managed to fit in. Usually, I'd love to hear him describe the big waves and look at the photos he downloaded from an on-site photographer's website. Usually, I'd be here for all the details about the new contracts he scored with major surf retailers and celebrity skateboarders.

But today is not normal. Today, my body hums with one thought—how to get Gracie into my bed for more than just one night.

At the same time, I'm dejected by how dismissive she was of last night. Like she didn't see any potential for more than a hookup. Granted, I know my reputation, so maybe she's not wrong to jump to that conclusion. And she made it clear that romance and work do not mix, and if she has to choose, work is the clear winner.

Yet…a part of me knows she was protecting herself from my reputation, guarding her heart a little bit. That's what gives me hope. All I want to do now is hear what Gracie was about to tell me in the car.

"So we spent a week together after the trade show just kind of bumming around on the beach, trying different surf spots and eating seafood every chance we got. It was the most fun I've had in ages." Kyler's thumb glides across his phone screen until he finds the picture he wants.

He slides it across the counter for me to see. It's a selfie of him with a blond guy who looks like a teenager. The two of them are grinning at the camera in front of a pristine beach with surfers in the background. I'm confused because I've only been half-listening to his story.

"You and he…" I scroll through the next few photos. They're pictures of surfers mostly, and I think I can identify Kyler and this dude in a few of them, but it's hard to be sure.

"Are partners."

The last I heard, Kyler was still dating women, so this is new. "And how did you two meet?"

"I told you. At the trade show."

I want to be supportive of his new relationship, but I'm also aware I missed about half of the conversation over the past half hour. I don't want him to know my mind was elsewhere, so I need to cover.

"Cool," I say. I catch Gracie trying to hide a smile. She looks down at the counter, where she has her pancake box open. She's managed to get through about half the stack. Kyler picks up a pancake, rolls it up, and takes a bite from the end.

"Yeah? Cool?" Kyler asks, tilting his head like he knows I'm not all here, and he's about to bust me.

"You two make a nice couple," I say, hoping it's the affirmation he wants. I'm ready to move on from this conversation and find a way to be alone with Gracie before she leaves to pick up her friend. She's definitely laughing quietly now, still looking down.

Kyler takes the phone back and looks at the pictures. "I'm not sure that was exactly the goal, but thanks?" He takes another bite of the rolled pancake and tilts his head again. He's starting to look like Bogie, and I wonder if I should pet him on the head so maybe he'll go off somewhere and take a nap.

"Well, I don't know what you wanna hear. He's hot? He makes you look young and hot just being with him?"

"What the fuck are you talking about?"

"Your boyfriend, or whatever. I don't know what you want to hear. I'm just being supportive."

Gracie pushes the box of pancakes toward me. There's still one at the bottom, swimming in syrup, but I tear off a corner. Maybe I need to shove something in my mouth instead of words.

Kyler's laugh sounds like the bark of a seal. "He's not my boyfriend. He's my partner."

"Okay, call him whatever you want. All good." I launch off the barstool and push past him to find something in the fridge to counteract the sickeningly sweet pancake. I land on a bag of carrots and go to the sink to peel one.

"I mean, he's my business partner in the new venture to sponsor surf competitions like I said fifteen minutes ago. What part of that did you not understand?"

I turn around, carrot peeler in hand, and look from Kyler to Gracie, trying to make sure I'm getting the real story now. Gracie nods almost imperceptibly.

"Sorry. I spaced out for a second," I admit. "Didn't sleep great last night, so I'm a little off my game."

Kyler laughs. "So all this time, you thought I was coming out, telling you about my little side dish?" He looks at the picture on his phone and nods. "I mean, I could do much worse, but come on, I'm not a cradle robber."

"How old is he?" Gracie asks, clearly still amused by my gaffe.

"Eighteen."

I slap a hand against my forehead and take a bite of the carrot. "Jesus. Sorry I wasn't paying attention."

Still smiling, Gracie excuses herself. "I need to shower and pick up Tatum."

Kyler high-fives her and continues without missing a beat. "Sorry you didn't sleep. Was it the blinds in the office? Sometimes they let in too much light."

I nod. "Yeah, the blinds. I think that's what it was." I don't dare look at Gracie, but I hear her giggle. Even though I know I'm the butt of the joke, my senses still light up at the sound. I need to get her alone, but I also need to be a better friend to Kyler. I owe him my full attention, at the very least. "Anyhow, forget that. Tell us more about the surfing. What's the biggest wave you caught?"

Kyler thumbs through his phone again. "Thirty footer. There's only one good one before I wiped out, but it's here someplace."

"Take your time," I say. It takes all my self-control to sit here and let him, but maybe it's good practice for gametime. All I know is that every minute I sit here, it's that much longer I have to wonder about what Gracie was about to tell me.

racie

"YAY! I'm so happy to see you!" Tatum runs the short distance from the sidewalk outside baggage claim to where I stand next to my car, bouncing on my toes and shielding my eyes from the afternoon sun.

It's hard to believe it took me an hour to get here from the Hollywood Hills, but that's LA for you, I guess.

Tatum skips across the bus lane and tosses her overnight bag into my open trunk before giving me a hug. "Me too," I sigh.

As soon as we're belted in, Tatum starts asking questions. "Who are your friends? What do you do outside of work? How's living with Ky working out?" I navigate us out of the busy airport and into the traffic on Century Boulevard on the way to the freeway.

At the first red light, I level her with a look. "You want me to answer all of those?"

"Of course I do, but not all at once. Is there somewhere we can grab a drink?"

I input the name of the hotel in Santa Monica where Tatum is staying, and we drive straight there.

Another trafficky hour later, I feel the cool ocean breeze kissing my skin as it travels east beyond the palm trees. It's nearly four in the afternoon. We're situated at a perfect patio table on top of the Proper Hotel, where couples and friend groups sit at a rooftop bar, gawking at the coastal view and basking in the late afternoon sunshine.

"This could not be more perfect. It was foggy when I left San Francisco."

"It's always foggy in San Francisco. I miss it." It's the first time I've said the words out loud since I arrived here, and I consider how well I've adjusted to LA.

"Aw, you just miss me." Tatum smiles and accepts a spicy margarita from our server, who puts an identical one in front of me.

"I do. Of course I do."

"But a job full of hot soccer players must blunt the blow a little bit." Tatum should know. She's been engaged to Donovan Taylor, a star player for the San Francisco Strikers soccer team, for a while now. We met in grad school, where we both studied computer science. She works for a virtual reality company and, a few years ago, she was put in charge of building a soccer game featuring Strikers players as avatars. This is where my knowledge of soccer started and ended, and Tatum has always been fine with that.

I've been needing the companionship of a friend who really knows me since I arrived in town. "I'm so glad you're here," I say, pointedly ignoring the opportunity to tell her about Hunter, mainly because his reaction this morning was so confusing that I'm not sure what to say about him.

Until I talk to him, I'll say nothing.

The view from the roof deck is exactly what I need after weeks holed up at my desk analyzing player stats and game footage. Looking toward the ocean, I inhale a deep breath and close my eyes for a moment to feel the breeze on my skin.

At the table next to ours, three guys laugh a little too loudly, and I wonder if they're trying to get our attention. I'm never good at sensing these things. Maybe they're just loud. "You ladies here for dinner?" one of them asks.

I turn to look at him, noting his blond hair combed neatly over his forehead and the clean shave. He's nice looking enough, but after spending so much time with my rougher, unshaven roommate, I realize my tastes have changed. I find myself checking his arms for tattoos, and when I see none, I'm even more disinterested.

"No, just having some girl time. Catching up, doing our thing," Tatum says before turning in her chair to more squarely face me. The guy's face falls, but he gets the hint.

I raise an eyebrow. "Just killed a man's dreams, right there," I say quietly.

She shrugs. "They needed killing. You and I have soccer players to keep us warm at night."

"Speak for yourself, sister."

"Oh, come on. I can tell when you're hedging. A month ago, you told me Kyler's soccer star friend moved in, and then you clammed up about him for weeks. I know what that means in Gracie-speak. You and Hunter have something going, just admit it."

"How? How do you know these things?"

She snorts a laugh. "Just tell me about Hunter."

I take a big swig of my drink and tell her everything about last night. The timing of her visit couldn't be more perfect because I actually need a download with a friend who can help me figure out how to navigate this new situation.

If it even is a situation.

"But then, it got really awkward this morning, and we haven't had a chance to talk it through. So basically, that's it." I want to say more, but I snap my lips shut like I need a physical barrier to keep from oversharing.

"I'm afraid I'm gonna need more details," Tatum singsongs as though this is all a juicy story and I'm holding out to build tension or something.

I sip my drink, which, when combined with the one last night, is more alcohol than I've had since that evening when Hunter introduced me to scotch. And now my thoughts are back on him.

"Come on. It's me, Gracie. You know I don't judge, and I can tell you're holding stuff in. Maybe it'll feel good to let it out."

I drain the last third of my drink and feel the warming effects of the tequila. Liquid courage I shouldn't need with my friend. "I don't know why it makes me so nervous to talk about him."

Tatum orders two more drinks. "Can I get you some bar snacks or anything to go with your drinks?" our server asks. I note that his voice is easily an octave higher than Hunter's low rasp, and there I go, thinking about him again. Apparently, I'm not capable of stopping.

"Bar snacks. Absolutely," I say, looking around and spying a chips and guacamole platter that would do a good job of absorbing some of the tequila from my margarita. I order that along with truffle fries, making all of my fried carb dreams come true. Tatum adds a plate of tuna tartare, and now we're basically set for the rest of the evening.

"You're staying here with me tonight, so don't even think about turning me down," Tatum says. I'm all set to tell her I need to be at Kyler's, but then I take another look at the blue Pacific and decide this is what my soul needs. Time with a good friend. A hotel room with a spectacular view. Some time to think about Hunter and what to say to him when I get back.

"Okay. Not gonna argue."

"Great. I hear they have fluffy white robes in the room. We can wear those later and order latenight room service. It'll be like when we were in the dorms, only without the crappy cafeteria food and the fraternity guys next door."

Another night in a hotel, this one equally awesome with its view of the ocean and proximity to the beach. How is this my life?

Two months ago, I was licking my wounds over torpedoing my job and my life in the Bay Area, and now I'm in a gorgeous place with gorgeous people, and my heart feels full.

I smile at the memory of our college years, grateful to have Tatum here. "So tell me again why you came without Donno?" The exhibition game between the Devils and the Strikers isn't for a couple weeks, so I know she didn't travel from San Francisco for that.

"I have some business here next week." She dismisses it with a flick of her hand like it's nothing, but the woman is the head of product development at a billion-dollar company, and she's solely responsible for growing its virtual reality gaming division into the powerhouse it is.

"So in other words, you're meeting with…"

"The head of Major League Soccer. And the guys from basketball and football."

"Just the top brass for every major sport in the country."

She tries to hide some false modesty behind her margarita glass, but I catch her grin. "Pretty much."

Shaking my head, I raise my full glass for a toast. "You're such a badass. That's awesome."

"Thank you. And…" She looks around us to make sure no one can overhear the conversation. "Just between you and me, I hear there's another deal in place. With your old company. There's going to be an announcement and a big launch event for the Devils partnership with AIFund."

Tatum explains that she heard the Silicon Valley rumor mill says AIFund is backing an artificial intelligence game with the Devils. I kind of miss being in the know about tech news, but also, it's kind of nice to be away from it.

I can feel the color drain from my face. "Well, I may work for the Devils, but I won't be going to that event."

"Why? Oh…" Tatum's eyes go wide because she knows exactly what I'm thinking—my ex-boyfriend will be there. The one who cost me my job and then dumped me. "Peter?"

"Yeah. No need to see him. Besides, the event is probably only for bigwig execs."

"I beg to differ. First of all, as the chief data analyst, you're about to get a whole new playground at work, detailing out the player specs and stats for the hottest game to roll out in years. That's totally your catnip."

My smile at the idea of the new work challenges goes so wide that my cheeks hurt. If she's right about the news, my job is about to become a hundred times better than my old one ever was. "That will be amazing, actually. I'd think about staying permanently for that."

"Okay, then. You need to hold your head high in your badass job, show up looking amazing with Hunter, and make Peter jealous as the icing on a very decadent cake."

"Hold your horses. First of all, no one at work can see me with Hunter. Peter is the perfect example of how I ruined a job over a guy. I'm not making that mistake again."

She waves a hand in the air like she's fanning away smoke. "So many problems with that thesis—Hunter isn't Peter, you're killing it in your new job, you aren't doomed to make the same mistake again—but we'll get to that later. For now, make Peter insanely regretful for breaking up with you."

"I guess I can hold my head high and show him that I'm absolutely ambitious enough to flourish without him. I would really like him to leave in tears, preferably mortified publicly, but that may be too much to expect."

"You need to look amazing. Be amazing. Show him how much better your life is without him."

"I will do my very best." *Guess I'll be giving my one black silk dress a run for its money.*

Our chips and guac arrives on a large platter, and I don't waste a second before scooping a heap of green goodness onto a chip and popping it into my mouth. Tatum does the same, and for a moment, we munch in silence.

It takes me back to this morning, when the conversation with Hunter ground to a halt after I tried to thank him for rescuing me. Still confused about why that would offend him, I describe the situation to Tatum.

She puts both hands on the table and levels me with a stern look. "You thanked him for sex? Like he was a paid escort or something?"

A wave of nausea hits me, and I taste bile in my throat. "That's not what I meant." But I realize it doesn't matter what I meant if it sounded that way to Hunter. "Oh god, do you think that's how he took it?"

"I hate to break it to you, sweet thing, but for a super-smart person, sometimes you have a startling inability to grasp the obvious."

I think back on the conversation and how quiet Hunter got.

You said you don't go to hotels for hookups. Well, neither do I.

"You think he was saying he wants more than a hookup?"

Tatum flicks me in the shoulder. "Well, yeah, because that's basically what he said! Why is this so hard for you to grasp?" She drums her fingers on the table impatiently, and I don't want to ruin our time together by being obtuse and clueless. I try to allow the thought into my head that Hunter sees me as someone different from the other women in his long dating history— someone he could hook up with more than once.

He may have alluded to that idea, but I still feel wary. I'm just hitting my stride at my job, and the last thing I need is gossip that I'm sleeping with a player. Or the impression that my analytics are biased. I need to make the right decision this time and think about my future.

But first, I need to apologize to Hunter.

CHAPTER 27

*H*unter

GRACIE IS STILL out when I stagger up the driveway after a punishing afternoon workout. Somehow, I deluded myself into thinking that starting late in the day meant Coach would go easy. Not a chance, and the afternoon heat didn't help.

I don't see her car when I pull up, and Kyler intercepts me before I walk in the door. He has Bogie on a leash and a ball in his other hand. "Hey, I was going to take this guy up to the reservoir. You wanna come?"

My aching legs want me to say no, but I haven't spent time with my friend since I've basically moved into his house, so I nod. "Yeah, lemme grab a coconut water and a bar or something. Coach killed us today."

He waits while I pull together my snack and slap a baseball cap on my hair that's still damp from the post-workout shower at the facility. When I return, he's tossing the ball across the drive-way, and Bogie is chasing it, dragging his leash behind him.

Half the time, he chases a ball in good faith, but then refuses to relinquish it. He'll roll onto his back, mouthing the ball and clawing at the air until the ball falls from his mouth and rolls away. He'll watch it and look at me with sad eyes until I relent and go pick it up.

He's on his back, wiggling on the driveway to scratch an itch, but he hasn't let go of the ball.

"You could've let him off the leash. He's not gonna run."

"Yeah? He knows where his bread's buttered?" Kyler shrugs. "I figured I oughtta be able to grab him fast if I needed to."

We watch the dog play a game with himself, batting the ball away, waiting for it to roll, and pouncing on it. He can entertain himself for hours, but there's nothing like getting him out on a hiking trail to tackle his pent-up energy.

"I don't see your sister's car. What's she up to tonight?" I keep my eyes on Bogie as though the question is a passing thought.

If Kyler suspects I have even a shred more interest in her than that, he gives no indication. "I think she's with her friend Tatum. They went out somewhere." He couldn't care less, so I let it go.

Bogie comes running when I whistle, and we pile into Kyler's truck. It's about a five-minute drive through the neighborhood to where we park and walk. Truthfully, we could have gone on foot, but given how cooked my legs feel, I wasn't going to suggest walking up a damn hill.

"You free after this for some food?" Kyler asks.

"Free as a bird."

"Thought we could barbecue. Looking like a nice night to be on the deck."

"Works for me."

We park and start moving toward the Hollywood Reservoir, where I can see a few dozen people on the same walk we're planning.

Bogie has his leash in his mouth even though I hold on to the other end of it. "He's a control freak," I explain. "Thinks he's in charge."

"Who're we kidding? He is."

When we reach the path, we let Bogie off his leash even though it's technically not allowed. I don't see anyone who looks like they'd care. The other people heading our way have a dog running loose as well, a big sheepdog with hair over its eyes. When Bogie lopes over, the sheep dog bounces along next to him. They sniff each other and circle and figure out whatever dogs do from those things.

I almost wish people were like that. Maybe then I'd be better at relationships.

Ky and I walk about halfway around the reservoir, catching up on his travels and my life in the weeks since I moved into his spare room. "I can't tell you how grateful I am for that," I reiterate. "My insurance will pay for a hotel or whatever, but we spend so much time on the road, I feel like I'd get hives in another hotel, but now that you're back, if it feels too crowded—"

He cuts me off. "Not another word. It's great having you." Kyler starts to laugh. "God, I don't think I've heard you string so many words together in a while. My sister must be rubbing off."

I don't look at him. I can't.

Instead, I jog over to where Bogie has grabbed hold of a large tree root and is trying to tug it from the ground, not realizing it's attached to a tree. Or maybe he does know. Just likes a challenge.

Like me, I suppose. Going after a woman who should be getting her mind blown by an astrophysicist, not a jock who didn't finish college.

When I manage to lure Bogie away from the root with a dog treat from the sack attached to his leash, Kyler is chatting up two women in sports bras with tanned, flat stomachs, wearing tiny, form-fitting shorts. Some things never change.

He waves me over. "Meet my friend Hunter." He introduces

the two of them, and I see a flicker of recognition from one of them, but she plays it cool, extending her hand.

We chat for a few minutes, and they make a big deal out of how cute Bogie is and how they're available if I ever need a dog sitter. Then they take off jogging, and we resume our walk.

"Hell, maybe I should get a dog," Ky says. "That happen a lot, women offering you favors?"

"Not really."

I throw Bogie's ball and catch Kyler's skeptical look. "Okay, fine. It happens."

"Good to be a soccer star."

Now I'm thinking about Gracie again and her insistence on calling me Soccer Star. No wonder she assumed last night was a "one and done" if she sees me as some celebrity athlete who rotates through women like it's part of my job.

And who am I kidding? For years, it was a nice perk of the career. "Do you ever feel old?" I ask, not entirely sure where I'm going with this.

Kyler laughs. "You mean because those two women looked like they were probably in college, and it was ten years ago that we were freshmen?"

"I hadn't even thought about that. No, more like the things I want now are different from what I wanted back then."

He mock-gasps. "Are you telling me you're growing up? Say it ain't so."

I follow Bogie down a side path, which takes us off the main trail. Kyler follows me, and we walk behind my dog, who wags his tail like a flag as he trots along the path.

"Seriously, man. Is everything okay? I know losing the house was a blow, and all the stuff with potentially getting transferred… we haven't really had a chance to unpack all that."

"Yeah, that stuff feels somewhat like I have it in hand, but it's more…everything else."

Bogie comes back to us with a stick he's found and drops it at

Kyler's feet. Tail wagging furiously, he looks from one of us to the other with pleading eyes. "Okay, buddy. Okay," Kyler says, hucking the stick down the path. Bogie scrambles after it and, true to form, lies down in the brush and starts chewing the stick instead of bringing it back.

"He's not good at this game, is he?"

I shrug. "Well, he's a retriever. He knows how to retrieve, not how to return."

"Ah, I see. Good to clear that up." We watch Bogie, who looks beyond happy gnawing on the stick in the shade. For not the first time in my life, I feel jealous of my dog, who knows what he wants and goes after it. Wish I could wring that much happiness out of a stick.

Just as quickly, Bogie has a change of heart, picks up the stick, and races past us toward the reservoir. We follow, and I ready the leash in case I need to grab him. Like if he sees a flock of ducks and decides they're dinner.

"So what's the 'everything else?' Relationship stuff? Family?"

I pretend to cop some dude swagger. "You know me, I don't do relationships. I do flings. I do hookups. I do meaningless shit that gets splattered all over the tabloids."

Ky holds up a finger. "Correction. You used to do that shit. The last few times I've seen you, it's like you're immune to every single woman in the room. They may not notice, but I do."

"Yeah. I'm not interested in shallow non-relationships anymore." I look over my shoulder to make sure we're not being caught in someone's social media feed. The last thing I need is my thoughts being broadcast everywhere.

Kyler smirks. "You're not gonna get arrested for that, don't worry."

I shove him off the path with my elbow. He returns the gesture, and I'm sure we look like two overgrown toddlers wrestling our way down the path.

I should tell him about Gracie, but what is there to tell? We had one night together, and she made it seem like we're one and done.

"Feels strange to have such a strong feeling about wanting a normal life."

"Doesn't make it wrong. Only new. Hey, just because you've been a player all your life doesn't mean you've gotta stay that way."

Leave it to my oldest friend to cut right to the chase despite everything I've done to mask my concerns and avoid the issue.

His assessment of me, although true, still cuts deep. It's not like I thought I was fooling anyone. I know how many women I've hooked up with for one night. But unlike some people's exploits, mine have been splashed all over social media.

The worst part is that it's clear that Gracie sees me the same way.

"Yeah, maybe."

"Well, you know what they say. Admitting the problem is the hardest part. I say, go forth and get thee a relationship. Nothing is stopping you."

If he only knew I had Gracie in my mind during the entirety of the conversation, he'd probably blow his stack.

Then true to form, Bogie finds his way into trouble, staring at a mud puddle and barking at it. I take off at a run because I know what comes next, but despite my speed on the soccer field, navigating around joggers and walkers gives me a different challenge. I reach Bogie about five seconds after he decides to slide into the mud, roll onto his back, and coat his entire body in filth. Then he runs, tries to stop, and slides across the damp grass.

When I turn back, I catch Kyler laughing his ass off. Reminds me of how Gracie did the same thing.

racie

The Following Morning

I knock lightly on Hunter's door, which has been closed since I got home after a lazy brunch on the hotel rooftop with Tatum. It was hard to leave that view behind, but the thought of seeing Hunter ignited a nervous thrill that I still feel now, standing outside his room.

"You awake?" I ask softly, hoping he'll sleep through it if he's lost in dreamland.

When he opens the door, it's clear from his look of concentration that he's been doing anything but sleeping.

Well, likewise. I didn't get a great night of sleep sharing Tatum's queen bed in the hotel room. Not for lack of room. And Tatum barely moved all night.

I was lost in my thoughts, replaying potential conversations in my head. None of them seems important now that I'm standing in front of Hunter, who's wearing only a pair of low-slung black sweatpants that hug his muscular thighs.

My eyes roam over his pecs and abs and I lose track of time. Again.

Must. Control. That.

Hunter catches me staring, and his bleary eyes crease at the corners. He smirks at my gobsmacked expression and crosses his arms, obscuring his magnificent chest, but giving me a great view of his sculpted biceps. It's a fair trade.

"Morning," he says, gravel in his voice.

"Afternoon, actually."

He pulls his phone from his pocket and checks the time, nodding. "How'd that happen?"

"Well, you see, time waits for no one. You may delay, but time will not. Time is the most valuable thing a man can spend." I spread my hands wide. "Take your pick from my useless mental encyclopedia of time quotes."

"Not useless."

It feels like our usual banter, and that calms me. But I still don't know what to say to Hunter, and that makes my heart race.

"I was thinking about a walk around the neighborhood. Wanna join me?" I ask.

It's a lie. I wasn't thinking about a walk. Kyler's neighborhood is hilly, and it doesn't have sidewalks, making it more of an urban hike with cars in danger of sideswiping us at every turn.

"Sure." He reaches for a tee hanging on the desk chair and pulls it over his head. From a neat row of shoes against one wall, he grabs a pair of flip-flops and slips them on before putting on a baseball cap and glasses. "Okay, ready. Let's walk."

Before we get to the front door, Bogie comes bounding through the patio door and tries to stop between us and the front door. His paws slip on the floor, and he goes sliding like Tom Cruise in *Risky Business*.

"I think someone heard the W-word," I say, laughing and giving Bogie a good scratch behind the ears.

"Yeah. Mind if he comes? He could probably use some exercise."

"No prob. If I get tired, he can pull me up the hill."

Hunter leashes up his dog and puts some water into a bottle, then we head out the door. He tips his head in the downhill direction, and I gratefully follow his lead. We walk in silence for a couple of minutes, letting Bogie sniff his way along the road and investigate several bushes and rows of flowers growing near the curb.

Every so often, he strikes gold, finding an In-N-Out burger wrapper that fell out of someone's trash can or a smushed lizard that bears investigating.

I wonder how long we could keep going in silence. Sneaking a look at Hunter, I can't tell much from his expression. As usual, he's wearing a baseball hat, but I can't see his eyes under the sunglasses, so I have no idea what he's thinking.

"Listen," I say at the same time he says, "Look—"

At least it breaks the ice. He tips his head toward me. "You want to go first?"

"Sure." I clear my throat even though it doesn't need clearing. "I wanted to pick up from where we went off-track yesterday morning. I could tell I made you feel bad when I kept thanking you for rescuing me, but I'm bad at these things, so I don't totally know why it bothered you."

He shoves a hand in his pocket. "Okay. Well, it's pretty damn simple." He blows out a breath. "What I was trying to explain was that I didn't come to the restaurant out of some feeling of pity or obligation. I came because I was jealous as hell when I saw you leave the house with that douchebag, and I thought…" He looks at the sky for a moment, finding the right words. "I want to be the guy taking you out. I want to be the one you kiss at the end of the night. And I thought that if there was a shred of hope that you felt the same way about me, I needed to show up there and find out. So if it felt like a rescue, I assure you my motives were a hundred percent self-centered. I fucking wanted you, pure and simple."

My jaw hangs open. I try to get it working, but it feels slack and weak. "I…that's not at all what I was expecting you to say."

His laugh heals me. "Well, what in the hell were you expecting?"

Bogie spots a squirrel and attempts to dart after it, but Hunter holds him tight. Bogie strains at the leash, but there's no question who's in charge. When he reels him back in, Hunter bends down and kisses the top of Bogie's head.

It's the sexiest thing I've ever seen.

"Good boy. No squirrels for lunch."

I think back on all the conversations in my head over the past twenty-four hours. They all involve a version of him explaining that he doesn't do relationships. He's been quoted as saying that, for heaven's sake. So it's taking me a minute to let this new information sink in.

"I guess I was preparing myself for you to let me down easy. Tell me you don't do situation-ships or whatever."

He presses two fingers against his forehead as though his brain aches. Or maybe that's me. "I don't even know what that means. But if you're saying you thought I was only into hookups, I guess I had that coming. I know that's what people think about me. I just didn't think it's what *you* thought." His voice breaks a tiny bit, and I feel how much it hurts him that I've jumped to a conclusion.

We reach a fork in the road, and he points us to the right, which will take us down Beachwood Canyon toward the flats. Bogie walks ahead of us like there was never any chance of a different decision.

"Hunter, you have to understand something about me. I live in a world governed by data. I use my instincts, but only after I've done a really good job of loading the deck in my favor. So I went with the odds—that you were interested in me for a fling. Because no offense, but you're known as a guy who dates a lot of women, so…"

He stops walking. "I hate that you know that."

"I'm sorry. I know I'm a scientist and all, but I don't live under a rock."

"Fair enough."

"It wasn't so much that I was judging you as much as protecting myself," I admit. Letting go of that information feels as cleansing as a long exhale.

Hunter's hand wraps around mine. "You don't need to protect yourself with me."

My heart skips a beat. It feels like the breath has been knocked from my lungs, and when I figure out how to breathe again, my heart races like a hummingbird.

"Thank you." It hardly feels like a sufficient answer.

"I don't expect you to take me at my word, but if you give me a chance, I'll prove it to you. I don't want something temporary with you. It's just hard to live down the past."

I cast him a side-eye, not wanting him to go overboard in protesting his old ways. "It's okay. I get what it must be like to be you. I'd hook up with a lot of women too."

He comes to an abrupt stop. Even Bogie knows not to continue, plopping himself down in the shade like he's happy to have a break while we adults sort through our miscommunications.

"Two years," he says flatly.

I give him a blank stare.

"I haven't been with a woman at all in two years. I don't care what you think you know from whatever social media bullshit is out there, but I want you to hear it from me. Two years, and that's because I haven't been interested."

I bite down on my lip, debating what to say.

He shrugs. "I'm not trying to impress you, in case that's why you look like you're about to laugh in my face. Just stating a fact."

Shaking my head, I lean against him, smiling to myself at the depth of our misunderstanding of each other. "Never," I say, finally. I'm diving in deep because this is what I do. I tell myself to hold back and protect myself, and then I have big feels and go for broke. "I've never felt like myself with a man as much as I did the other night. Not ever. Until you."

He can't fight the boyish pride in his smirk. "Well, that's maybe the best thing anyone's ever said to me."

"Don't let it go to your head." I playfully try to swat him, but his reflexes are too fast. I end up with my arms pinned to my sides in his tight embrace.

"Oh no, you don't. You can't say something like that and get away from me."

I wriggle in his arms but have no real intention of escaping. "I don't want to get away."

"Good. Because we're doing this."

"We are?"

He nods slowly, deliberately. "Yes, we are."

"Okay." I grin at him like a groupie, and I don't care if I look like a fool.

He wraps his large hand around my rib cage and pulls me against him. I revel in the feeling of being pressed against his body. Without second-guessing, I stand on my toes and loop my arms around his neck.

Hunter swivels his baseball hat so it's backward and cups my cheek in one hand as he leans in to kiss me. There's none of the hesitance from the other night, no light brushes of his lips against mine. This is a kiss that claims me as his, leaving no question about where I stand.

I savor the taste of him as our tongues tangle. The flavor of coffee mixed with raspberries. I want more than I can have on the side of a road, but for now, it's enough.

When we break the kiss, Hunter looks me over and nods as though he's satisfied. "So you'll go on a real date with me?"

I laugh because it sounds like he's proposing a tennis match. "I'll do all kinds of things with you. I like you, soccer star."

"You hear that, Bogie? Gracie likes me." The dog's ears perk up when he hears his name. "And that makes me really goddamn lucky." Bogie starts circling Hunter's legs. Whether it's because he understands the words or he wants to start walking, I can't be sure. But I prefer to think he understands.

"Kyler is going to lose his ever-loving mind," I say. "Do we have to tell him?"

"I, for one, can't fucking wait."

Hunter releases his tight grip and moves his arms up my back and up to the nape of my neck. He turns my face at an angle and floors me with a kiss that feels like nothing I've ever experienced. It's needy and hot, and it communicates everything that can't be put into words. I feel like Hunter is digging deep into my soul and connecting to me on an elemental level. My body arches into his, and I'm oblivious to any cars driving by.

We're wrapped up in each other in the shade of a sprawling live oak, tucked into the nook of a side street. Bogie sprawls like a seal on his belly. No part of me wants to leave this corner or step away from Hunter.

Our kiss deepens, and I wrap a leg around him, urging myself closer even though closer may be physically impossible. He lifts me easily, and I encircle his waist with my legs and cup his face in my hands. Tipping my face down, I kiss him like he's essential to my very survival.

Reaching down, I feel how hard he is, and it matches my own hunger for him.

"God, Tink," he bites out. "I'm not fucking you on a street corner even though I want to."

His course words send a ripple of heat down my spine, and I picture myself pushing his pants down and having him rail me against a tree. The surprising image makes me smile against his lips.

"What?" he asks, adjusting his grip and digging his fingers into both cheeks of my bottom.

I shake my head. "I was imagining the PR fallout if you were caught on social media with your pants down in the Hollywood Hills."

He laughs and lets me slide down his body until my feet are on the ground. He kisses my temple. "Wouldn't be the first time," he mutters, more proud of himself than embarrassed. I kind of like that he doesn't shy away from his past, even if he's telling me that's no longer who he is.

"Such a player," I tease.

"Former player."

"If you say so."

"I do. Can you trust me on that?"

Even though it doesn't come easily, I decide I do trust him. "I can."

"Good."

I stand frozen on the corner, debating whether to ruin the moment. "But what about work? Dating you goes against company policy."

He frowns. "Are you sure? Does it apply to players or just corporate execs?"

"Ha. Not specified. But players are probably even worse than corporate types. I'm running player data and making recruiting suggestions. It's more of a conflict of interest than, like, dating someone in the PR department."

"I guess that's true."

"Even worse, I advocated for keeping you on the team. I'd look super biased."

"But that was before you even knew me."

"True. But people think what they think."

"Okay, then. We can call it off or try things out and keep

everything under wraps, see how we feel."

I know what the right decision is—the clean, clear decision that's best for my career.

And I know what my heart wants. I've let it make decisions for me in the past, and it hasn't worked out, but it's begging me to trust it one last time. I have a good feeling about Hunter.

At the end of the day, instincts beat out data as the deciding factor.

Otherwise, we're not human.

"I don't want to call it off. I want to try. But please, promise me you'll tread lightly here. I'll go to my bosses if the time is right."

He kisses my temple. "I promise."

Interlacing our fingers, Hunter starts walking again, making sure he's on the outside so I'm out of the way of cars. Bogie seems glad to be on the move again, trotting in front of us with his nose to the ground, on the scent of the next squirrel or leftover hamburger wrapper.

We've almost reached the bottom of the hill, and I look up at the steep climb ahead of us to get back to the house. "That doesn't look too fun. I'm gonna be slow, just warning you."

"Tell you what. Let's get a couple of smoothies and give Bogie a chance to slurp some water, and then we can get a ride back to the house. Pick up where we left off on the corner." His eyebrows bounce behind his sunglasses.

"That all sounds perfect."

CHAPTER 29

$\mathcal{H}$unter

BEING with Gracie now already feels different.

The next fifteen minutes are an exercise in self-control.

Sitting across a table for two on the front patio of a Kreation Juice place on Franklin, I have a perfect excuse to stare at Gracie for as long as I want.

But what I want to do is anything but stare.

I'm already calculating that we'll grab a rideshare to ferry us up the hill so I can get her into my bed with minimal detours. And so help me, if Kyler is home and feeling like a long chat, I might throw him off his own balcony.

Bogie laps up water from the collapsible bowl from his hiking harness and seems content in the table's shade. I'm antsy, drumming my fingers while we wait for our car to arrive.

"I don't mind walking. It's only, what, fifteen minutes?" Gracie asks, seeming as eager as I am to get back to the house.

"All uphill, but I'm game if you are."

She chews on her lip, debating. "When's the car supposed to come?"

I look at the app, which has been giving me the runaround for the past ten minutes. "Ugh, it's looking for a new driver again. I guess it's peak hours."

"Let's go. I can handle a hill." She's up before I have a chance to argue and untangling Bogie's leash from the leg of the table.

"Wait, there's a new car coming in two minutes. Can you wait two minutes?"

"I can definitely wait two minutes."

I tug Gracie against my side and nuzzle her neck. Can't keep my damn hands off her.

Out of the corner of my eye, I'm vaguely aware of movement that I've learned to spot over the years. Someone notices me. There's some surreptitious pointing and maybe an attempt to take a picture that looks like a selfie, but the phone is really pointed at me. In my sunglasses and hat, I'm barely recognizable, so I doubt there's much social media currency in whatever she's capturing.

All the same, I shift so Gracie is out of view, tucking my head down a little more so only the brim of my hat is visible. No point in mentioning it to Gracie because she'll worry unnecessarily. This kind of thing happens all the time and is mostly a big noth-ingburger.

Our rideshare pulls up, and I shuttle Gracie and Bogie into the car, and a second later, I disappear behind tinted glass as the car chews asphalt, taking us up the hill.

Kyler responds to my text, saying he's at the beach for the afternoon. Perfect.

Gracie leans her head on my shoulder, and I brush her hair away from her neck. Her skin looks milky and soft. I press a kiss to her temple and run a finger along her cheek. Gracie smiles up at me, and for the first time in a long time, I don't have any regrets about the past or worries about the future.

I didn't think anything rivaled the feeling of snapping a soccer ball away from a striker and saving a goal. But this right here is it.

~

A FEW LAZY HOURS LATER, we're still in Gracie's room, which looks like a tornado blew through it. Clothes strewn everywhere, pillows chucked from the nicely made bed, reading light knocked from the bedside table.

Gracie reclines on the bed, hair splayed across an overstuffed pillow, lips red and swollen from being kissed for an hour straight. I'm on my side, propped on an elbow, enjoying the view. She looks good like this—scant makeup, messy hair, eyes glazed. Behind them, that fire of fierce intelligence still burns bright, but she's spent, and it softens her focus. I like it.

"Are you coming to the game this weekend?" My ego wants to impress her, but I know I need to keep my focus on the game.

"I'm definitely watching, but I like TV better." She cringes as though afraid of my reaction.

"Really? You are one of one, Tink. Most people love the rush of action and the crowd at a game."

"I get that, but it's hard to focus when people are screaming all around me. Especially in the team box when everyone wants to know my opinions, like I can do analytics on the spot."

"You can. It's your superpower."

She smiles. "Shh. Don't tell."

"Noted. No live games for Gracie Albright."

"We don't have to be so extreme. How about fewer live games?"

"Deal."

I pull her against me and run a hand down her arm until I hear the tiny sigh that gives me life.

"Mmm. I've gotta say, I was not happy about moving to LA, but you're looking at a total convert." Her smile is easy, and the post-sex haze has her blinking up at me slowly like I might disappear if she makes any abrupt moves.

I laugh and point between the two of us. "Yeah? You're crediting LA with what we've got going here?"

"Totally. All LA magic."

"Good to know." My hand takes a slow trip down the length of her body, starting at her shoulder, following the swell of her breast, nipping in where her waist contours, and settling on her hip. I can't help the way my fingers dig into her flesh there, gripping her possessively. From the way her eyes seem to melt, I know she likes it.

"Mm hm, magic," she whispers.

Leaning over to brush her lips with a kiss, I roll against her side and feel myself start to get hard again from barely touching her. This woman. She has a hold on me like I've never experienced, and I don't even think she realizes it.

Maybe it's better that way. Until I figure out what this thing between us is, and whether there's any hope of a future, I don't want her to know how quickly my heart is sliding into quicksand, pulled deep by how much I want her for more than stolen hours or nights.

Much as I'd love to spend more time with her like this, the comment about LA gives me an idea. "How long have you been in LA? A month? Two tops?"

"Split the difference. It's been about six weeks."

Six weeks of falling for her.

"So you still kind of look at this place like you're a tourist."

She tips her head from side to side, considering. "More or less. I didn't come here thinking it was permanent, if that's what you mean. So I guess I haven't dug in and thought of myself as an Angeleno."

I don't like hearing her talk about her time here as finite, even if I know it's true in the recesses of my brain. Easy enough to push the thought aside in favor of what I want in the moment.

It's how I thrive on a soccer field. Everything is about the here and now and the goal at hand. If I think, if I dwell on the past or the future too much, I lose the moment. That's often the difference between blocking a shot and letting it slip by. Between winning and losing. Between success and failure.

I don't want to fail here, so I force myself to stay in the present.

"I was thinking maybe I should give you a tour. Not the well-known spots like Venice Beach. I'm talking about the 'Hunter Reyes inside LA' spots. The ones that aren't on the map.'"

She perks up instantly at the idea, pushing herself to sit and swiveling her legs to cross them. Eyes bright, she looks as eager as a kid who's been told about a spontaneous trip to Disneyland. Come to think of it…

"Or we could go to Disneyland. Your pick."

She leans back as though I might trap her if she's too close. "No, not that. I don't do scary rides."

I can't help but laugh. "Scary? Five-year-olds go to Disneyland. It's the 'happiest place on earth.' You watch soccer players try to kill each other for a living. Trust me, I think you can handle a ride or two."

She shakes her head. "I mean, I'm sure you're right, but I like the idea of the 'Hunter tour.' I want to know you better. Show me what you love about LA."

I can't say no to that. My brain fires up, and I start thinking about where I want to take her, all the things I want to do with her in the hours we have before sunset. It's early afternoon, so that gives me a roadmap.

"Okay, Tink, get dressed and grab shoes you can walk in, a few layers, and something you'll want to wear to dinner later. Leave the rest to me."

She puts her hands on my chest and lowers herself down until her breasts push against my body, and it's all I can do not to cage her in and keep her here for the rest of the day. Her gentle kiss immediately deepens, and I'm a hairline away from flipping her over and taking her one more time before we leave.

But then she breaks the kiss with a disappointed moan. Pushing herself away from me, she shakes her head. "Too good, soccer star. Promise me our night will end right here?"

"I promise."

Easiest promise I'll ever have to keep.

*H*unter

"I BARELY KNOW my way around. I swear I won't be able to guess where we're going." Gracie sits in the passenger seat of the Range Rover with a bandanna I tied over her eyes. "Can I take this off?"

"Nope. I want it to be a total surprise."

"It will be. How can it not? I told you I've been to like three places since I got here, most of them within a stone's throw of work."

I can be a stubborn son of a bitch when I want to, and right now, her protests are only egging me on. "Nope. Sorry."

Even under the bandanna, she has the sensory ability to elbow me in the side. "You're not sorry. Not even a little."

"Correct."

Her hand goes to the bandanna but mine is quicker. I take her hand and keep it wrapped in mine. "Patience, grasshopper. I promise, it will be worth the torture."

A few minutes later, I pull onto Pacific Coast Highway from

Kanan and everything changes. The serene Pacific sprawls to our left, blocked by intermittent houses that pop up along the drive, and the scattered restaurants and shops to our right. "Okay, you can take it off now."

Gracie squints for a moment as her eyes acclimate to the light, but she immediately smiles when she sees where we are. "I'll take a view of the beach any day. This is gorgeous."

She's right. It's a bluebird sky day, and the few fat, white clouds look like they were painted there to make the sky look better. There aren't a lot of cars on the road. We glide past the occasional cyclist in bright spandex, but it feels like a world away from where we were earlier.

"This isn't just the beach. This is Malibu. Nice, clean water, not super crowded, lotta surfers. I come here when I need to get out of my head." I point at the water, which is closer to the highway along this stretch. "When I stand on the beach there and look at the water, I can let everything else go."

She puts the window down and inhales deeply. "I can imagine. That ocean air is cleansing."

I put my hand on her knee. "Have you ever been stand-up paddleboarding?"

"What's that?"

"You've probably seen people doing it. Standing up on what looks like a big surfboard and paddling along on top of the water?"

She nods. "Oh, yeah. People do that at Shoreline Lake, near my house in the Bay Area."

"Good stuff. It gets you onto the water, super chill. I had a couple of boards at my house, but the fire took 'em."

Her face falls like it does every time I mention the loss of my house. "Sorry to hear that. Would've been fun to try it."

I cough out a laugh. "You're such a bad liar. In no universe do you think it would be fun to get up on a board on the ocean, but we're going to do it, Gracie. You need to trust me."

She presses her lips together, brows furrowed. I feel like something set off a land mine in her brain, and I'm not sure it's the idea of standing on a foam board.

Grazing her chin with the tip of my thumb, I tip her face up to see the confidence in my eyes. I'm not sure if it's confidence in her ability to handle a paddleboard or confidence in her ability to handle me, but I need her to see and understand it. "You can trust me, Tink."

Her almost imperceptible flinch tells me I've hit the nail on the head. She's having a hard time trusting me. Fair enough. I need to earn it.

"I promise. I won't let you get hurt. And I don't just mean the paddleboard."

Her eyes flicker, and she sucks in a breath. I wait for her to exhale, grateful to see some of the resistance leave her expression. "I...I didn't bring a bathing suit."

I slip a finger under the hem of her white denim shorts and caress her skin. "These'll work fine. We'll go in a little cove where the water's gentle. You probably won't get anything wet besides your feet."

"I know a big fat liar when I see one," she says. "But you're also a sweet talker. So...I trust you."

It feels like a victory. It's all I can do not to dance.

WHEN WE'VE PARKED at the cove, I walk Gracie over to my buddy Ricardo, who's loaning us two of his boards and oars. Leaning against his pickup truck, he runs his thumb and finger over his beard.

"Nice to meet you," she says politely, extending her hand.

Ricardo holds both of his hands up like she's pulled a gun. "Oh no. We'll have none of that." He pulls her into a bear hug and lifts her off her feet.

Gracie shrieks and giggles until he puts her down.

Ricardo takes off his straw hat and pops it onto Gracie's head. "You'll need this in the sun. This character should know better than to bring you out here without sun protection."

"I told her to bring a hat and she has one. Don't you think for one second that I'm not taking care of my girl."

My girl.

The words come out before I can stop them. Ricardo doesn't seem to notice, but Gracie does. I look at her apologetically, ready to backpedal, but her cheeks warm and she puts her hand in mine. If she likes being called my girl, I have no intention of quitting.

"I'm new at this," Gracie admits. Ricardo doesn't waste a second, putting his arm around her like an old friend and guiding her over to the two boards he has laid out on the sand. He gets down on his knees on one and points at the other one for Gracie to do the same. Then he picks up an oar and places it on the board next to him.

"This is all you need to do."

Sitting on her heels, she gives Ricardo a side-eye. "Isn't it called *standup* paddleboarding? Seems like I'm missing the point if I stay down here."

"She's a sharp one." Ricardo points his oar at me, and I swat it away.

"Smart-ass. You gonna teach her right, or should I?"

He stands up and hands me the oar. "Thought you'd never ask." He winks at Gracie. "This guy knows more than I do, if I'm being honest. I was messing with you two."

Ricardo slaps me on the back and goes back to his truck, where he's stashed some other gear. He'll probably take out a kayak or swim while we're doing our thing.

It's a perfect day for paddling. The water is always calm in the cove thanks to the breakwater built just offshore, but today it looks especially glassy.

I get down on my knees next to Gracie and walk her through the basics of paddleboarding. "You start on your knees. You're super stable like this, so you can push out into the water and get away from shore. Then when you feel comfortable floating, you get up onto your feet. Crouch first, then stand." I demonstrate, holding the paddle in my hand.

She watches me studiously but nothing in her expression says she likes the idea of this.

"Uh-huh. And when in this process do I lose my balance and belly flop into the freezing ocean?"

"I'm not gonna lie. It happens. But the worst thing is maybe you get a little wet and you scramble back onto your board and try again."

"Scramble? I don't scramble."

It occurred to me that she might feel this way, and I don't want to force her out of her comfort zone. So I turn and march back to my truck, returning a moment later with a pristine beach chair and a towel.

"That's it? You're giving up on me?" She sounds outraged, but the relief on her face tells a different story. "So I'm going to watch while you paddle? Come on, soccer star, at least make me feel a little bit lame for copping out. It's only fair."

I grin. "You're not copping out."

"I'm not?"

Shaking my head, I put the chair down and wrap her in my arms. Leaning down, I kiss the tops of her cheeks and then her lips.

"Nope. We'll go together. And I promise you'll stay dry." I unfold the beach chair, set it on the front of one of the boards, and put the towel over it, making a nice, comfortable passenger seat. Extending my hand, I invite her aboard.

"Milady."

She takes my hand, and I escort her to the chair. Then I lift the board, carefully balancing her on top, and tote it on my shoulder, enjoying Gracie's squeal when she's hefted high. I balance the board carefully so she doesn't fall.

Once we get to the water's edge, I ease the board onto the water.

Gracie looks like a princess, bobbing in her chair at the helm. I push the board along as I wade into the water. Once we're a hundred feet from shore, I hop on and start paddling, staying on my knees at first.

The afternoon sun is starting to dip, so I'm paddling directly into the glare, but I don't care. I'm happy to be here with her, happy that she went along with my crazy plan. Happy she trusts me.

We get farther out, and I push myself up to stand on the board. She peeks behind her to see my oar sweep through the water. "See? Nothing to it."

"Easy for you to say. You're an athlete with impeccable balance and strength."

She wiggles forward in her chair so she's lounging now, tipping her face toward the sun.

"You could do this, but there's plenty of time for that later. Enjoy the ride."

It's so quiet out here, so removed from the bustle of LA. Anything that could possibly crush my vibe is literally behind me as I paddle atop the deep blue water. A couple of gulls circle in the distance, eventually diving down when they spot a fish. But otherwise, we're alone.

"This is so nice." Gracie stretches her legs to the tip of the board, and her hair whips lightly in the breeze.

"Right? It's one of my happy places."

"I can see why. Now I'm excited to see more of them."

The only sounds out here are the swish of my paddle and the lap of the board on the uneven water. We move in silence for a while, and eventually, I turn the board so we're parallel to the shore, which makes for an even smoother ride.

I continue navigating around the cove until we're back in shallow water. Gracie looks so content in her chair that I decide to leave her be. No reason to insist she try paddling if she doesn't want to, not when we're having such a perfect time as it is.

That's why it shocks me when she turns around and confidently says she's ready to try paddling on her own. "What's the worst that could happen? I could get wet. I'm waterproof."

"Yeah?" I can't help grinning at how chill she is. The power of the ocean, I guess.

"Yeah. Let's do it."

I hop off the board and hold it steady while she shifts out of the chair and gets into position on her knees in the center. "You good here for a sec while I get my board?"

The board shifts beneath her when I let go, and she panics for a second, grabbing onto the edges and humming anxiously. "Yeah. Okay. I can do this."

Moving as fast as I can, I hold the beach chair overhead and slog through the shallow surf. I chuck the chair onto the sand and grab the other board. In under a minute, I'm back in the water.

Her look of relief when I'm next to her makes me feel a hundred feet tall. I hold on to her board to steady it. "I've got you. Want to try popping up?"

We're deep enough for her to try standing, but shallow enough that she won't get soaked if she falls. Gracie puts one foot and then the other one beneath her and stays in a squat for a moment, white knuckling the edges of the board.

"That's great. Now use the paddle to steady yourself and see if you can stand. If it feels wobbly, you can drop back to your knees."

She does as instructed, wobbling as she slowly rises. I think the wobble is more about her shaky knees than the motion of the water, but I'm not about to distract her with that information.

"Okay, I think I'm up."

I laugh. "You're definitely up. Now try paddling."

She carefully puts her oar in the water, and once again, I marvel at the care she takes in everything she does. Her oar moves through the ocean methodically. Twice on one side, twice on the other.

Watching her sail out toward the horizon, I feel so proud of her that I forget I'm supposed to be paddling along next to her. She turns to look at me before I can tell her to keep her eyes forward.

I catch the round-eyed look of fear right before she topples off the board and falls into the water, which is still only waist-deep. Drops cling to her face and hair. Cringing and paddling quickly toward her, I half expect our excursion to be short-lived.

"I'm sorry," I say when I reach her. Her tee is half soaked as she stands with both hands on the board. "I got so distracted watching you that I didn't stay next to you. Are you over it?"

"Over it?"

"Want to call it a day?"

"Are you kidding? I can't get much wetter. Let's do this."

Before I can give her a boost, she pushes herself atop her board and gets back onto her knees in the center. She blows out an impatient breath. "Are you ready, or what?"

I give her a little salute. "Ready, boss. Let's go."

For the next half hour, we paddle side by side as the sun teases us with a sunset that's still at least a few hours away. And that's a good thing because I have a lot more planned for us before our sunset kiss.

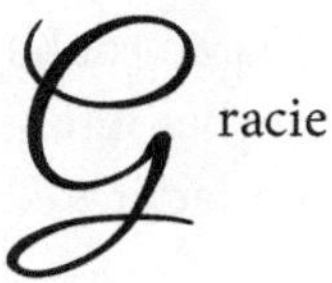racie

"WELL, THAT WAS AWESOME!" I'm practically bouncing in the passenger seat, and I'm not a bouncer. I'm calm and methodical and measured.

But not when I'm with Hunter. Somehow, the time we spend together has me reaching into a reservoir of joy I didn't know existed. I'm the girl who always has a plan, always knows where she's going.

And today, I'm also the girl who got up on a stand-up paddleboard and rowed out to sea next to a hot athlete and made out with him on the sand afterward. I like this version of me.

Now we're parking again, this time at the Malibu Lagoon, which seems to be mainly a destination for bird-watchers and nature lovers. Hunter introduces me to a ranger after he finishes pointing out a good birding area to a couple of parents and their little kids.

"This is Gracie. She's new to town, and I thought she oughtta know about this place," Hunter says, pointing a thumb over his shoulder at the sculpted marine habitat where signs explain the preservation efforts underway.

"Glad to have you, Gracie. Hunter's got a good eye for spotting some of our shyer species, so stick with him."

"I plan to." I tip my head against Hunter's shoulder, and he wraps his hand around mine. It feels natural to be with him like this.

Like a girlfriend.

I don't know if that's what I am, but maybe I could be. I'm not sure if Hunter "does" girlfriends or relationships. But I'm okay not knowing.

The ranger, a guy our age with a full, dark beard, round glasses, and a parks service badge around his neck, fishes into a gear box and retrieves two pairs of binoculars and a laminated list of birds, complete with photos.

"You'll see a lot of these." He points at a crane and a sandpiper on the sheet and then tips his head toward a flock of them on the wet sand. "But lemme know if you spot any nests in the grasslands. We need to mark those."

"Sure thing," Hunter says, taking the binoculars. I grab the birding guide, and we walk toward a grassy area where the tide is rolling in.

"We looking for nests?" I point at the grassy areas.

"Yup. Where there are nests, there are often really cool mama birds keeping their eggs warm. And like he said, they need to be marked and cordoned off so they don't get trampled."

I press my lips together to keep from smiling when he calls them "mama birds." The sun warms the back of my neck as we poke along in the waving grasses, submerged in ankle-deep water.

"I'm getting the impression that today's theme is getting wet," I say as my flip-flops squelch in the wet sand.

Hunter leans close, his short beard grazing my cheek when he growls against my ear. "If this is getting you wet, I'll consider my work today done."

My skin blazes at the suggestion, and a jolt hits my core. If I wasn't wet before, I am now. "Um, I…" I sputter.

"Good," Hunter whispers before kissing my cheek. I look around to see if anyone notices him being openly affectionate. Even if he doesn't seem concerned, I am. Not interested in being a part of some beach bunny's social media post.

We're all but alone in a section of sand and grass, so I relax. Hunter grabs my hand and puts a finger to his lips. He points, and we tread softly toward an area in the sandy grass where he indicates I should use my binoculars. He does the same, and we zoom in on two birds with blue plumage fussing around three minuscule babies in a small nest.

He squeezes my hand as we stand silently, taking this miracle of nature. I'm dying to ask how he knew where to look, but I don't dare disturb the birds. We watch for a good five minutes as the birds communicate with each other, one plodding through the grass while the other feeds the hatchlings, beak to beak.

Hunter taps my shoulder and indicates the shore behind us. I nod, and we silently back away from the birds.

"That was amazing," I say.

Hunter's voice is low, and I can barely hear him over the lapping waves a hundred feet away, so I lean closer. "You might be sensing a theme…all of my favorite LA places are about perspective. Getting away from the crowds and finding a little peace."

"I'm glad you figured out a way to do that. Thank you for sharing it with me."

"Aw, Gracie, it's my pleasure. We all need a little peace, don't we?"

Hunter wraps an arm around my shoulders, and we stroll along the sand, every so often raising our binoculars to track a bird in the air or zoom in on another grassy area with potential for babies.

I can't help feeling like I've found my little bit of peace right here. With him.

~

OUR DAY ENDS with a casual seafood dinner at a spot I'd never have noticed without Hunter pointing it out as we continued north on the highway.

We stopped at a beach club on the way so we could shower and change, so I'm now wearing the outfit I chose earlier, before I knew where we'd go to dinner. I've ditched the tee and shorts for a yellow cotton sundress with spaghetti straps and a fitted bodice, and the flip-flops have given way to sandals.

The beach club was stocked with every imaginable hair and skin product, so I feel halfway decent sitting across from Hunter, whose tanned skin glows and his dark, damp hair is perfectly tousled, as usual. I don't think he could look bad if he tried.

We're sitting against the railing of the restaurant patio, which is empty except for our table overlooking the ocean. The view is spectacular, a wide stripe of dark blue beneath the orange rays of the setting sun. I swear, Hunter must have timed our afternoon down to the minute because we arrived here about fifteen minutes before sunset, and we've been sitting here watching the light fade from the sky ever since.

"Why isn't half of LA clambering for a table here? This place is going on my top ten list."

"Yeah, you have a top ten list?" His interest piques at the opportunity to get information, and he breaks his gaze from the ocean.

"I'm making it as we speak. Best hidden gems in LA."

"What else is on the list?"

Our server brings over a bottle of wine I don't think we ordered. Hunter nods at the label, and the wine is opened and poured. "Did you order this?"

"No, but I trust them. Been coming here a long time."

Our server watches Hunter taste the wine. He's appropriately friendly, reciting a few tasting notes and waiting for Hunter to nod in approval before filling our glasses. But something about his manner intrigues me. He seems nervous like he's at a job audition or like he'll be rated at the end of the meal. He leaves without a word, and once again, we're wrapped in the sound of ocean waves and solitude.

"Thanks for letting me be your sidekick today."

Hunter holds up his glass. "Are you kidding? It was my pleasure. You are rapidly becoming my favorite sidekick."

I hold up mine. "To my favorite tour guide."

"Who knew, right? After all these years."

Our hands brush with the musical clink of crystal, and Hunter's eyes lock on mine. I'm mesmerized as he brings the glass to his lips and sips. His tongue moves inside his mouth as he swirls the liquid before swallowing it down. His Adam's apple works in his throat, and I've never seen something so hot in my life.

Hunter stares at me for so long that I'm almost afraid to drink my wine under his intense gaze. "Everything okay?" I ask, finally.

He nods. "Everything is great. But…I feel like I need to be honest about something." He inhales a deep breath and looks up.

"This seems dire."

"No, not at all. I…this isn't a new feeling for me, wanting to be with you. I've always had a thing for you, Gracie. Always."

"You mean…?"

"Back when we were younger and you used to come home from college. I was crushing hard and totally intimidated."

I grin and reach for his hand. "I had a thing for you too."

"Yeah?"

I nod.

"And now?"

"Better than I ever imagined."

"So much better." He takes a long sip of his wine. Then he holds up the glass, looking at the liquid like he has a lot to think about. When he puts the glass down, his eyes return to my face, and his smile spreads wide. "You were worth the fucking wait." His eyebrows bounce above a wolfish grin.

I smile and try to drink my wine. The first sip goes down easily, but when I look up at the molten heat flaring in his eyes, a shiver rolls over my skin. He looks like he wants to devour me.

I could easily let him.

"So I feel like maybe you like this place?" He can't keep the satisfied smile off his lips. Leaning back in his chair, he picks up his wineglass and surveys our surroundings. Small tables set with simple white tablecloths and blue flowered napkins. The chairs are bamboo and blue wicker, making them look like they belong on a café patio in Paris. A vintage-looking crystal chandelier sheds enough light from its dimmed bulbs to allow us to see each other. And a small candle burning in the center of each table adds romance without detracting from the real star of the show—the ocean lapping just beyond the sand and the moon already hanging high in the sky. A light breeze filters through the open spaces above the painted wooden railing.

"I like it a lot," I say, playing with my menu, which is a single sheet of paper clipped to a stiff board. "What do you feel like eating?"

He doesn't answer. Instead, he takes my hand across the table and leans in. "You." His voice crackles like electricity in the damp air.

I feel a full-body shiver as my focus goes hazy. I can't help chomping down on my lip.

Reaching over, Hunter frees it with his index finger and runs the pad of his thumb over my trembling lip. "But I intend to feed you first."

His eyes are so dark I can barely see his pupils, so I nod, hating how easily he can unnerve me. And loving it equally.

"Okay." My hoarse croak makes him smile. Clearing my throat, I try to regain some of my composure, but as I lean on my elbow, it slips off the table. His sharp reflexes have him catching me before I fall.

As he rights me, he keeps a hand wrapped around my elbow possessively. "Not gonna let you go."

I look over the menu. Lots of plant-based options and seafood with simple preparation. No heavy sauces or fried food. No wonder he likes this place. I don't have a chance to think about the menu anymore because our server shows up with two appetizers and plates for each of us. "Hamachi crudo with Sicilian peppers and jalapeño poppers stuffed with spiced cream cheese."

I do a double-take at the second item, but the server disappears before I can confirm that the dish sitting in front of me is really one of my go-to bar food staples. And now, I'm starting to understand Hunter's little game here. "This place doesn't really serve jalapeño poppers, does it?"

Hunter tries to give me his best impression of bafflement, raising his eyebrows high, but then he relents. "Yeah, no. I asked for those when I let them know we were coming."

"Did you also ask for the place to be utterly deserted?"

He nods. "Do you mind?"

"Do I *mind*? This is the single most romantic day I've ever had. I can't believe you managed to make all this happen between the time you offered to show me around and the time I said yes."

"When I'm motivated, I can get shit done." So smug. So damn handsome.

If I don't let some air into my lungs, I might crawl over and straddle his lap. Sneaking a look around us at the empty space, I feel emboldened. I take another sip of wine for courage and focus on breathing. Then I push my chair back.

Hunter watches me and slides his own chair back as though he knows exactly where I want to be. I hike up the skirt of my dress above my knees and sink onto his lap, dropping my arms over his shoulders. His hands grip my hips, but he lets me take the lead.

"Thank you for bringing me here. I love it."

He nods, his eyes moving slowly over me.

"So you're the kinda guy who knows the owners of restaurants," I tease.

It may be my imagination, but I think his lips twitch before he admits, "Something like that."

I pick up a jalapeño popper and bite it in half. It's blazing hot, and the cheese oozes out of both sides. Rookie mistake to eat it before it's cooled, but this man is throwing me off with his romantic gestures and heated looks.

The corners of Hunter's eyes crinkle in amusement as he watches me try to get control of the fried little thing. He lifts his napkin to my lips while I chew to dab away the oil that's no doubt dripping everywhere. I never pretended to be elegant.

"Good?" he asks, leaning back in his chair and watching me with crossed arms.

"Mm-hmm. Very." I push the plate closer to him. "Are you going to try one, or does a greasy pile of cheese go against your lean-protein regimen?"

He picks one up and examines it like he's never seen one before. "Oh, I'm trying one." He pops the whole thing in his mouth and chews. He can't feign indifference. By the time he swallows, he's licking his lips and reaching for a second one. "Oh my god. I'm doomed."

I grab another one too, leaving the beautiful shards of yellowtail in their perfect sauce untouched. We devour the remainder of the poppers and wash them down with wine.

Sliding off his lap and going back to my chair, I sigh. "I think my life is complete. Jalapeño poppers, the best guy, and a moonlit night at the beach? It doesn't get any better."

"The best guy?" His voice is low, repeating my words.

I nod. "The very best."

I should say more. I want to say more. I want to tell him that I'm falling for him, but I'm afraid of that look I know so well. I've seen that look with other men I've dated, the one that says he's flattered, but he doesn't feel the same way. The look that says he likes things the way they are and really wishes I wasn't thinking about the future.

I don't want to see that look on Hunter's face. I like what I'm looking at right now, how he seems happy to be here. That's enough.

After dinner, he walks me out of the restaurant and onto the sand. Down the beach, a pale blue lifeguard station beckons with what look like fairy lights. As we get closer, I see that, in fact, someone has hung a string of tiny lights on the railing.

"When did you do this?" I gasp, taking in the twinkling bulbs that usher us up the ramp and into the small structure, perched on stilts in the sand.

"Had a friend do me a favor."

"You mean a friend who works for you at *your* restaurant?" I tease.

"Something like that." He dips his head to nuzzle my neck, and I shudder as chills roll down my spine.

We stand at the top of the ramp, taking in the view of the nearly full moon, its reflection dancing in the waves of the ocean. The surf breaks in a calming rhythm. Like breathing.

"You impress me more and more every minute, soccer star. I thought this was supposed to be a rambling sort of drive through town so you could show me some things."

"I don't want to leave anything to chance when it comes to you. I want it to be right."

Inside, he's managed to have the lifeguard tower outfitted for us. A large floor cushion sits inside the doorway of the wooden structure, and a small lantern with a single bulb lights the inside in a warm glow.

"It's right," I say. "It's perfect."

unter

I WRAP Gracie in my arms, and we stand on the ledge of the lifeguard tower.

Did I have to scramble to make things happen after I invited Gracie to spend the afternoon with me? Yeah. Would I do it a hundred times over again just to see her delighted expression at every turn? Hell, yeah.

Way too many women in this town expect things. It's like they think they've done the heavy lifting to stay fit and look hot, so everything else should come their way. Eventually, it felt like too much effort to find the needles in the proverbial haystack.

And then, Gracie found me.

It's not for nothing that I want to make every minute we spend together better than the ones that came before it. It's not an accident that I want to make her forget about that ex of hers who did more damage than good, as far as I'm concerned.

So I have no problem showing Gracie exactly how much she

means to me. Starting with everything I've been thinking about since she slithered onto my lap, and I had to contend with a hard-on for the rest of dinner.

"Are you upset we skipped dessert?" I back us up slowly until we're inside the tower, out of view of anyone nearby. But there's no one nearby. Not a point of light on the water, no movement on the sand. We're alone, and the soft jazz from the restaurant still plays in the background, barely audible over the crash of the waves.

She nods slowly and brings her lips to mine, making up for dessert with a kiss that devours all the air in our midst. Lips, teeth, tongue, everything she gives me I want to return, and then some. I pull her down until she's sitting on the feather bed and blankets that cover the floor of the tower.

There are pillows behind her, pressed up against one wall, and I position her against them. The moonlight shines through the open door, dancing in the waves of her hair and flickering in her eyes. This is how I imagined the moment when I concocted it in my head hours ago, only it's better—brighter and more vivid.

From the small takeout bag I've been carrying, I extract a round plastic container and a spoon. "Can't have you upset," I say, lifting the lid from the container so she can see the chocolate mousse inside. Handing her the spoon, I sit back on my heels to watch her face as she scoops the spoon in and takes the first bite.

Her eyes flutter shut. "Mmm, oh my god, that's so good." Her tongue darts out to lick the spoon and get every last bit. If I wasn't already hard, that would finish me off. "Here, you need to try this," she says, offering me a spoonful.

I shake my head. "No way. That's all yours. I have my dessert right here." I slowly push her dress up to her waist, watching her skin pebble as the breeze hits her skin and she clues in on what I plan to do.

"So I'm going to eat this while you..." Her cheeks flush, and she chews her lip. She starts to sit up from the pillows, as if she might actually protest my decision. I know she has a rational mind and some part of her probably thinks this situation is unfair, so I need to assure her that she's right. Only I'm the one getting the better end of the deal. I gently push her back, and her head sinks into the pillows.

"Shhh," I tell her. "Eat your dessert, Tink. I'm busy."

Peeling her panties down her legs, I peek up to see that she's taken another spoonful of chocolate mousse, as instructed. "Good girl," I growl, letting my hands move where they want to go, higher inside her thighs, where her skin is soft and warm.

My tongue finds her slick, wet, and hot, and I suck hard on her clit. Her moan is so loud and satisfied that I have to fist myself to keep from coming as she gasps my name.

"I'm right here, baby." I slide a finger inside her and continue working her with my tongue, too focused now on the prize to bother looking to see if she's still eating the dessert.

"Hey, stop," she pants. My head jerks up for fear that something's wrong, and I see the wicked smile on Gracie's face. She swipes her index finger through the chocolate mousse and runs it straight through her center, coating herself with the creamy dessert. Then she licks the rest from her finger with a pop.

"You are something else," I groan, making short work of licking off every last damn drop. By the time I'm done, she's moaning and arching beneath me, gasping her way to her climax, convincing me she's the woman of my dreams. As if I didn't already know.

She's glistening, glowing, and wasting no time in unbuttoning my pants and sliding them down my legs. "C'mere." I barely get the condom on before she pulls me on top of her and guides me exactly where she wants me.

And the moment I'm inside her, I'm already gone. My body shudders hard, and I give in.

racie

ONE WEEK Later

IT'S nice to have Kyler back in town, but I'm surprised at how much it feels like Hunter and I have developed a rhythm without him. He knows I'm not exactly a morning person, so I appreciate being able to stumble around and drink my coffee in peace before I pull myself together in the bathroom.

And in the evenings, when I don't work late and Hunter doesn't have a team dinner, we've settled into a friendly routine of sharing cooking and cleanup duties. And then going straight to my room.

"Who got lost in Sicily?" Kyler asks, holding his nose in the air and sniffing the aroma coming from a saucepan on the stove. "That sure smells better than what I ate on my trip to Bali."

"Seriously? This is sauce from a jar." Hunter joins us in the kitchen in his customary outfit of barbecue apron over shorts and workout tee. "What are they eating in Bali?"

"Fish, mostly," Kyler says, going over to investigate the contents of the saucepan. "Actually, the food was awesome. All fresh, caught daily. The surfing is epic. Beaches couldn't be more gorgeous. I could move there, no prob."

"Maybe you should." The words come out before I realize how they sound. "I-I mean, not that I don't love having you here. I'm so grateful for the place to stay, and I'm not saying you should move to Bali, though it sounds pretty nice—"

Hunter steps closer to me and puts his long index finger against my lips, effectively shutting me up and making my pulse race. My gaze shoots to Kyler, who is busy tasting the sauce and oblivious to us.

"Okay, I call bullshit. There's no way this came from a jar," Kyler says.

Hunter puts up a hand. "Guilty. I knew you'd pester me for the recipe, so I was trying to let you down easy."

Kyler goes to the fridge, grabs a beer, and offers it to Hunter, who declines. I hold up my glass of sparkling water and orange juice when he looks my way. "Wow, you guys are no fun. Okay, I'll drink alone."

Hunter sweeps a leg over a barstool and sits, grazing my thigh along the way. A few butterflies take flight in my chest. "Tell us about the trip."

I don't know how he can be so casual with his tiny touches when they knock me off my feet every time. He seems desperate to find any excuse to brush against me while being equally unaffected by it. Meanwhile, I'm trying to keep myself from panting and turning the color of a pomegranate.

Fortunately, Kyler seems as hungry as he is oblivious. He slices off a hunk of baguette and dips it into the small dish of olive oil on the counter. "Hope you made enough for three. I fell asleep on the flight and missed the meals, so not only am I starving but I'm wide awake in time for night."

"Jet lag's gonna be brutal," Hunter says. "With all the travel you do, I'd think you'd know better than to sleep on the plane."

"Oh, I knew. But my body had other ideas. I was go, go, go the whole time I was there. Client meetings, surf demos, and I met a girl." His dimples dig in deep when he smiles.

"Okay! Do tell," Hunter says, motioning for Kyler to slice him some bread.

Kyler shrugs. "Not much to tell. She was fun. Sweet. Twenty-three…"

Hunter hums a Taylor Swift lyric about being that age, while I go all schoolmarm on him.

"I hope you didn't give her the wrong idea. Does she know you live half a planet away?"

"Of course. And trust me, what I gave her made her very happy. Not saying there's a future, but at least it'll give me something to look forward to if I need to go back there."

"Good for you, man. Great to hear." Hunter raises his hand for a high five.

"Guys, seriously." I shake my head, mock-disappointed in their caveman ways.

Hunter checks his phone and goes over to the stove. After turning off the pasta pot, he stirs the sauce and ladles the noodles into the pan, adding some pasta water at the end. He grabs a hunk of Parmesan cheese and shaves a healthy amount over the noodles.

I whisk together vinegar, mustard, lemon juice, and oil. I add a dash of salt and pepper and pour the dressing directly onto the arugula and tomato salad before giving it a toss in the bowl.

After Hunter plates the pasta, he hands the dishes to me. I add a heap of salad and drop a few basil leaves on top of the pasta. Then brush olive oil onto several slices of bread and pop them into the toaster oven.

Kyler watches in amazement as we assemble the dinner on his round kitchen table. "You two have got it down. Impressive."

"We do," I say, looking at Hunter. "We've got it down."

Kyler doesn't notice the looks that pass between us or the tiny touches, but a part of me wants him to notice. A part of me needs my brother to be a part of this, whatever it is.

"Hunter and I are dating," I blurt. Then I go to the cabinet to search for more olive oil, even though there's some on the counter.

I have my back to Kyler, and I'm waiting for him to answer before turning around. But he doesn't say a word. Then I realize I've sort of abandoned Hunter by dropping the bombshell and retreating. So I turn around and slowly look from one of them to the other.

Kyler is glaring at Hunter. "I warned you, man." He sounds angry, but he can't stay in character. He claps his friend on the back and hugs him. "And I couldn't be happier if this is legit."

"It's fucking legit," Hunter rasps. "I'm crazy about her."

Kyler smiles. He's not just grinning in amusement but flashing the widest smile I've seen from him in a while. He snaps his fingers. "I thought something might have been going on. So tell me. What's the deal?"

I'm so stunned by his reaction that I don't have a ready follow-up. "Um, we're dating and it's good." Now I smile. "Things are really good."

He shuts me down with a wave of his hand. "Okay, cancel that. I don't need details. I'm glad to hear it. For both of you."

Walking over to him, I extend my arms, and he pulls me in for a hug. "Thank you for being cool about it. I didn't mean to keep things from you."

He releases me and shakes his head. "I get it. We're sibs. It's weird. But like I told you, you're a catch, Gracie. You deserve to be happy, and if this brute does it for you, well..." He points at

Hunter and shrugs. "Then I'm happy." He looks at the table, which is laden with food. "And I'm starving. Can we eat?"

"We can eat," Hunter confirms, pulling my chair out while my brother nods, impressed.

"Look at you with the chivalry," Ky says.

"Not another fucking word." He points a finger at Kyler, but he can't suppress his own smile. So we sit there, the three of us, grinning like loons. And I love it.

CHAPTER 34

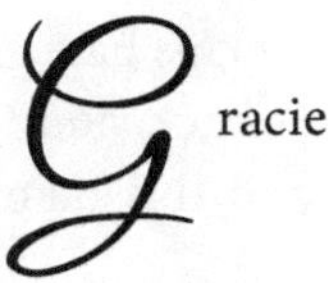racie

One Week Later

Three brownie pans sit on the stovetop, each batch undercooked because I was impatient and convinced myself that people will eat brownies that are practically liquid in the middle. And by "people," I mean me.

I dig into the coolest pan and remove a square from the center, where it's practically goo. I catch a drip on my tongue as I shove a corner into my mouth and bite. The chocolate and sugar hit, and I feel slightly calmer.

I let out a big exhale and take a swig of my coffee, thinking about the Devils event with my former company tonight, where I know I'll run into my ex.

I realize that for the first time since my breakup with Peter, I feel ready to face him.

I'm more fulfilled by my job with the Devils than I was at my old company. I love it in LA despite my affinity for the Bay Area. I'm in a good place in my life. I want to show him that he didn't end me despite how I felt when we broke up.

And Tatum is right. I should try to look good. I should walk into that room with an air of confidence and show him that I'm fine. He didn't break me. In fact, he did me a favor, leading me here.

Another bite of brownie confirms it.

This is the earliest I've been up in a while, and I can almost see why Kyler likes waking up before dawn and heading out with his surfboard. It must be nice on the ocean as the sunlight illuminates the sky and the cool morning air feels still.

"Is it…morning?" Hunter comes up behind me, puts his hands on my shoulders, and nuzzles my neck. My head falls back, and I let out a little moan of approval. One tiny touch, and this man has me at his mercy.

"Mm-hmm. Go back to sleep. But don't because that feels too good." He kisses my cheek and then my lips.

"Chocolate. Smells like a bakery in here."

"Yeah, sorry. Did I wake you?"

He stretches, and I take note of his bare torso, the lean muscle of his abs, and the V leading into his low-slung plaid pajama pants. "Not really. I was reading. There's a new Karin Slaughter book out."

"You love a good thriller."

"I do. I'm halfway done already. Why are you up?"

I debate telling him the real reason. I could say I had an early phone meeting, and he'd believe it. But then I decide that I want a real relationship where I'm open and I trust my partner.

"The event tonight with my old company. I'll know people there. And I feel like I'll be judged."

He studies me, nodding. "Your ex? The one who cost you your

job?" Hunter grabs a green apple from the bowl on the counter and bites into it with a juicy crunch.

"Probably," I say, trying to sound as though it's not the focus of an hour of stress baking.

"That going to be okay?"

I nod, probably too enthusiastically. "Sure. I probably won't even cross paths with him. Totally fine." I wish my voice didn't shake as I say the words.

Hunter puts an arm around me and pulls me close. "You're better off without him. And better here with the Devils. You're doing good work. Tonight is part of the job, nothing more. Fuck him."

"I know. Thank you." I nestle into him. "Any chance you'll be there?"

"Nah. Most of the players aren't going. Just a few for photo ops, I think. Apparently, Ashley thinks I'm too controversial. Or that I'll send social media tongues wagging by doing something dumb."

"Ha, well, she needs to get an updated idea of you."

He rubs a hand through his hair, making it stand on end. Somehow, it looks even better. "Yeah, maybe. I'm not bothered." He holds me away and assesses me. "You doing okay?"

"I am. Thank you. Get back to that book. You can probably finish it before training later."

He kisses my cheek and shuffles back to his room, while I decide what to do with three dozen brownies. People at work will probably inhale them, so I start wrapping them up.

I pack a bag so I can change after work without coming back here. I don't have a lot of fancy options, so I pull out my black dress. It's slinkier and more revealing than anything I wore when Peter and I were together, but maybe that's the point. I'm different now. If I have time after work, maybe I'll stop by Sephora and have one of the women there do my makeup.

I want to look like I'm miles away from the plain nerd girl who lost her job over a mistake with a guy.

And then I want to come home to Hunter and show him how much I appreciate him. Maybe even surprise him with a healthy dinner I'll cook myself. If I get the timing right, I can be at the event for an hour and still have enough time to cook before Hunter gets back. I assume he has training as usual, so I'll ask him to meet me here after eight.

I text Kyler, knowing he'll be able to voice text from the car, and ask him for cooking advice.

Me: SOS healthy vegetarian cooking help

   Kyler: Assume you're feeding Hunter?

   Me: Yes. Please don't make it weird

   Kyler: Make something with pulses

   Me: See? Weird

   Kyler: Trust. Pulses

   Me: Hold please while I look up WTF pulses are

   Kyler: Haha. Beans. Lentils. Easy to make a one-pot dinner with some whole-grain bread and a berry bowl for dessert. Boom.

   Me: That doesn't sound delicious, but I'll trust you

HE SENDS me a bookmarked list of recipes that makes my job easy, and one or two actually sound decent.

Later, I text Hunter and tell him the plan.

Me: Meet me at the house later? Anytime after 8

   Hunter: Sure. Everything okay?

   Me: Yes

   Hunter: Awfully brief response for a woman of words

Me: More words not needed. See you later
Hunter: Ok

I'M PURPOSELY VAGUE. Better if Hunter walks in tired and hungry, and then I'll blow him away with my dinner of pulses. That's a sentence I'll never say again.

Everything will go according to plan, and I'm a woman who likes a plan.

CHAPTER 35

*H*unter

SOMETHING'S BEEN BOTHERING me all day, but I can't put my finger on it. Practice was uneventful. Coach felt the need to kill us with drills, but that's nothing new. The closer we get to the league season, the better shape we need to be in. He doesn't mess around, and neither do I.

Gracie's text doesn't do anything to alleviate my edgy feeling. Maybe it's that she isn't specific about why she wants to meet at the house. I know I'm reading way too much into a text exchange, but it feels cold and distant. Like something's different.

I can't imagine what, given that last night I'm certain I took care of her, and she fell asleep in my arms. But that was before Ashley came down to the field and pulled me aside before training.

"Hey, I wanted to talk to you about tonight, the big press announcement with AIFund. Not sure if you were thinking about being there, but please don't. We only need a few players to represent."

I wasn't thinking about being there, but her outright exclusion stings. I'm used to her guiding me away from public showings where she thinks my "vibe" isn't right. In other words, she doesn't want a hothead saying the wrong thing to the wrong person. Normally, I acquiesce.

I know tonight kicks off a big splashy deal, and everyone on the team is falling all over themselves because we'll be the prototype when the AI company rolls out its next-generation gaming console. But I only want to be supportive of Gracie. I'm thinking about a guy she mentioned, the boyfriend she loved and recommended for a job. Then he turned tail and acted like the ultimate dick.

I know how badly he hurt her and how their relationship cost her a job. I'm worried about how she's going to feel if she runs into him tonight.

"Why not me?" I ask.

"We have enough players is all. This is about a great deal for the team, Reyes. Don't make it about anything else."

Message received. She doesn't want me there, but I'm tired of being viewed as an unhinged troublemaker.

I don't plan on making tonight about me, not at all. But I would like to be there for Gracie. Offer her a shoulder to lean on if she feels flustered at the sight of her ex. And who am I kidding? I'm hoping that, just for a minute, she'll parade me around in front of him like a prize so he'll see he was a fool for letting her go.

Of course, I know that'll never happen because it's a work event, but the caveman in me wants to beat his chest and show the world she's mine.

By the end of the day, I've convinced myself I need to be at the event.

I tell myself I'll only stay for as long as it takes to make sure she's okay and support her. If she's holding her own, I'll obey Ashley's advice and get the hell out, go home, and wait for the rehash when Gracie comes back. Maybe that's why she texted and asked me to meet her at the house. Perhaps I should respect her request and go home instead.

But I'm my own worst enemy when it comes to making impulsive decisions. So I put on a sport coat and drive to the event.

As I'm mulling yet again whether to abort the mission, the elevator doors slide open and I'm greeted by Dario Conner, our genial striker, who seems glad I showed up. He grabs me by the arm and drags me over to where Dave Ryan, the head of AIFund, stands off to one side in his trademark baggy jeans and a pale blue shirt with a button-down collar.

"Reyes, come hear about how your avatar is going to be new and improved with AI."

Ryan introduces himself and immediately launches into a lengthy explanation of how his company's computer interface will revolutionize gaming. I don't understand a lick of it, but he reminds me of Gracie, so passionate about what he's telling me that he doesn't seem to notice I'm not following along. But Dario notices, and he follows my roving eye around the room.

"Sounds great, sir. I'm grateful to be a part of it. Please reach out anytime if I can help."

"Oh, will do. Will do."

Dario tries to steer the conversation away from techspeak, but Ryan is impassioned about AI's potential, so he keeps talking. I excuse myself and roam through the crowd, which is mostly corporate execs mixed with media people and a few players for authenticity, I imagine.

I don't spot Gracie right away. For a moment, I worry that her nerves got the better of her, and she isn't going to show up. All the better reason for me to get the hell out of here and go meet her at home like she asked.

Dario catches up to me, looks at my ragged face, and nods. "Hey, man. I don't know what's going on with you tonight, but if you ever need to talk, my door's always open."

I nod absently. "Thanks, man." I'll never take him up on it, and I want him to leave me alone.

This was a bad idea. I catch Ashley glaring at me from across the room, but I dart between a few executives, earning some slaps on the back and praise over how the team is looking. I nod and thank people, moving toward the exit. I'm about three feet away when a swish of hair catches my attention across the room.

It could be any one of the women who works for the team, but it's like I have a radar for Gracie Albright, and I'm drawn to her like a homing pigeon.

She looks goddamn amazing in that black dress she was wearing the night I took her to the Château Marmont. Even though she wore it for her date with douchey Captain Bart, I heaped so much praise on her that night that she knows how much I love it. I'm sure she's wearing it tonight for my benefit.

But wait. I didn't tell her I'd be here.

A second later, I notice who has her attention. I've googled pictures of her ex out of curiosity, and that's definitely him. He's taller than I would have expected, tucking his head down when Gracie speaks and bringing his face close so he can hear her.

But let's be real. It's not that loud in here. He's doing what any guy would do and taking the opportunity to be closer to her. A pit forms in my gut as I can imagine him inhaling the scent of her lavender shampoo and the grapefruit oil she dabs on her neck.

A fire burns low in my gut. It's familiar. The same feeling that launches me toward a player on the field like a puma on the hunt. I want to claim her.

When I see her there with that guy, it's all I can do not to march up and take a swing at him. I know how he made her feel, and I can't quell the anger burning in my chest. It's primal, the need to defend my woman from another man, especially one who hurt her.

Although she doesn't seem like she needs rescuing. Doesn't seem unhappy when he puts a hand on her arm and takes a step closer to her. Doesn't step away from him.

I start to spiral. On the field, I can channel it properly. Here, I'm a loose cannon, swinging wild and loaded with ammo.

She hasn't looked in my direction, so she probably doesn't know I'm here, but now that feels like a good thing. I don't want to know what she'd do if she saw my watchful eye. I want to know what she really wants when she's not enjoying the physical pleasure of being with me.

That's all I am, after all, a plaything who's a good defender on the field and a good lay off it.

Might as well stop denying the truth.

The sex may be off the charts, but I'm not marriage material. This guy, with his dark suit, his computer science degrees, and his fancy job—he's the kind of guy someone like Gracie should be with. Someone smart and cultured. Someone who understands what she does for a living and doesn't need a tutorial. By the way, I still didn't understand data analytics after the tutorial.

Ashley seems to sense what's going through my mind. She shows up in an instant and shuttles me toward the bar, where Mick, one of our defenders, is sipping a drink. "Mick, do me a favor and take this guy out of here. I'm buying."

"Whatever you've got on draft," I tell the bartender. "And I'll take a shot of vodka too." Why the hell not? It's an open bar, and the drinks are flowing. Looking around the room, I see pretty much everyone holding a drink and a cocktail napkin with passed canapés. It's a party, one I wasn't invited to attend. So far, I'm behaving, and I catch a few photographers grabbing candid shots of me with Mick as we chat at the bar. I shoot the vodka and take a sip of my beer.

As the alcohol hits my brain and starts having its way with me, I instantly feel better and worse.

When I look over at where Gracie was a few minutes ago, she's gone. So is the guy.

Mick finally succeeds at steering me away from the bar. "Let's get that drink Ashley suggested." I definitely shouldn't have a third drink. That one is always the dividing line between good decisions and bad ones. I'm going home like Gracie asked me to.

"What the hell, why not?" I tell Mick.

This is the kind of shit I do. Self-destructive, repetitive shit.

Why would tonight be any different?

And then a new idea occurs to me. "D'you think she figured I'd show up here tonight?" I ask Mick as we walk down the block to a sports bar where the red neon sign beckons.

"What now?"

"She asked me to be home at eight. Maybe she thought I'd come to the event and need to be escorted out of the place before I jeopardize the deal with AIFund, just like Ashley. Maybe they all see me the same." He doesn't know I'm talking about Gracie, so I doubt he understands my word salad.

I'm making this shit up as I go, but when I hear the words, I start to believe them. "She works for the Devils now. She's part of the corporate team. So her job is to look out for the good of the club, but she still believes I'm the angry asshole positioned to fuck it all up. I could make her come from now until the end of days, nothing's gonna change that. It's who I am."

Mick stops cold in the middle of the street. We're lucky no one is driving by, or we'd both be roadkill. "What the fuck did they put in your drink?"

I shake my head and continue walking. Mick can follow or not. I don't care.

He keeps up as I stride toward the bar, determined to believe the thing I've been pushing away from the time I laid eyes on

Gracie Albright. Before I pull open the door, Mick grabs my shoulder. "Hey."

I turn, aggravated that he's not letting me have my way. "What?"

"Just…don't do anything stupid. Okay?" I glare down at his hand, and he lifts it off.

"Not going to do anything stupid at all. I want to have some fun without anyone busting my chops for once. Is that alright with you?"

"It's fine," he says as I pull open the door and the din inside the bar assaults our senses. "As long as you make it to training tomorrow morning, have your fun. You know the drill."

I roll my eyes. Yes, I know the drill.

There's no shortage of women in the bar, and within moments, two of them are talking me up, telling me they're fans. I order one more drink, but I nurse this one. I'm not going to jeopardize training tomorrow, much as I'd like to order six more beers, just to show Mick I can handle it.

I don't plan to take any of these women up on their offers. That's the last thing on my mind. I have no interest in anyone but Gracie, but getting a little attention from these willing fangirls blunts the ache in my chest from seeing her looking so friendly with her ex.

racie

Hunter is a no-show.

At first, I welcomed the fact that he didn't get home right at eight because I ended up staying at the event longer than planned, leaving me scrambling to pull out my ingredients and get everything into the pot before setting the table.

But now it's after nine. I look at my phone. Actually, it's closer to ten. He didn't respond to my text asking for his ETA, and that didn't worry me at first. There have been lots of nights when he stayed late after training to work with the keepers and their coaches. He doesn't have his phone handy when he's at practice, and he can easily lose track of time.

Or so I thought. Now, it's plain late. I've called Hunter twice, but both times the calls went to voicemail.

I look back at our earlier texts, now second-guessing my decision to be vague about my plan for tonight. I should have let him know I wanted us to have dinner. Maybe he took my request to come after eight to mean that he could show up any time after eight. Nine, ten, midnight.

By ten thirty, I realize my plan is a bust, so I change out of my black dress and into a soft pair of gray sweatpants and a long-sleeved tee, immediately feeling more like myself. Curled up in an armchair in the living room, I pick up a book I started a month ago, but I can't really focus.

As much as it was nice to see the pang of regret on Peter's face when he realized how well I'm doing without him, I felt silly for needing that proof. Seeing him felt the same as seeing an acquaintance, and after a few minutes, we barely had anything to say to each other. I couldn't wait to come home and tell Hunter how good it felt and how lucky I feel to be with him now.

"There she is." Hunter's gruff voice is softened by the fatigue in his eyes. He looks as lost as he did when he showed up that first night after his house caught fire, and I worry that something happened.

"Hey. You okay?" When I stand and wrap my arms around him, I can tell from his breath that he's had a few drinks. He's not sloppy drunk. Just mellow and maybe a little sad. He told me he doesn't drink much during the season, but tonight, he seems like he's had a few.

He's rumpled and messy, the arms of his shirt rolled to the elbow, revealing his muscular, tattooed forearms. His eyes are a little bleary and dazed, but they still burn hot when he looks at me. I still love it and everything about him.

"You wore the dress." The accusing words sizzle in the quiet of the room. "The dress I fucking love. You wore it for him."

"What?"

"Your ex. You wanted to impress him?"

How does he know that?

Before I can form the words to ask, he explains. "I went by the event. Figured your ex might be there. I wanted to be supportive if you felt awkward." His face contorts like he's bitten into a raw onion. "Clearly, you didn't."

I rack my brain, trying to remember what he could have seen that upset him. But more than that, I'm surprised that he came there for me. And confused by why he left without saying anything. "You were there?"

He nods. "Not for long. But a few things fell into place." He taps his temple and sways to one side. He covers by moving to the couch and letting the cushion take his dead weight.

"I did wear the dress. But not for the reasons you obviously think."

"What do I think?"

"That I was—I don't know—trying to seduce him or get back together with him?" All of those ideas sound ridiculous, but I can't discount the fact that I did want to prove something to a guy who isn't worth it. And I feel ashamed.

"You're saying none of that was on your mind."

I look him dead in the eye, hoping he'll see my conviction. "Correct."

"Why, then? Why the dress?"

Through the shock and surprise of learning that he was at the event tonight, a more important realization hits. My heart fills at his touching gesture. "You came to support me?" My voice cracks on the last word as unexpected tears fight my will to push them back. I wipe the at my eyes.

Hunter's face softens. "Hey, don't do that. I didn't mean to... god, I'm an asshole."

"No. You're anything but that." I slide across his legs and straddle his lap, holding his face in my hands. This beautiful face of this complicated man who gets in his own way right when he's on the path forward.

He looks unsure of what to say, his mouth opening and then closing tight. He shakes his head, eyes closed. When he opens them, they're soft, so vulnerable that I have to fight back a new wave of tears.

"I can't help thinking…" He takes a deep breath and lets it out slowly. "That you should be dating someone like him instead of me."

Once the words are out, he looks almost relieved. And resigned. Like now that he's given me permission to leave, I'll take it.

"Someone smart? Thoughtful? Someone who sees me and makes me feel valued?" A single tear slips down my cheek and he dabs it away with his thumb. "I am with someone like that. I'm with you."

He swallows hard like there's a lump in his throat. "It's nice that you see me like that, but—"

I cut him off the same way he's done with me, by putting a finger against his lips. "No buts. It's happening," I say, echoing the words he said to me that day on our neighborhood walk.

He looks at the ceiling, but his hint of a smile doesn't escape me. "It's happening," he agrees.

"Hunter, I love that you came there for me. And I'm sorry if it looked like I was trying to get my ex's attention. You're not entirely wrong, and I'm not proud of it, but I did want him to see how much better I am now without him. But that's because of you. I love you."

I haven't said these words, though I've thought them. If ever there was the right time to risk my feelings for Hunter, now feels like it.

His jaw goes slack in my hands, and his brow creases. For a second, I worry I shouldn't have gone that far, but something pushes me to go further.

"What I realized tonight is that his opinion means nothing. Less than nothing. The only one whose opinion matters to me is you. In the time we've been together, I've started to trust again because you're trustworthy. I believe in us. Don't let some guy from my past take that away."

I lock on Hunter's eyes and try to make him believe me. I feel like he'll see my conviction, and that will erase any doubts he has. He seems relieved. Maybe convinced. Definitely emotionally spent.

"Come to bed with me?"

"Yes, please."

"Let me prove how much I missed you tonight."

I nod and follow him into his room and try not to dwell on the fact that he may not love me as much as I love him. I try not to worry about what it means for us.

CHAPTER 37

*H*unter

THE BIG EXHIBITION game against the San Francisco Strikers has been sold out for weeks. Tickets on resellers are going for exorbitant fees. Our teams have different strengths and weaknesses, so basically anything can happen.

In some ways, it feels like any other home game. Fans are tailgating in the parking lot. Lines at concession stands are epic. The roads are jammed with cars trying to get to the stadium before kickoff. But this game is different.

Fans love a rivalry, and this one is legendary. Even though this game doesn't count because it's still preseason, people have been talking about it as if it were the World Cup.

We can feel the fierce competitiveness the moment we enter the stadium. Fans are on their feet and shouting before we leave the tunnel. It sounds like an ocean roaring and crashing, and that kind of game lifts me to another plane. It's electric. My adrenaline races in my veins.

As we prepare to take the field, I swear the crowd cheers louder than I've ever heard. They're waving flags and shaking their fists. Looking up at them always lights a fire in me.

I start feeling the aggressive need to prove something on the field. The fans want a win. I want it more.

The Strikers came out before us, and they're doing warm-up drills and getting ready for the coin toss.

I'm standing in a line of players in the hallway from the locker rooms to where we'll enter the field through the tunnel, when something catches my eye. It's not any fan wearing a Devils jersey, it's *my* fan.

Gracie is walking down the hall toward the physical therapy room, which isn't unusual before a game because player health stats are part of her analytics, and she's thorough about gathering up-to-the-minute data from the trainers.

I'm more amped than usual, super fired about my feelings for her, especially since she told me she loves me. Like the dolt I am, I'm waiting for the right time to say it back instead of telling her I've loved her for longer than she fucking knows.

It's not the first time Gracie has passed by the team on our way out to the field. But it's the first time I've felt so charged and impulsive that I loop an arm around her waist and pull her toward me. One kiss on her temple. I need her positive energy to meld with my own. It feels right to claim her for a quick second before a high-octane game. A kiss for luck.

Her eyes are as wide as dinner plates when I release her. She straightens up and keeps walking down the hall. I hear a "Good luck, guys," in the distance as she retreats.

Dumb idea? Probably.

But I'm too gone for her, too high on my own vibes to worry about it. Or to notice if anyone besides the couple of guys near me saw anything. It's not like I did it on camera.

"And the home team…the Los Angeles Devils!" The

announcer cues us to exit the tunnel, and all thoughts leave my mind except soccer.

～

WE PLAY A NEAR-PERFECT GAME.

We win with an impossible shot in the last three minutes, and the fans absolutely lose it.

We beat our rival.

And all anyone wants to talk about is my personal life.

"Hunter! Hunter, one question! You've been spotted canoodling with someone new. Your fans, especially the female ones, want to know if it's serious."

"I don't comment on rumors about my personal life," I say. It's what I was taught to say after going through a media training seminar Ashley held for the team. Normally, it's enough to get people to move on and take no for an answer.

"I understand she works for the team. Can you confirm that?"

Are they talking about the kiss from earlier? Impossible. No one even saw it.

I need to control the narrative, like Ashley always warns me. Now I'm wishing I hadn't always been so smug about knowing how to handle myself because I'm not certain what to say now.

"If someone has a question about the game or the Devils defense, I'm happy to oblige. Otherwise, I think that's it for questions," I say, leaving the podium and moving toward the door of the press room.

The issue should be dead now. I've made it sound like a rumor that isn't worth commenting on, or at least I think I have.

Apparently, this reporter hasn't received the memo. Or she smells a story where there doesn't need to be one. She persists, shoving her tiny, fluffy mike in my face and walking alongside me as I exit the room.

"Hunter, a few more questions. Are you in a romantic relationship with someone working for the Devils?"

Her camera guy points his little setup toward me and backs down the hallway as I walk forward. I look away from him, annoyed that someone from Ashley's team hasn't swatted him away like a bug.

I'm about a second away from smacking the camera out of his hand, but I work to restrain myself. I don't need a new fiasco where I'm in the flames for messing up a guy's face. I pick up the pace and lengthen my stride, making it harder for the reporter to keep up and for her camera guy to keep his footing. He's forced to step aside so he doesn't fall over, and I move past him.

"No comment. Are we clear?"

She does a good job of staying on my heels. If I wasn't so damn annoyed, I might be impressed. "Not quite. I'm also hearing that the woman in question is Gracie Albright, the data analyst who some people credit with saving your job. Sure you don't want to comment?"

Fuming and desperate to put the issue to rest, I whirl around and put a finger in her face. I make sure to position myself so the cameraman gets me in the middle of the shot as I spit out the words.

"I told you, I don't comment on relationship rumors, and that's the entirety of what this is. Gracie Albright is an employee of the Devils organization, and as such, we are occasionally photographed together. But any rumors about a romance between us are exactly that—rumors. Whatever anyone thinks they know or saw means nothing. Zero."

Pushing past them, I continue down the hallway toward the locker room, still fuming that I let her get the better of me.

But before I make it halfway to the lockers, Ashley comes speed walking down the hallway in that way she does when she's angry but doesn't want to run. She looks like a corgi moving on tiny legs with her tail on fire. "Hunter!"

The fiery expression on my face should tell her not to mess with me right now, but Ashley has never been afraid of me or anyone else. It's probably what makes her so good at her job. Arms crossed, I turn and face her.

"Yeah?"

She presses her lips together and shakes her head. "Follow me."

I don't want to follow her orders when I'm dying to head into the locker room and take a cold shower. That's the only thing that will begin to temper the hotheaded ire burning in my veins, and I start to protest. "I don't—"

"Goddammit, Reyes, for once do what I'm asking."

I blow out a breath and let her lead me outside the clubhouse. She doesn't say a word until we're alone in the empty training room. "What the hell were you thinking? How hard is it to say 'no comment' and keep on walking?"

"I did that. Maybe you didn't hear, but I did that three fucking times, but that woman wouldn't take no for an answer."

"She's not in charge! You are!" It's not the first time she's shouted at me, but I can see now why she wanted us to be alone. Her face is red, and she looks like she'd like to take a swing.

Ashley cracks her neck and exhales her frustration. "She can ask all the questions she wants, and they're all bullshit until you go spouting your mouth off, and now people have something to talk about, and it has nothing to do with soccer."

I nod. She gives this speech multiple times a year because, apparently, we are a bunch of dundering meat heads who don't know enough to shut our traps. Or maybe that's me.

"I know."

"You do?" Her eyes take on an incredulous roundness.

"Yes."

My rage has cooled in the couple of minutes since my confrontation with the reporter, and now I'm no longer seeing red. This is the problem with being a jock and not someone who thinks things through. Gracie always has a plan when surprises arise. I guess it's part of her job to think everything through and play out all the possibilities in order to analyze what could happen with specific players.

Unfortunately, I don't think that way.

I go on instinct. Block the shot, move before my opponent knows what hit him. If I wait that extra second to think things through, the moment is lost. The ball is in the net.

Instinct is all I have.

And today, it's fucked me.

"What do I do? Tell me what to say and I'll say it. I'll blow out the smoke before it catches fire." I start pacing the room, thinking. "Can we get that reporter back in here? Offer her some other story if she doesn't go live with what I said?"

Ashley shakes her head. "She'll never go for that. If we start protesting, it'll convince her even more that she's got a scoop. Best thing you can do now is go silent. Stay home other than coming to training. I'll instruct Gracie to make a statement putting the rumor to rest, and if you behave yourself, it should go away."

"You need Gracie to make a statement? Why?"

"Because she's the one whose job is on the line. No one's gonna fire you for parading around with yet another woman, but she's new here and has a high-profile position. The fact of the matter is that she did basically save your job on the team, so the optics are pretty bad if now you're thanking her with your dick. She's a wonky numbers girl. Even the idea of you dating someone like that gets tongues wagging, so we need to shut it down. Shut. It. Down."

I scrub a hand over my face as the enormity of the situation hits home. Gracie could lose her job. I know how hard she's worked to get where she is, and the idea that I could torpedo that because I can't control myself makes me feel worse than ashamed.

Ashley is right. We need to handle this properly for Gracie's sake. "Tell me what to say and I'll say it."

She nods. "Good. You need to get ahead of this. The sooner you're 'caught' on camera with another woman, the sooner this whole thing goes away."

"Wait, what? I thought you said I needed to stay home and let Gracie make a statement."

Ashley snaps her fingers as she paces the room, as if ideas are popping up like popcorn. "No, no, this is better. Cleaner. We live in a visual world. People believe what they see. So let them see you with another woman. Two within a week, even. That'll cool the other rumor right down, and Gracie will be off the hot seat. Better for her anyway. She's not media trained."

"Yeah? You really think that'll work?" I'm too confused to know what's right. I need to talk to Gracie, at least before I commit to this crazy plan. As long as she's in on it, I'll do whatever is needed to save her credibility.

"I really do. And Hunter..." She shakes her head at me. "Don't fuck this up."

I close my eyes, regretting how much I've already done to throw things off the rails. "I won't. I promise."

CHAPTER 38

$\mathcal{H}$unter

I WISH I'd filled the refrigerator with Yoo-hoo. Or stress baked. Or done any of the things Gracie seems to do to keep herself calm. Because one thing is certain—blurting out Ashley's advice when I get home after the press conference is not a calming activity.

"She wants you to get photographed with other women?" Gracie's doe eyes look especially round and innocent, and I remind myself that she's a numbers girl. All the camera shots and bright lights are foreign to her. Not foreign, awful.

She takes an apple out of the fruit bowl and carries it to the couch, shining it on her shirt. I almost make a comment about her eating healthy fruit, but something in my brain tells me it's not the time.

"As a stunt, mainly. To keep focus away from us. From you."

She shakes her head. "No."

"What do you mean? We have to do it. Otherwise, my stupid

stunt of kissing you before the game and all the media questions will blow out of proportion."

"I already put that issue to rest. I covered for you, don't worry. Rolled my eyes and told people at work you think I saved your job and were just pumped before the game."

"Oh. Well, great. Does Ashley know that?"

She shrugs, but I can see from her turned-down mouth that something's bothering her. "What's wrong?"

"I hate myself a little bit for lying."

"What? Why?"

Gracie puts her hands on her hips. She looks like a superhero or a girl boss or something. All I know is that it's different. "I didn't fight back. Before, when I lost my other job, I just took the hit and walked away. It wasn't fair, and I wish I'd fought harder for my job."

Something hollows out in my gut. If she'd fought, maybe she'd still have her old job in the Bay Area, which is what she's been saying she wanted since she got here. She regrets coming here. At least, that's how it sounds to me.

She doesn't give me time to sort through the ugly feelings, the reality that she wishes she were someplace else.

"I don't want to lie down and wait for someone else to decide my career fate. Maybe it's time for me to do the right thing and talk to my boss. Maybe if I'm honest and clear, it will be okay?" She doesn't sound convinced. "I don't think anyone really cares about who I'm dating as much as you think."

"No, but they care who I'm dating."

It's a dumb thing to say, but my ego is bruised by the idea that she doesn't seem to want my suggestion. That she doesn't want me.

Gracie reacts like I've dropped a torpedo through the ceiling. Her face falls. I've never seen such a look of disappointment. No, it's more than that. She looks gutted, but she has ice in her eyes.

"People care who you're dating," she repeats. "Yeah, I'm sure being with me doesn't make for social media-worthy shots. Is that it?"

"I just don't want you to ruin your career over a guy. Isn't that how you put it before?"

"I was talking about a very different guy." She bites out the words, and I can see the hole I'm digging is getting bigger. Good. I deserve to fall into it. My dad was right—I'm only good at one thing, letting my brutal side guide the way if I can find the right place to use it. That place is soccer, not love.

"This is why I don't do relationships. I don't fucking know how. I say all the wrong things," I lament.

Gracie bites into her apple and chews slowly. I'm desperate for her to say something. Anything.

"So say the right ones. Tell me what you want. Do you want to be photographed with a bunch of women?"

"No, of course not, but—"

She cuts me off with a shake of her head and another crunch into the apple. "What do you want, Hunter?"

More than anything, I want to give her the answer she's looking for. So she'll know I'm doing this for her, even though I keep saying it wrong.

"Tell me what to say and I'll say it." I look her in the eye, needing to convey how serious I am about doing the right thing. I expect her to react the way Ashley always does, grateful that I'm willing to play the game and do what's expected of me.

That's not how Gracie is looking at me. She looks disappointed. Disgusted. She shakes her head sadly.

"I'm not going to do that."

"What? Why?"

"Because I shouldn't have to tell you. You should know. All I asked was what you want."

I feel the same frustration that used to spike when a teacher would tell me I was "bright but not meeting my potential." I took it to mean that I was too useless to understand how to be as smart as I should be. "Maybe I'm not that smart. Give a guy a helping hand."

"Oh, come on. Don't cop out and pretend you're not smart because you didn't go to a fancy college. You read more than anyone I know. You're intuitive enough to handle any player on the pitch without thinking twice about where the ball will be. Stop being so hard on yourself. I think you can figure out what to say to me without me feeding you lines."

"But I want to make sure I say the right thing."

She leans in and makes her voice low. I'm not sure if it's because she's getting emotional or she wants to drive home her point. Either way, it gets my attention. "If I give you the words to say, they don't mean anything."

I'm out on a ledge without support. This is where I always fuck things up.

I feel the slow creep of anxious tension fill my muscles, the blood heat in my veins. It's exactly what happens when I'm in a game situation, facing down another player, and something tells me to go hard and take him down, even if it results in a penalty or a red card. It's a "fight or flight" instinct, and I always want to fight.

Not with her.

It's true. I don't want to fight with her, but I don't have enough other resources in my arsenal. I'm not good enough with words to make my case for why she should be with me instead of a guy with fancy degrees. I only have my instincts, and they're flawed.

"I want you," I say.

Her expression softens. "Why?"

I swallow hard, worried I don't have a good enough answer. "Because I love you." She inhales a shaky breath, and I think I'm doing okay. But then I look at her, really look at her.

This beautiful, brainy, capable woman is offering me her

heart. And with one stupid action in a hallway, I could tear it all down. And she'd let me because she loves me.

I can't do that to her. She deserves better.

She's encouraging me to use my words, so I'll use them. Let's see how she likes it when all my thoughts spill out unfiltered. All the messy ones, full of doubt and lack of trust. The things I should keep to myself and bury deep. She's telling me to open up, and I know she won't like what she sees.

Maybe that's what urges me on. The desperation to convince her that she's wrong about me. "I love you so much, Gracie. But that's an albatross for you, not a gift. I can't be the one who ruins your career. I'm not worth it."

Her eyes fill with tears, and her mouth turns down. She tosses the apple on the couch and wraps her knees in her arms. "I hate that you believe that. I can't be the one to convince you it's incorrect. You need to know it." She wipes her tears, but more take their place. With the pad of my thumb, I try to help. She doesn't fold into me like she normally does.

She sits rigid, protecting herself.

So I back away. "Maybe it's best if we...cool things off for a bit."

I don't know what I'm saying. I don't know what I'm doing. But somehow, I'm in motion, going to Kyler's office and throwing a few things into a bag. I'm walking over to Gracie and kissing her temple. And I'm moving to the front door.

I'm walking away.

"I think you're worth it." Gracie's voice is so quiet, I barely hear it. "So I hope you figure it out."

CHAPTER 39

racie

Two Weeks Later

Something looks different when I pull in the driveway, but I can't put my finger on it right away. It's probably nothing. My thoughts have been unfocused in the weeks since Hunter and I broke up, so I've been missing a lot of details.

At work, I'm generally able to fix my mistakes because the math insists on it. Otherwise, I'd be more worried about turning in bad analytics reports. But my team seems to have their wits about them, and right now, that's saving my bacon.

Exiting my car, I give the front of the house a once-over. What's different?

Unable to land on anything other than maybe a few plants that are in bloom now, I'm baffled.

My laptop bag hangs from my shoulder, and my purse, heavy

with uneaten granola bars and computer glasses, hangs from the other shoulder. At least, I'm balanced. I unlock the door and push it open with the toe of my low-heeled bootie.

The moment I'm inside, Hunter's dog is on me, sniffing me and licking my hand. Kyler comes up behind him with a treat. "Come on, good boy. Let her at least get in the door."

Seeing Bogie pulls at my heart, unleashing a mixture of emotions. The furry bear-dog is so full of unconditional love that I can't help but feel my spirits rise around him, but then I think about Hunter chasing Bogie around outside and the couple I almost believed us to be, and I get sad.

"Sorry, sis. I didn't expect you to be here." He checks the time. "Why are you here? Did you get fired or something?"

It's so like my brother to ask that question without sympathy because he knows it's probably not true. "I left early."

"I'm sorry. Who are you?" He squints his eyes in mock concern and taps at my cheek as though testing to see if I'm a real human. "Funny. You look like my sister, but you're surely an alien pod person because she doesn't leave early. If you must eat me, please spare the dog."

I roll my eyes. "If only you were actually funny, you might have a girlfriend."

"Ouch."

"Sorry."

He bends to pet Bogie, whose ears perk when Kyler talks directly to him in a serious voice. "Okay, buddy. Here's what we're gonna do. I'll hold her down and you lick her within an inch of her sanity, and then maybe she'll tell us who sent her to take over the earth."

Shaking my head, I walk into the kitchen. I guess that's what looked different—the sunlight bouncing off the glass in front of the house, because Kyler is right—it's the middle of the day. I'm never here, home from work, in the middle of the day.

In the fridge, I find Kyler's glass container of cut-up carrots and celery and pair it with my jar of Skippy on the counter. Taking a big swipe of creamy peanut butter with a celery stick, I plop myself onto one of the barstools and munch my snack. If Kyler wants to give me a hard time about being home early, I'm not going to listen to it on an empty stomach.

My brother looks from me to the dog, who has managed to find his leash and now holds it in his mouth. "Easy, buddy. I think Gracie needs our attention for a sec."

Kyler takes a couple of sticks of celery and starts to take a bite, but then he thinks better of it and swipes it through the peanut butter. Taking a seat next to me, he swivels my stool to face him. "What's going on? Real talk."

I shrug and focus on breathing. And another bite of peanut butter on celery.

Kyler hops off the chair as quickly as he landed there and hooks the leash to Bogie's collar. "Come on, let's go."

Bogie sits, tail wagging. Both of them stare at me expectantly until I give in. "So go."

"I was talking to you. Let's go."

I'm too mentally drained to argue or ask questions, so I follow the two of them out the door and into Kyler's truck, where he lets Bogie ride shotgun. "I promised him," he explains.

Folding myself into the back seat, I wait while Kyler runs back into the house, returning a moment later with a pile of sweats and towels. He drops them on the seat next to me, hops in the driver's seat, and speeds down the hill.

It seems pointless to ask where we're going because it's not like Kyler is going to change his plans if I object. Twenty minutes later, we've navigated the hills in Griffith Park and stopped at the observatory, which is perched atop the tallest peak in the area. Kyler lets Bogie out and sets him free to run off the leash while we walk behind the whirling dervish of a dog, who looks like he's been caged up for a month.

"Why do you have him?" It's the question I've been trying to articulate since Bogie ambled out and started licking my hand, but the thought had a hard time fighting through the emotional fog.

"Hunter's out of town."

I wait for him to elaborate, reminding myself of the Devils schedule, which doesn't have any away games before the season opener. "Vacation?" I ask, feigning mild disinterest.

"Mental health day." He turns to face me, and the weight of his stare tells me he wants to talk about Hunter, even if I don't.

"Oh. Good for him. We all need those." The words sound hollow. I know I'm probably the source of at least some of his mental pain.

"Right." Kyler stares off at the view, which is tremendous. Today is one of those clear days in LA right after yesterday's wind blew every trace of smog and haze into the ether. The tall buildings and houses down below look like they've been carved in sharp detail out of glass and stone against the clean blue backdrop of sky.

It takes me back to the afternoon of paddleboarding with Hunter, when he said that anything bothersome was behind him when he stood at the ocean. I feel like that now. Like nothing can touch me up here. Nothing except the sadness swirling inside me because I take that everywhere I go these days.

I wait for Kyler to tell me more, but he says nothing. I hear his deep inhale, and it prompts me to do the same. All the while, Bogie races around in circles on the grass, occasionally coming back to us as if to check in before sprinting off again. His capacity to entertain himself amazes me.

"So...why'd you make me come here?"

"Isn't it obvious?"

I look at Bogie, who is pure joy in a fluffy golden body. "Because Bogie needed exercise?"

He makes a jarring buzzer sound. "Wrong."

I blink longer than necessary. Or maybe it is necessary to

stem the sudden prick of tears and swallow back emotions I didn't plan on feeling.

"Because *I* need a mental health day." I barely get the words out before my voice cracks.

"Bingo."

He doesn't ask what happened between Hunter and me. The two of them are lifelong friends, and I imagine Hunter told him his version. No place for me in the middle of that. It's enough that he brought me up here to look at this view and maybe start to pull myself back together. We stare over the city, each in our own space.

"Do you need one too?" I ask. "Not saying you need to spill your guts if you don't want to, but if you were looking for an opening..."

My brother smiles. "I'm good. I have what I need, and I'm happy you're living in my city for once. You think you'll stay?"

"I'll see this job through. I'm not going to let my dating life get in the way, if that's what you're asking. Eyes on the prize, right? I know how to stay focused."

"D'you...think this could be home?"

The question startles me, and my mouth pops open. Kyler waits, but it takes me a minute to sort my thoughts.

"Hunter asked me the same thing once."

"What'd you tell him?"

"I said that, yeah, maybe it could. But that was—"

Kyler holds up a hand. "Just leave it there. I'd like it if this was home for you."

Bogie comes back and circles our legs, panting and making little jumps in the air. Ky takes out a water bowl from his backpack and fills it with water. The dog slurps with such gusto that I can't help but laugh. When he's finished and brings his head up, a trail of water pours from the sides of his mouth. Then he sees a white dog with a curled tail and takes off again at a run.

Kyler stands in front of me, so I have no choice but to look at him. "You never talk to me about stuff—your job, relationships, whatever's happening in your life—and you should. I'm your biggest fan."

I take in this image of my brother, his rumpled hair blowing in the light breeze, his fierce blue eyes riveted on me. He's twenty-eight. He's traveled the world and runs an impressive business. He's lived life. For maybe the first time, I see him as an adult who knows more than I give him credit for, and I feel like a jerk.

"You're right. I'm sorry."

He blows out a laugh. "I'm not asking you to be sorry. I'm asking you to be a little less absolute in your thinking. Less black and white. Come to LA for the job, leave LA when you have what you need to get the other job… Fall for the guy, give up on the guy when he gets in his own way… Don't tell me about any of it, and make me read the tea leaves. Maybe something to be said for the gray. While we're not talking about our hair, anyway."

My response starts as something between a gasp and a laugh, but the sound of it is more like a sob, which leads me to a full-on crying outburst I didn't see coming.

I feel the urge to walk. Standing here with my brother feels too heavy, so I start following where Bogie is running. That leads me in a zigzagging line, which frustrates me, and by the time I give up, I'm standing in front of a bust of James Dean on a concrete pillar. It seems like as good a place as any to stop and let myself have the cry I've been holding in since Hunter walked away.

My brother comes over gingerly because this is still a new kind of moment for us. He reaches over and gives me that awkward sibling hug from the side, but I turn into him and dampen his shirt as the tears stream forth. He leaves his arm in place and lightly pats my hair while I lose my shit.

Seeming to sense he's needed, Bogie ambles over and nuzzles the backs of my legs. It forces enough levity for me to stop sobbing. The tears still dribble from my eyes, but I wipe them away and dare a look at Kyler. I expect him to be freaked out. I'm his older sister, after all. I've always kept it together in front of him.

But he actually looks relieved.

"Finally," he says kindly.

"What is that supposed to mean?"

"You let me in. Finally. Thank you."

This makes the tears roll again, but this time my feelings are laced with appreciation for the boy who became a man when I wasn't watching and now wants me to lean on him. So I try.

We amble over to a bench and sit with the view sprawled out in front of us. "There's no escaping the majesty of this," I say.

"Kind of the point. A little perspective."

I nod. "Listen, it's not that I don't want to share things with you. I...don't really know how. I'm used to solving problems on my own."

"And how's that working out for you?" His wry tone is answer enough.

"Did Hunter tell you where we left things?"

He stretches his arms over the back of the bench in that way only guys can do. His knees splay open, and he looks as at home here as Bogie. It's a gift to be able to find that Zen space anywhere, and I wish I had more of it.

Slouching down a couple of inches, I try to get more comfortable, but I end up failing. "He's not ready for a relationship," I say. "I feel like I've come a long way in the time since we met. I let my guard down. I started to trust him to say he loved me and mean it. But he still walked away."

"That's on him."

I sit up and turn toward Kyler, so he sees my face. "I know. A hundred percent, I know that. I won't let myself doubt that trusting him was the wrong idea. It's not my fault that he doesn't know what he wants."

"He does know. He just won't let himself have it."

"What does he want?" My voice is quiet because I almost can't ask. Maybe Kyler doesn't hear me.

"He wants you." Kyler nods to himself. "But…"

He doesn't have to finish. I know what the problem is. He's in his own way.

"Exactly."

unter

YOU KNOW those moments when you know you're making a terrible decision, but some part of you can't turn the car around, take the fastest route in the opposite direction, and shut down the urge?

That's how I found myself knocking on the front door of Dario Conner, the Devils striker.

Maybe it's that he offered himself up if I ever needed to talk. Perhaps he gets it. We've always been friendly, but never friends.

He's too sure of himself, too optimistic, too level-headed to understand someone like me, especially on a night like this one when darkness is my chief personality trait. Or at least that's what I always thought.

But I've already bent Kyler's ear, and there's only so much I can talk to him about his own sister. He's a good friend, but no one is that good. The best thing I can do for our friendship is stay clear of Gracie, so I don't hurt her more, which is why I'm holed up at a hotel near the Devils training facility. Might as well lessen my commute while I'm ruining my life.

It's where I should be right now, eating room service off a tray and watching some cooking show on TV. I tried it for about ten minutes, but the chef started making stuffed baked potatoes, which reminded me of Gracie, and in two seconds, I'd lost my appetite.

So now, thirty minutes later, here I am at Dario's door, which I can't help noticing is painted a nice shade of green. The door swings open, and my teammate holds out a cold beer as if no other greeting is needed.

"You have a green door," I say, following him inside. I've never been here, so my head is on a swivel, taking in the details of his craftsman bungalow in Santa Monica. Even though it's nighttime, there's an open feeling from skylights overhead, glass revealing treetops and maybe even a few stars.

"Yes. Painted that myself. Otherwise, I can't take much credit for the place."

His furniture is simple. A large mirror above a console loaded with framed photos of his son. A white-painted kitchen outfitted with pale wood cabinets and stainless steel appliances, a few comfortable-looking tan couches in the living room.

Right when I'm about to marvel that the place is spotless for a person with a kid, I see the massive pile of board games, a train table with tracks and trains covering its surface, and a full-sized camping tent, which I can only imagine is full of more kid stuff.

Dario points at the empty couch, which sits at an angle from a worn brown leather chair with an open beer next to it on a side table. He drops into it and waits for me to tell him why I came to talk.

"I'm not sure why I'm here," I admit. The beer goes down easily, and I decide that maybe that's why I'm here. For once, no one's giving me a hard time about empty carbs, and I can enjoy a cold beer and wallow in peace.

"You called me. And I have nowhere to be, so take your time." Dario takes a swallow of his beer and waits. I see he's not going to make this easy by slinging small talk.

Fine. I guess I don't deserve easy.

"I guess I have some questions." My eyes sweep over the toys and trains, and it hits me that he faces the same professional stresses I do, only he does so as a single dad with a kid in his full-time care. I feel exhausted from my own thoughts. I can't imagine how he manages the actual exhaustion that comes with raising a human being.

I rest my forehead against my palm and close my eyes against the world.

"We don't have to talk. We can drink a beer, enjoy a moment of peace. Lord knows I don't get a lot of that with a five-year-old," he says.

"Where's your kid?"

"Asleep. Which means this is the time I have for *this*." He gestures between me and his beer before picking up his phone and tapping something on the screen.

I shouldn't have come here. He's got better things to do than give me a couch to wallow on, so I stand from the couch, planning on thanking him for the beer and heading home.

A chill Alabama Shakes song starts playing from the surround-sound speakers, and Dario adjusts the volume on his phone. He looks at me standing there and raises an eyebrow.

"If you're planning on going anywhere, it'd better be to the fridge for the next round."

I do as instructed and put the unopened bottles on a tray sitting on the glass table and return to my seat on the couch.

"Okay, spill," he instructs, waving me forward. "What is eating you up? I can start guessing if it makes it easier. The team? Coach? A woman?" He watches me, and something must change in my expression because he nods. "Bingo. Who is she?"

Shaking my head, I again regret that I came here. I detest the thought of letting another person know about my screwups and getting wind of my weaknesses. I let out a long breath and consider whether I can make up a lie and pretend I'm here about something else.

"Jesus, man. Stop torturing yourself," Dario says. "Whatever it is, it can't be as bad as the hell storm you're making it out to be in your head."

I close my eyes and ratchet up the courage I didn't think I needed to talk to another dude. "I fucked up my relationship with an incredible woman I never deserved in the first place, and the worst part is that I can't stop trying to figure out how to fix it, even though the best thing I can do for her is stay far away. She deserves so much better than me, but I'm having a hard time letting her go."

When he doesn't say anything, I keep going, giving him more details about all the ways I screwed things up for myself. It's like I want to lay out all the evidence so he can tell me I'm right to feel as shitty as I do right now.

I guess I'm hoping for some tough love and proof that I did the right thing. Who better than a guy who's a lone wolf? He sees how hot-tempered and stubborn I am every day, so I leave to him to explain that some people are meant to be alone.

The song changes to Springsteen, and I feel oddly comforted by the Boss singing about his desire for a woman.

When Dario finally speaks, it's to tell me something I already know. "Sounds like you love her and don't want to lose her."

"Yeah, that's true. Though irrelevant to the situation."

"Why? Seems very relevant. Fix your mistake. Tell her how you really feel. Make things right."

He says those things like they're easy.

"Or I could be alone. Simpler, right?"

"If you're a coward, maybe. But that's not you. And look, I get what it's like to have a dad who fills your head with shit, and then that becomes the narrative. 'You're not good enough.' 'You're not smart enough.' 'You're never successful enough.' 'You don't deserve to be happy.' It's bullshit, man. There's no way out, unless you agree to stop listening."

I sit dumbfounded because I can't remember ever telling him about my dad.

"He used to come to games, I remember," he explains, as though he knows my thoughts. "Tough nut to crack. Always looked a little angry, even when you played your ass off and I never knew how that could possibly be, except that my dad was the same way. Used to tear me up. I thought about quitting the sport just to spite him."

"Would've been a waste."

He looks off as though remembering. "You got that right. Only took me years of therapy to figure it out and stop doing it."

"Do what?"

"Not letting his voice become my own. Not making his opinions more important than what I know about myself." He shakes his head. "Shouldn't be so damn hard, but there you go."

He takes a swig of beer and leans back in his chair, listening to the music with his eyes closed, silently mouthing the words to "She's the One."

It feels like a revelation, the idea of not letting my dad's opinions be my narrative. "Maybe I need some therapy."

"Maybe you do." He makes it sound so simple. Perhaps it is.

Could be that I'm the one who makes things complicated by being stubborn. It's my choice to let my dad's opinions define me. The idea of *not* doing that makes me feel lighter, almost gleeful.

I want to share this new sliver of wisdom and talk about it. Of course Gracie is the one person I want to tell. I have to earn her trust again, and it will be harder this time.

"I'm sorry about your dad, man." I wish I'd been more aware of what he was going through.

"Yeah, it's in the past. Now my job is to make sure I don't fuck it up for that one in there." He points a thumb over his shoulder toward his son's room.

"You won't. I'm an instinct player, and I have a good feeling," I say.

He gives me a tired smile. I can't imagine how he manages everything on his plate.

"I'm gonna choose to believe you because I want to." He says the words calmly like he's a normal guy having a normal conversation, but I know he's been through some shit. He split from his wife a year ago, and I remember it being messy, but he never brought his emotions onto the field.

Now probably isn't the time to ask him for details, but I make a mental note to be a better listener and a better friend to him in the future. "Thanks, man. And even though I've been a self-centered asshole up until now, I hope you'll let me return the favor if you ever need one."

His laugh is so quiet that I have to look at him to be sure it's what I'm hearing. "I think you're the only one who thinks you're an asshole. Maybe try being a little less hard on yourself. Start that today."

"Feels like I've heard that someplace before." I shake my head.

"Lemme guess, Gracie isn't just a brilliant analyst, she's also emotionally intelligent?"

"How'd you know it was her I was referring to?" I wondered why he didn't bother asking her name or anything else about her. Guess it's because he already knew.

He levels me with a stare. "The kiss, for one thing. Then you lost your shit when you saw her with some dude at the AIFund event. Couldn't have been more obvious if you tried."

I nod, resigned to the fact that I'm not good at hiding my emotions, especially when I get riled up.

I finish my second beer and do the smart thing and call a ride share to get me back to the hotel.

Dario walks to the front door and yanks it open when the car arrives. "Don't be a stranger. I'm here most nights by myself after Hayes goes to bed. Always happy to have some company."

"Do you not date?"

He shakes his head. "Nope. Too complicated. So feel free to come on over here and join me anytime."

I look around his tidy space, which is so quiet right now, even though I know he has a noisy five-year-old. He looks drained in a way only a dad can. He also looks content. I want that with Gracie. I want it all.

"Good vibes here, man. I'll take you up on it."

CHAPTER 41

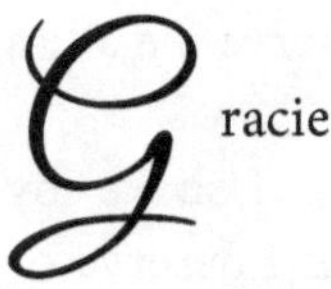racie

"How many texts has he sent you?" Tatum asks on our FaceTime call.

"So many. I've lost count." I bustle around my office, where I've pushed my desk toward the center of the room so it no longer has a direct view of the practice field. I couldn't stop myself from glancing out at the players every five minutes and debating what to say to Hunter.

"And you're freezing him out?"

"No. I'm not a 'freezing out' type of gal. I'm responding politely every few times he texts."

"So you're freezing him out, but being polite about it. I like it." She laughs, and I can hear her typing. Her phone is positioned against her computer screen, so even though it seems like she's looking at me, I know she's also working. I'm doing the same.

I scan the recent string of texts to see if she's right.

. . .

HUNTER: **I'm so sorry, Gracie. I love you.**

Hunter: Not much to add, except that I hope we can get through this

Hunter: I know I have work to do

Me: Glad you know

Hunter: I do

ONE TEXT TO HIS FOUR. Does that qualify as freezing him out? I don't think so. It would give the wrong message if I were bantering with him when he needs to sort through his issues without my influence.

I didn't respond at all to a drunk, rambling message where he professed his love for me and told me he didn't deserve me all in one long, slurring sentence.

"You should have betterrr, Tinnk. I know that." I shake my head at the memory, hoping he doesn't believe that I deserve or want anyone other than him.

"He texted this morning and I was a little more effusive," I tell Tatum, recounting our exchange.

HUNTER: **Thinking about you. I'm always thinking about you. Have been since I was sixteen, FFS**

Me: Me too

Hunter: We can get through this. I'm working through my shit. Started therapy

Me: Glad to hear it.

Hunter: I know I need to be a better man for you

Me: No, you need to be yourself

Hunter: I love you

. . .

I SHOULD RESPOND and say I love him too. But it's almost like I'm holding back a tiny piece of my affection, urging him to love himself so I can give myself over fully. It's too much to explain in a text, but I know Tatum understands because she knows me so well.

"He needs to feel like he's worthy of you, and you can't do that for him."

I nod and stare at my phone screen, wishing Tatum were here in person. She'd get me out of this office and away from the players distracting me beneath my window.

Then again, I shouldn't need someone else to do that for me. "Hey, Tate. Lemme call you later. I just remembered something I need to do."

After straightening up my desk, I leave the building, heading for a soccer gear shop on Wilshire where I know they sell team jerseys with player names on the backs. I want my very own Reyes jersey to wear to the game this weekend. I want a tiny connection to Hunter, even if he doesn't know about it.

racie

Two Days Later

Whenever I enter the Devils stadium, I think I'm overhearing noise from an outdoor concert. As I make my way through the hallways in my jersey and jeans, I feel like it's the only explanation for the coordinated roar of instruments and singing voices.

Then there's The Wall.

Some teams have them, others don't. The Devils have a legendary one. The Wall is a special section for superfans. It sits at one end of the field—not exactly prime seats unless the home team happens to be scoring a goal—but it doesn't matter.

The superfans are there to support the Devils, rain or shine, with drums, coordinated songs and chants, horns, costumes, masks, and beer. Lots of beer.

The sound I hear while walking through the tunnels rises to

full volume when I emerge in one of the team boxes high above the midfield. The rest of the stadium is still half-filled, which is normal given that it's a half hour before game time, but The Wall is packed and jumping with energy.

Shielding my eyes from the sun with my hand, I stand in the box and watch the superfans do their thing. Jumping, singing, dancing, all coordinated by a few leaders at the front. They're having a better time than most people have in a lifetime.

It makes me appreciate my job and the sport a tiny bit more every time.

The team boxes never disappoint. Plush seats, refrigerators filled with drinks and snacks, and a server clad in Devils gear standing by to bring more food or drinks. It's quite the luxe setup, so I'm not surprised to see the WAGS, wives and girlfriends, one box over, chatting with drinks in hand.

Our box, reserved for team executives and their guests, is still empty, but that will change by the time the game starts. Wandering over to the fridge, I feel the nervous anticipation of seeing Hunter on the field. I also feel sad. The past few weeks without him have been lonely. I feel gutted like I'm missing an integral part of myself. I'm mad at Hunter for making me feel that way, but I love him for making me feel.

When I open the fridge, I'm startled to see it filled with bottles of Yoo-hoo. That's right. The entire thing is dominated by bottles of chocolate milk, something I've never seen anywhere at this stadium.

"No, he didn't…" I mumble, looking around the empty box and thinking about all the times Hunter managed to clear a room for us.

But when I lift the lid on the first tray of hot food, I know that, yes, he did. It's an overflowing display of bar food—jalapeño poppers, potato skins, nachos, and tater tots.

Under the next lid, I find a plate of cookies. "I stress baked these for you," reads a card on top. Next to the plate is a bowl of fruit, with a note clipped to a sheaf of papers on top that reads, "Get your vitamins."

I open the first card to find a simple note.

"I love you. I want to be with you. Please say yes."

The din of the crowd falls away as I absorb the words I've wished Hunter had said to me that day when he walked away. I know enough to understand that words aren't a guarantee that he won't freak out again. But he's working on fighting his self-doubt. He's going to therapy. And the words are a sign he's doing what I asked. He's trying.

Hunter knows I don't like to watch live games in a room full of people asking me for magic tricks with player stats, so he cleared the room. It also ensures my focus will stay on him. He's put some thought into this.

The second note makes me laugh out loud.

The card is blank, but when I remove the paperclip, I see a title across the sheaf of papers, reading, "Fake Analytics Report."

The pages are ridiculous lists of statistics—basically gibberish —lots of red arrows pointing to a conclusion: "Gracie and Hunter are a perfect match."

He really is trying. And I love him for it.

I load up a plate with bar snacks and an apple and sit down to watch the game in my private box.

CHAPTER 43

unter

EVERYONE HAS LEFT the locker room, but I'm lingering here staring at the wall, waiting for I don't know what. Divine intervention? Some excuse for why I can't play today?

The rational side of me knows that neither of those things is going to happen. It's the opening game. I'm the starting center back. It's not an option for me to sit out unless I've suddenly vomited up my left kidney. And even then.

I picture Gracie's face when she realizes I've cleared a team box for her to eat her favorite snacks and watch the game. I hope she likes the gesture, but the bigger part of me thinks it may be too trite and simple. She deserves more than text messages and big gestures.

But this is what I have.

I untie my left shoe and pull the laces tighter. They were tight enough before, but I'm stalling. The moment I go outside, there won't be time for the self-loathing that still has a grip on me. Indulging it for a few more minutes might fight it out of my system before it swallows me whole.

Gracie's face flits through my head, and I allow it to take over. Images of her lying in my bed, her hair messy and cheeks flushed. Memories of her laughing with me, at me…no matter. The gentle sound of her laughter stirs me like a warm breeze. Thoughts of the last time I saw her, disappointed in how stubborn and near-sighted I was being.

That image takes over, and I feel like I might actually puke up a kidney. There's no one else to blame for the utter loneliness I feel, even when I have a team full of guys who have been my friends for years. Guys who have my back. I'd trade them all for one more night with her.

The emptiness in my gut feels like someone's blown a hole straight through me. There's a cavernous, hollow space where there once was warmth. Where there once was love.

I did this. I know I need to take responsibility for the ache in my heart. For a short while, I had everything I wanted. Gracie opened herself up to me fully and I turned her away, pretending it was for her own good.

If this is what I do when someone offers me her whole heart, maybe I deserve to be alone. I deserve the sadness I feel. I don't deserve her. Never did.

No, that was the old narrative. I'm better than that.

There's a tiny part of me that can't give up. It's what propels me on the field, and it's maybe what Gracie's analytics identified in me when she felt so strongly that I'm an asset to the team, despite my shortcomings.

Maybe she can still believe I'm an asset to her.

I shouldn't be thinking any of these thoughts on game day. I'm a professional, for fuck's sake. I've trained for difficult situations. On top of therapy, I started sessions with the team psychologist to help me get my head straight on the field.

It was the last thing I felt like doing, believe me. Having someone crawl inside my brain and tell me how to "manage my feelings" never ranked high on my list of fun ways to spend my time.

"You know what you need to do, but you're letting in distractions," Bern told me yesterday while I lay on a table in the physical therapy suite. My eyes were closed, and my body felt limp after an easy training day designed to keep us loose while enforcing the muscle memory of every move we'll make on the field.

Jimmy had finished stretching out my limbs and working his knuckles into the sore knots of muscle. I should have felt restored and game ready. Instead, I felt spent from relentless hours of fighting the thoughts that keep intruding into my game focus. Then, Bern set me straight. I'm certainly not the first guy to get the yips or find himself in the middle of personal drama before a game. Sports psychology is an entire industry for a reason.

"I know what I need to do. Doesn't mean I can do it," I told him, prepared to be aggravated if he was going to tell me what I already knew.

He made me stay still on the PT table, with my eyes closed, while he talked me through how to channel my frustrations into something useful in a game. I work to remind myself of those things now.

"If you feel a wave of sadness, outrun it, go faster," Bern said.

I get a little revved up, all the stored glycogen in my system pushing sugar into my veins. I'm like a kid at the end of Halloween night with energy to burn.

"If you get angry with yourself, take it out on the ball."

That won't be a problem. I'm so angry, I'm going to need to pull myself back unless I want to split the ball in two and send it into the stands.

"If you find thoughts creeping in that don't belong on the

field, tell them to go fuck themselves and find an opponent who needs roughing up." My eyes popped open when Bern said that one because he never tells me to take anything out on another player. He knows it barely takes a salty look for my temper to dial from one to a thousand. But he said what he said.

I run through the mantras and a few more in my head. Soon, I'm muttering them out loud, exhaling hard with each word until I feel ready.

Then I take the field with the rest of the team. My thoughts are only on soccer.

~

"Fuck!" I spit the word out under my breath and out of range of the referee. I didn't expect the Michigan striker to dive in when I stood in his path. I know how he thinks. He always chooses a side. This time, he went hard, I miscalculated, and that's all it took for him to have a clear shot at the net.

He took it. And now we're down a goal.

The fans are aghast. My teammates walk with their heads hanging, heading back to the centerline for kickoff. Our keeper is shouting at me to corral my defenders. Someone should have been covering the middle when I went to the side. It's as basic as it gets. But I'm so sure of myself that the other guys had a false sense of security.

I should have read the situation instead of the player. This is on me.

Jamming a toe in the turf, I get back into position. A bead of sweat rolls off my forehead, and I wipe it with the back of my hand. I don't dare look into the team boxes to see if I can spot Gracie. Not only would that take my focus from the game, but I'm not sure what seeing her there would do to my emotional state, and I'm already tearing up grass like a feral bull.

The whistle blows, and we kick off, playing it back in a drill that always works for us to set up the offense. It plays back to our midfield, then our defenders, then back up the field as our opponents position themselves and wait for opportunities to turn the ball over. We can't give them any, not if we want to even up the score.

We take a shot, but the keeper is fast and dives for the corner, saving it to the cheer of the crowd. Our fans are fired up that we got a shot off. Their fans are happy about the save.

They take the ball up next, and I track it, calling to our midfielders because they need my perspective from the back. *Defend, defend.* We do our jobs. Take possession. The fans go wild.

We start pressing forward, moving the ball on the ground, getting close enough to shoot. Everyone's in sync, calling to each other, getting in position to get a rebound off a shot that hits the post.

The play gets closer to the Michigan goal. We're pressing hard, pressuring the defense. It's getting crowded, more of our players moving up, our keeper well out of the box behind us, all of us watching and waiting.

Dario gets the ball and charges hard, taking two steps before firing off a shot. The Michigan defender slide tackles a second too late, catching his foot instead of the ball. The shot goes wide, Dario goes down, and the ref blows the whistle.

The fans are booing and yelling at the Michigan defender. It's a pretty clear penalty, but they're going to look at replay footage to be sure. Dario stays down, waiting for the medic to come over and assess his ankle. No reason to get up too fast and risk injury. Better to have the medic run through the tests and clear him. If he comes out of the game, he can't go back in.

I pace around, feeling like a caged animal. Watching our guys get fouled boils my blood, and I was already running hot. I know the defender wasn't trying to hurt Dario, just like I know my slide tackles aren't meant that way, but we all play it close. Too close. And in the first game of the season, maybe I want to hurt an opponent a little bit, enough to warn him not to be reckless.

Dario gets cleared and stands up. The crowd cheers, and he goes to the corner for a penalty kick. We've practiced set plays like this a thousand times, but there's always a wildcard element. The sun at a certain angle, a defender who's an extra inch taller, the tiniest bit of spin on the ball when it comes off Dario's foot.

But this time, everything goes right, and we get the point. Tie game.

Maybe that's why I lose a tiny bit of focus. Maybe knowing Dario has made up for my mistake earlier allows me to pull my mind off the accelerator for the time it takes to look up at the team box. I shouldn't be able to discern one person in the crowd, but Gracie isn't any person. She's the salve to my aching heart, and I'm certain it's her standing in front of her seat looking down on the field. It's not like we can make eye contact at this distance, but I convince myself that we can.

"If you feel a wave of sadness…" Bern's advice jumbles in my brain, and I can't remember whether I'm supposed to outrun my feelings or put them into the game. All I know is that the Michigan team is playing the ball up the field on three passes, and our midfielders are chasing their dust.

I back up, moving closer to our keeper, watching how the ball is being played, looking for the first opportunity to head it off if someone takes a shot. One pass to the wing, another back to center, I move forward. The ball goes back to the winger, who takes his shot.

It's clean, but it hits the side post and ricochets back to our defender, who tries to clear it. But a Michigan attacking mid clips it, and it heads back toward our goal. I see red. I see Gracie. I run at the ball and the player who's getting too close to the goal.

Slide tackle.

All ball.

But the attacker loses his footing and lurches toward me, taking us both down right at the side post. I feel the harsh scream of metal against the back of my head mingled with the din of the crowd, a tangle of cleats, and the smell of close-cropped grass.

And then everything goes dark.

racie

"HE'S GROGGY, but he's awake."

I take my first deep breath since I saw Hunter go down. Even from a few hundred yards away, I heard the sound of his head hitting the metal goal post. I can still hear it.

My first thought was that no one hits their head that hard and survives. My second thought was that if anyone could survive, it's Hunter. Purely out of stubborn determination.

And then the thought that has been ricocheting in my brain ever since—I didn't respond to his last text to say I love him. If he never recovers from the crushing blow to his skull, he won't know that I've never wavered in my feelings for him. That thought has haunted me ever since.

As I've sat here around the clock, I can't stop the barrage of awful images. How the blow knocked Hunter out cold. How he had to be carried off the field on a stretcher with the entire crowd holding our collective breath, watching his unmoving body, which is normally so strong and full of vigor.

How I tried to block out the chatter I could hear in the stadium—or maybe I was projecting my worst fears—people wondering if he was okay, if he'd ever be okay, if he'd open his eyes only to stare blankly, if he'd live to play in another game.

How I pushed through the crowd and used my team credentials to get access to where the medical team was assessing Hunter before an ambulance took him to the hospital. How I stood there with all the other concerned members of the Devils and understood that keeping our relationship under wraps meant I had no claim on him. Maybe I never would.

It didn't stop me from driving to the hospital and planting myself here until I could get a definitive word about his condition. Kyler, who left on a last-minute work trip to Bali, has been blowing up my phone for information. I keep telling him I have none.

"Ms. Albright?"

The male voice from across the room has a quiet, lilting tone, as if from someone accustomed to delivering bad news.

"Yes?" I look up, ever hopeful.

"I'm Dr. Sanchez. I've been monitoring Hunter's condition since the accident. He has skull fractures and severe bruising, but no internal bleeding. He made a big improvement last night. He's awake in the ICU."

"Really?" I light up with the thrill of hope. But it leaves just as quickly. "What does that mean? Like, he's awake physically, but what's going on mentally? Would he know me if I went in there? Am I allowed to go in there?"

The neurologist, a kindly woman in her fifties who's been out here twice before to tell me Hunter was still undergoing testing, smiles patiently while the questions fire from my brain to my mouth. I'm sure she's answered them numerous times for the

Devils managers and teammates who have been here around the clock, checking on Hunter's condition. I'm the only one who hasn't gone home, though. I can't. I need to know if he's okay, and I need to lay eyes on him rather than hearing the news from someone else.

"We'll be doing another CT and an MRI, but I'm optimistic. He asked about you."

"He did?"

She nods and motions me in the direction she came from, and we walk down the sterile hall of the hospital silently while I figure out what I want to know before I see him.

"Is there anything to know about his…condition?"

"He has a bad concussion, and because he took the blow to the back of the head, it caused bleeding that pooled in the soft tissue around his eyes. It's common to get raccoon eyes from the type of hit he took, but don't let that concern you. It looks worse than it is. All the neurological tests came back fine. As I said, no bleeding in the brain."

I've been here at the hospital for nearly twenty-four hours while they stabilized him and ran all the neurological tests needed to check for brain damage.

Brain damage.

My first thought when I heard that was regret over our last conversation. I didn't want it to be the end for us. I still thought maybe we'd have a chance down the road of learning from what went wrong, but if Hunter's injuries are severe…

I've tried so hard to stay in the present and keep myself from spiraling into worry and fear. I know who he is. He's the kind of man who reserved an entire team box so I could watch the game without having to make idle conversation. I want to be with that man. I want to make sure he knows it.

"So there's no brain damage," I confirm.

"No evidence of that. Like I said, we'll take another MRI tomorrow before we release him and monitor him for several weeks. But your guy has a hard head. A few skull fractures, but nothing that won't heal."

A chill runs down my spine at the mention of skull fractures, and not the blissful kind of chill I loved when Hunter touched my skin. I shake it off and tell myself to buck up and prepare to see the man I love with raccoon eyes and machines hooked up to him.

The fact that he asked to see me makes me brave.

The doctor shows me into the room, which has a curtain drawn around the bed for privacy. I hear the door close behind her when she leaves. Inside the curtain, I find Hunter sitting up, head reclined against a pillow. He's hooked up to monitors emitting a steady chorus of beeps and squawks, and there's an IV taped to his forearm. But other than the dark circles around his eyes, he looks pretty much like himself.

His features lighten and relax when he sees me, but only for a moment. Then the creases in his forehead dig in, and he frowns. "What's the matter?"

I shake my head, unable to form words or explain the tears that have sprung free from the corner of my eyes. So many emotions rushing forth. How much I miss him. How sorry I am for letting him walk away without fighting harder. How much I love him.

Moving to his bedside, I open my arms to hug him, and he does the same, pulling me against his chest and burying his lips in my hair.

I push back, aware he's bruised and battered. "I don't want to hurt you."

"Then don't leave." His voice is a sexy command. "Ever."

My senses flood with dopamine, and for once, I let it happen without thinking about the physical processes are happening in my body. I let them happen and revel in this feeling that I've missed over the past few weeks.

"I missed you." I know he may not be ready to hear how I feel about him, but I'm not willing to take any chances in case he lapses into unconsciousness again. "And I—I haven't stopped loving you."

He closes his eyes, and for a moment I worry that he's zoning in and out, not really awake. When his eyes open, they're watery. "I love you so fucking much, Gracie. I'll do whatever it takes to make sure you always know that." His voice is gravelly and gruff from disuse.

Hunter tries to sit up, but from the way he winces, moving seems to hurt his head.

"Don't," I instruct, leaning closer so he doesn't have to move. "Or let me help you."

He nods and I grab an extra pillow, folding it in half to bulk it up. Hunter takes my hand, and I pull him forward enough to stuff the pillow behind him. It props him upright enough that we're sitting face-to-face.

"Thank you." His voice sounds strained and weak. I'm about to tell him not to talk, but he beats me to it and begins talking. "I fucked everything up so badly by walking away from you, and—" He starts to cough, and I grab the cup from a tray next to the bed and hold the straw up to his lips.

"We don't need to have this conversation right now. I'm so relieved you're okay. That's enough."

He shakes his head. "It's not enough. There's so much I want to tell you—" He coughs again, his throat probably dry from the hospital air. After another sip of water, he nods. "I guess it can wait until I can form a full sentence without choking to death." He tries to laugh, but it comes out like another cough. "But know this—I love the fuck out of you, Gracie Albright, and I'm not letting you go."

CHAPTER 45

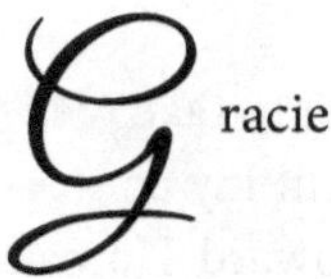racie

Two Days Later

"Hunter Reyes and I are dating. I'm aware it's unprofessional, and I promise that it has in no way affected my objectivity or ability to do my job, but I want to be aboveboard and give you all the information so you can make your decision."

I've barely made it past the threshold of Gerald's office, but nerves are balled up like a tangle of electrical wires. I can't bear to make small talk or, worse, pretend I'm here to give him a player assessment. Not until I unburden myself with the speech that kept me up all night rehearsing it in my head. Side note—what I said to him bears no resemblance to what I planned to say.

I'm dressed in my usual black pants and low heels, and I have a Devils scarf wrapped around the neck of my red sweater to

273

show team spirit. I'm hoping that will demonstrate my devotion to the team, despite my obvious lapse in professional judgment.

Leaning back with his hands flat on the desk, Gerald observes me as I shift from foot to foot. Lifting a finger, he beckons me closer.

I take a step forward, inching away from the comfort of the doorway, which makes for an easy escape if I need to run away in shame.

Using his whole hand, he waves me in. "Come sit down, Gracie. I won't bite."

I slide awkwardly around the arm of one of the chairs facing his desk and plop onto the seat. There's no mistaking the sharpness in his gaze, and I force myself to look him in the eye and accept my fate.

He cracks a smile, but that could mean he's going to take pleasure in sending me out on my ass. After I blurted out my confession, I've been half expecting him to point me toward Human Resources without further discussion. I've read the company handbook back to front, and I'm aware of the no-tolerance policy for sexual harassment.

I certainly haven't harassed anyone, but if a player who was hoping for a better analytics report wants to claim favoritism, it's a slippery slope to unemployment for me. Not to mention the optics. Ashley's voice rang loudly in my head as I was planning what to say.

Don't date a player. That never ends well.

Shifting in my seat, I know better than to keep talking. I'll only make the situation worse if I make excuses or protest, and I've already told Gerald as much as he needs to know to send me packing.

"Does Reyes know you're here falling on your sword?"

Oh. I guess I didn't tell him everything.

"Um, no. But I promise you the relationship is consensual, if that's the concern."

"It isn't."

"Oh, so…" I should know what he's getting at, and it annoys me that I don't. I should also have a way to finish the sentence I began, but I don't have that either.

"Gracie, relax."

He looks unconcerned, sitting there behind his big glass desk in his big corner office. Of course, he's not worried about his job, and he holds all the cards pertaining to mine. I shift in my chair, but it's only a movement from one clenched ass cheek to the other.

Gerald laughs again. "Do you know how to do that?"

"Sorry?"

He reaches for a jar on the console behind him and brings it to the desk, then slides it across to me. I can see the Reese's Peanut Butter cups through the glass, and my stomach does a little backflip.

Lifting the lid, Gerald nods at the container. "Help yourself."

I take two of the foil-wrapped goodies and put them on the desk in front of me. He retrieves one from the jar and unwraps it. I do the same, and we both pop them into our mouths like we're in agreement on the need for sugar.

The rush of sweet carbs hits the sensory receptors in my brain, and I relax a tiny bit. The sugar will do some of the work now.

Seemingly satisfied with the snack, Gerald covers the jar but leaves it on the desk. "Gracie, this is not a crime, dating a player on the team."

"Sure, but it's unprofessional." I snap my lips shut. Why am I adding fuel to his case? I unwrap the other peanut butter cup. Better to keep my mouth busy. Otherwise, I might fire myself.

"Maybe. But it happens. You're not going to lose your job because you fell for a player on the team. I'm going to tell you what I told Reyes when he came to see me earlier."

"Wait, what?"

I lift my head, trying to see if I can spot the players on the field below our offices, but I can't see anything from where I am. Hunter didn't tell me he was cleared to come back to practice. And he definitely didn't tell me he had a meeting here this morning.

For a second, I fear the worst, that he wanted to beat me to the punch, talk to Gerald before I have a chance to defend myself. He wouldn't throw me under the bus. He wouldn't. But a tiny voice in my head starts to protest otherwise.

Stop it. He asked you to trust him, and you gave him your word.

I nod and wait for Gerald to tell me the rest. "He offered to put himself on the trade list if it would save your job. I told him that you're the best head of analytics we've had, which means we're keeping him. And you. Who you date in your personal time is your business. But all the same, you two had better sit down with Ashley and get your ducks in a row. There will need to be some kind of social media control, and that's not my purview."

I'm so filled with unexpected relief that I can't find words. Again.

Gerald solves that problem by pushing the jar of candy back toward me. "Take a few for the road, Gracie. And don't sweat it so much around here. You have job security. And the fact that you showed me your ethical core only ups the ante."

"Thank you. I'll, um, get back to it, then."

"I know you will."

CHAPTER 46

*H*unter

The Next Day

My plan for tonight is a real date with Gracie—one where we don't have to sneak off to a corner of the city to hide from roaming smartphones and watchful eyes. The social media firestorm has been fierce since we became an official item, and Ashley loves it. She says fans are invested in our romance and that makes her job easy.

Nevertheless, Gracie hasn't gotten used to the spotlight, so I try to keep our outings low key.

I tell her to be ready at six but don't offer any further details. Well, except that I ask her to wear that goddamn black dress because I can't wait to watch her slink through a room in it before peeling it from her body later.

When I get back to the house after training, I call out in the direction of her room. "I'm home, Gracie. I'll be ready in fifteen."

I get no response, but I figure she's probably in the bathroom and didn't hear me. I hop in the shower, dress quickly, and rap my knuckles on her bedroom door. There's no answer.

"Tink?" I wait for an answer or any kind of a sign she's in there, but I'm met only with silence.

Twisting the handle on the door, I push it open and peek inside. The room has the shades half-drawn, which isn't unusual in the hot afternoon sun, but there's no sign Gracie has been here. No dripping water in the bathroom, no whoosh of perfume lingering in the air.

Did she forget our date?

I wander into the kitchen and grab a green juice. Then I take out my phone. No texts or voice mails from her. It makes no sense.

But then I spot a folded note perched on the counter like a tent. It has my name scrawled on the outside and only one line on the reverse. "Change of plan. Meet me on Main Street." She's scribbled an address in Culver City. I don't waste time looking up the location. I get in my car and drive straight there.

The traffic gets slow once I'm in the small downtown area, so I pull my car into a public lot and make my way to the Main Street address on foot. Passing by a Starbucks and several trendy restaurants, I make mental notes about places I should take Gracie for dinner sometime.

I didn't bother putting on a hat or sunglasses, but the last thing I'm concerned about is someone snapping a picture of me walking alone. Couples pass me on the sidewalk, and I barely notice whether anyone seems to recognize me or not. I have one destination in mind, and I've been reciting the street numbers to myself during the fifteen-minute drive over here.

I don't even bother looking to see my endpoint, only concerned that I've reached it. When I grab the door handle and swing it open, my sole focus is on finding Gracie and making sure everything is okay. I must look like an unhinged maniac because her eyes go wide when she sees me, and her hand darts out and wraps around my forearm.

Under the soft warmth of her skin, I relax. All of the self-annihilating thoughts in my head calm down, and I let myself believe that everything is okay.

"You alright?" she asks, taking a step toward me. I notice that she's wearing a red version of that black dress I love so much, and if it's possible, I love this one even more.

"How do you do that?" I ask, baffled.

"What?"

"Look even more gorgeous every time I see you?"

The worry on her face falls away, and her face warms at the compliment, which is always my intention. She smiles, and the room brightens.

That's when I take my first look around and notice the books. Everywhere I look, books on shelves and in little displays, and a lot of them have covers with women in ball gowns and dapper, smoldering men who could be dukes or counts.

"Are these all...romance novels?"

She nods, her smile not dimming a bit. Gone is the apologetic woman who worries about whether she's up to the task of "seducing an athlete," as she put it that night at the Château Marmont. She knows exactly how much power she wields over me, and I love it.

A large sign on one wall says "The Ripped Bodice," an apt name for a bookstore filled to the rafters with steamy books.

"I know you lost your library in the fire, and I seem to remember you saying you'd like some books about dashing Scottish heroes on your bedside table."

"Pretty sure I was talking about the sexy heroines, not the dudes. And I also recall that I was flirting with you."

"Really?" she asks innocently, looking up at me with round doe eyes. "I thought you were trying to get into my reading list."

"Oh, Tink. I was trying to get into something, but it wasn't that."

Her face goes a deeper shade of scarlet, and I pull her toward me. Her body hits my chest, and I wrap her in my arms. Right now, I don't give a shit who else is in the store or what they feel like putting on social media. If the world sees me kissing the woman I love, all the better.

I kiss her softly, but that's never enough when I get started with her. Never will be. Within seconds, my hands cup her face, and I deepen the kiss. Probably too much PDA for normal circumstances, but we're in a romance bookstore for fuck's sake. Anyone in here gets what it means to fall so hard for a woman that the outside world falls away.

It's the fairy tale. The happily ever after. Only I'm lucky enough to be living it.

Well, except for one thing, but our evening isn't over yet.

Gracie pulls away and smiles up at me. "Let's do some shopping. When your house is done, that bedside table is going to need some new books."

I follow her around the store, grabbing a book every time I see her look longingly at a cover. "You really want to read that one?" She raises an eyebrow when I pick up something about being romanced by a regal.

I shrug. "Maybe I'll have you read me the good stuff."

She laughs. "If it inspires you, I'll read whatever you want."

We spend a few more minutes shopping until I'm weighted down with a stack of books, a few of which I actually intend to read. The rest are for her. We drop them off in the trunk of my car, and I run through a visual map of places I noticed in the area for dinner ideas. I'm still determined to have the date I want with her tonight.

Then I have a different idea. "Trust me?" I ask, opening the passenger door and taking her hand to guide her into the car.

"More than I trust anyone."

I freeze.

My therapist has taught me that certain trigger words evoke feelings, but this is next level. Knowing she trusts me hollows out a space in my chest that lets my heart swell with so much love that it hurts. My breath catches in my throat, and I feel leveled in a way that no blow on a soccer field could ever match.

Looking at Gracie sitting in my passenger seat, I've never felt more certain that everything in my life was somehow perfectly synchronized to bring me to this moment.

Every penalty that led to me almost getting fired. Every mistake and emotional miscue that made me finally get my shit together so I can be the man she deserves.

I'm the sum of all my failings, only now they look like successes.

"I love you, Gracie Albright. That's it. That's all I've got."

I kiss her hand before closing the car door and going around to my side.

"It's everything," she says, and it's true.

She tilts her seat back a few inches and rolls down the window. The light breeze immediately has its way with her tangle of wavy hair, but it doesn't stop me from seeing the contented smile on her face.

racie

THE CITY SLIPS by in a blur outside the car, but for once, I don't find myself clocking all the details of my surroundings or wondering where we're going. It doesn't matter.

I meant it when I said I trust Hunter. Everywhere he's taken me so far has been better than I could have imagined, and it feels good to open my heart and trust that wherever we're headed now will be good.

Things at work have been a little awkward as word has passed around the office about Hunter and me. Once Ashley finished giving me a hard time for keeping it from her, she told me she was impressed that I'd kept things under wraps and not let anything slip, even the night of the game when he grabbed me in the hallway and I played it off like I was as surprised as anyone. "If the computer science doesn't work out, you should be a spy," she told me. "And remember, I'm your friend. I'd have kept your secret and even given you good advice. You can trust me."

One more person urging me to let my walls down. One more reminder that there are good people out there worth trusting.

Hunter drives west, and the sun shines bright through the windshield. He pops on a pair of sunglasses and smooths a hand through his hair. The wind from the open windows blows it back from his face, and I marvel at how beautiful he looks as the sun kisses his skin. Without taking his eyes from the road, he brings his hand to my knee and softly pushes up the fabric of my dress until his hand is on bare skin.

I put my hand on his and lean back against the headrest. "I wouldn't even care if we don't have a destination. We could do this for a while," I say.

"Agreed. But I have a destination in mind. Are you hungry?"

"Yes. I was going to have us walk up the street to this market-place area that has some food stalls and a roof deck where we could hang out."

He nods. "We'll do that next time. Promise."

He pulls the car into an alley that leads to a parking lot. "Don't move," he instructs, coming around to open my door. At least, that's what I think he's doing. But then I hear the trunk open. And close.

When he comes around to my side of the car, he's wearing a sport coat over his tee and faded jeans, and he presents me with a giant bouquet of daisies. I don't know why pinpricks of tears hit my eyes, but I pretend it's the sun and accept the bouquet.

"Thank you. I love them."

He takes my hand, and we walk under a dated-looking sign that looks like it belongs on an old drive-in. Inside the squat brick space is a classic steakhouse with red booths, a long, ebony wood bar, and a fireplace burning in a corner. It's cool and dark inside, and as soon as the door closes behind us, I feel transported to a bygone era.

A host leads us to a table in the back, near the fireplace, and takes my flowers to put in a vase for later.

"This place is awesome," I say. "The fabulous tour of Hunter's haunts continues."

"I have so many more places I want to go with you."

"Good. Because I have a relatively open calendar. That's the good thing about being an introvert."

He laughs. "You keep calling yourself that, but you don't seem that way to me."

"You bring out another side of me. I like it."

We order martinis with olives because it's that kind of place. When they arrive at our table, Hunter lifts his for a toast. I'm expecting something short and sweet. "To us," or another variation on the theme.

Instead, his expression goes serious, and he asks me a question.

"Do you know why I was at the airport that day?"

"Which day?"

"The day we ran into each other at the bar, before your flight."

It's funny that I never asked him about it. At first, I was embarrassed for not recognizing him, and later, it seemed like a blip in time. But come to think of it, I have no idea why he was there.

"I assume you had to fly someplace."

He chuckles. "That would be a reasonable assumption at an airport. Yeah. I was going to visit my mom. For an indeterminate length of time."

I feel a tiny pang of panic, and I don't know why. Is he telling me there's something he needs to do back home? Is his mom okay?

"Why indeterminate?"

"Because I thought I was getting dropped from the team. Traded to some god-awful place I probably didn't want to go. I'd been warned enough times. Even though the fans like seeing me dump guys on their asses, I knew my days were all but numbered with the Devils, and I wanted to beat them to the punch. I was going to leave town and not look back."

The idea hits me hard. He and I never would have crossed paths in the kitchen, never would have felt the chemistry that now seems irresistible, never would have found ourselves here.

"Why didn't you go?" My voice is quiet, but so is the room. It suddenly feels like we're the only ones here, and the moment hangs heavy like a wet bag of sand.

"You."

I blink hard. It's not what I was expecting at all.

"But you didn't know me. You said you didn't recognize me."

"I know. I had no way of finding you and really not a snowball's chance in hell of tracking you down, except..." He looks guilty, pressing his lips together like he might get in trouble.

"What?"

"I looked at your credit card receipt and saw your name. I know that's probably illegal or whatever, but I was a man on a hunt. So I immediately figured out you were Ky's sister, even though you didn't bear any resemblance to the girl I remembered from high school. And that felt like a sign. I didn't get on the plane. And when my house burned down, I took your brother up on his offer to put me up, even though I didn't have to."

"Wait, I thought you had nowhere else to stay?"

He chokes a laugh. "Really? My insurance was willing to give me thirty grand a month for alternate accommodations. I could've stayed anywhere in town."

"Oh," I say, looking away because I feel foolish.

"Hey." He redirects my gaze back to him with a finger beneath my chin. "What I'm saying is that once I saw you again, this was never going to end a different way. I've always had a thing for you, Gracie. Always."

My breath hitches as he draws a line from my chin to my lips. Leaning in, he replaces his finger with his lips. It's a kiss that rips through me, sealing every feeling I've ever had about Hunter Reyes into a permanent record.

"Thank you," I say when we have to break for air. "For telling me that. I love you even more, if that's possible."

He nods, cupping my cheek in his hand. "I know how you feel."

He places a gentle kiss on my temple and sits back in his chair.

"I think back to that day, and it seems like a year ago. How much my life has changed. Back then, I was convinced my time with the Devils had come to an end. I lost my house. I was mentally preparing to leave LA and never look back."

"Glad you didn't bolt out of town."

Hunter shakes his head like he can't believe his luck. "I'd have missed so much if I'd gotten on that plane. I have no idea where the road will take me, but I don't care as long as I can walk it with you."

At that moment, I realize, for maybe the first time in my life, that some things don't warrant overthinking. Some things just are.

This is one of those things, the love I feel between us. It's as close to perfect as any mathematical puzzle I've ever marveled over. Right there with the biggest mysteries of the universe. As pure as the elements and as durable.

I pick up my glass and propose a toast. "To you and me and the long road ahead."

Our glasses clink.

EPILOGUE

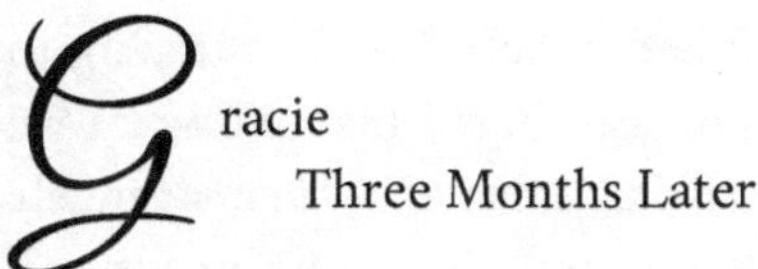

racie
Three Months Later

"So, what's on the menu?" Hunter sits on a chaise longue on the grass with an arm behind his head and a book in his hand, looking relaxed and just a tiny bit cocky. He's wearing a pair of workout shorts and nothing else, his tanned chest beautifully sculpted.

"Not sure, since you're cooking," I say in a cheery voice.

"Um, no. It's definitely you."

"I really don't think you're correct on that one, hate to break it to you." I stand on the deck behind the Santa Monica bungalow Hunter and I are renting until his house is finished being rebuilt. As much as Ky protested and said he liked having us as roomies, we decided to give him his space.

As soon as we did, my brother got a dog. With as much as he travels, we'll be dog sitting quite a bit, but Bogie won't mind the company, and I'm probably more excited than anyone. I've officially become a dog person.

But I'm not cooking dinner. I put my hands on my hips and give Hunter a fierce staredown, but he only laughs.

"I wish you could see how adorable you look when you try to pretend you're angry at me." The dimple in his cheek taunts me, and he gives me his very best smirk. I wish he wasn't so damn hot. No, I don't.

But he is very good at using his charm to get out of cooking duty.

So I stomp down the steps to where he's being lazy on the chair and stand directly between him and the late afternoon sun. His expression dims a tad.

"Are we back to that silly bet again?" I ask.

"What's that?" Ignoring my question, he points to a radish I've plucked from the soil in a raised bed, where I've been trying to grow vegetables. Of the two dozen seedlings I planted when we moved in, this is the only one that has survived. I feel strangely proud of it, even though I barely did anything to ensure that it flourished.

"A radish. I grew it."

He laughs. "I see. And will you be using it in the dinner you're cooking?"

"I'm not cooking. You are. You lost the bet. You brought me back to Ky's house for a hookup, not the other way around."

We've been arguing about this for months now, trying to determine who won the bet we made in the early days of living at Kyler's house over who would hook up first. I'd long ago accepted that neither one of us won or lost because we ended up together. And since we stayed at a hotel that first night and agreed that it wasn't really a hookup, it nullified the bet. That made sense to any rational person, or so I thought.

Apparently, my boyfriend is not a rational person. He keeps insisting that I owe him a home-cooked meal, and even though he probably cooks more often than I do, I've made my share of dinner.

Today, for some reason, he has a bug in his muscle-hugging britches and won't let it go.

"If you want me to rustle up some stuffed potato skins, just say so," I tell him, holding the radish close enough to his nose for him to smell the fresh dirt. He grabs me around the waist and pulls me on top of him, which causes the book he was reading to fall on the grass. I glance at the title and see that he's back to the classics.

He nuzzles my ear and squeezes me until I laugh. "I don't want that. I want you."

His lips find my neck, and he trails kisses from my ear to my collarbone before flipping me around so I'm lying on top of him. He kisses my lips softly, which immediately makes me press into him, wanting more. It only takes a minute for him to go from playfully nipping at my lips to diving in for a kiss so deep I feel it down to my toes.

I moan and wrap my arms around his neck as our tongues delve deeper, and I lose myself in the kiss. Which happens every damn day. By the time we come up for air, my brains are so scrambled that I feel like a robot programmed to do his bidding.

Rolling to the side to lay on the chaise next to him, I run a hand over his tattooed arm, remembering the conversation about him wanting to be more Zen. He's come a long way toward that goal in the past few months. Still fierce on the field, he's been able to separate his playing style from his judgment about himself. He seems lighter. More free. It's good to see.

"Okay, I'll make you a deal. I'll cook tonight if we agree that it has nothing to do with winning or losing any bet. It's just me cooking."

Hunter kisses my temple and agrees. "Sounds fair, Tink. I'll come in a few minutes and help."

I take my radish into the kitchen, cradling it like a tiny friend, and consult a cookbook from the stack we bought at our local library's used book sale. Hunter has made some good progress at replacing some of the books he lost in the fire, and I've been slowly threading the needle between recipes that aren't too healthy or too much like fast food. It isn't easy, hence the big stack of books.

Settling on a roasted chicken dish I can make in one pot with rice and vegetables, I put on Taylor Swift's new album and go to the fridge for ingredients.

Except that the refrigerator is inexplicably empty, save for one large brown box, even though I went to the grocery store earlier and Hunter put everything away.

"Don't worry. The food is in a cooler in the garage. No perishables were harmed in the making of this movie."

"What movie?" I turn and find Hunter no longer in the shorts he wore a few minutes ago. He's changed into a dark suit, looking impossibly handsome with a white shirt unbuttoned at the collar and his hair perfectly rumpled. Bogie sits next to him with a black bowtie around his neck.

My mind races, trying to remember if we're supposed to be somewhere that I've forgotten. In my sweatpants with my hair in a ponytail, I'm no match for his style, and it would take me a while to get there. "Do we—?"

Hunter steps closer and reaches for my hands, wrenching away the cookbook I've been white-knuckling without realizing it. I shake my head, so confused. "Is this—?"

He interrupts me with a finger against my lips like he regularly does when I'm about to talk before figuring out what to say. Hunter puts his phone on the counter, positions it so the camera can record a video of us, and turns it on. "You're not cooking," he says.

"Well, no. Not when you confiscated all the ingredients." My brain stops spinning out because I can see he has something planned, and all of his plans have worked out well in the past. So I'm along for the ride now, wherever he wants to take us. "What's with the video camera?"

He glances at it, adjusting it slightly so we're centered in the frame with Bogie, who hasn't moved. "I thought you might want to remember today."

"Is this the day you admit you lost the bet?"

He starts to nod, but then shakes his head with a grin. "Never. But this is the day I give you this." He points to the box in the still-open refrigerator and slides it out, exaggerating the weight of it and making me glad he's the one carrying it. He pulls over a barstool and puts the box on it so it's in view of the camera. "Go ahead."

Casting him one more quizzical look, I shake my head, confused and delighted by his constant surprises. I'll never get tired of them. Or him.

I pull the tape from the top of the box and it springs open to reveal a small shopping bag from a boutique I've never been to and plastic bag filled with pale sand. It I lift it out and understand why the box was heavy. There's a note taped to the bottom.

I read it out loud, mostly so it's caught on the video. "I love you. Please have dinner with me at the beach."

Smiling, I marvel at this man in front of me who always goes the extra mile to make my life special. "I would love to," I say.

Hunter tips his head toward the shopping bag, so I dig in and find a simple but elegant black dress. It's short and backless, tasteful and sexy at the same time. I look down at my sweats and back at Hunter. "You want me to put this on now?"

But Hunter isn't where he was a moment earlier. He's in front of me, kneeling with one more box. He pops it open to reveal a sparkly solitaire diamond ring. "I want you to put it on after you're wearing this ring. After you agree that we're meant for each other, Gracie Albright. I knew it when I was sixteen, and I'm even more certain now."

I nod. "We are."

"Then, let's make it permanent. Will you spend your life with me? Because I love you more than anyone and I want to fucking marry you so much it hurts." He squeezes his chest with one hand, and I know exactly how he feels. I get that same ache when my heart floods with love for him, like it can barely contain the wealth of feelings.

"Yes," I say. It's the easiest decision I've ever made. "I love you. So much."

Hunter stands and takes the ring from the box. I extend a shaky hand so he can slide it on my finger. Bogie yelps like he understands the significance of the moment. We both laugh and Hunter slips him a treat.

I glance at the phone and see the two of us in the frame, now engaged, and I love Hunter even more for knowing I'll want to watch this moment again and again. For always knowing what I need. And for wrapping me in his arms for the best kiss I've had in my life. And I've had some good ones. Each time, with him.

THANK you so much for reading Gracie and Hunter's story—I hope you fell for this couple the way I did while writing them!

I have a special glimpse into Gracie and Hunter's happily ever after for you—just jump on my mailing list for your BONUS EPILOGUE! I'll only send you the best stuff—new release info, exclusive sales, and a monthly free romance from one of my author friends.

Next up in the series, PLAYING TO WIN is a single dad, brother's rival romance between Dario and Julia—you can preorder it now!

ACKNOWLEDGMENTS

I love my romance readers so much. Mic drop.

I had a moment after my last book when I thought I might be done writing romance. And I thought maybe romance was done with me. But it's the sweet notes from you that made me sit back down at the keyboard and find this new soccer world - and I think it's my favorite yet. So, from the depths of my heart, thank you!

Jesse and Oliver, you are my support squad and I love you.

Thank you, Jenny, for top-notch edits in record time. Leah and Amy, I'd be a mess without your beta reads and brilliant notes.

Val at Books and Moods killed it with this cover - thank you.

Valentine and the VPR family—you are the absolute best!

Bloggers and bookstagrammers—thank you for embracing my books and helping me find new readers. I couldn't do it without your help.

And to every writer who was afraid to put pen to paper for fear of rejection, I see you. You've got this.

Stacy Travis writes sexy, charming romance about bookish, sassy women and the hot cinamon roll heroes who fall for them. Keep the coffee coming, and she'll keep writing.

When she's not on a deadline, she's in running shoes complaining that all roads seem to go uphill. Or on the couch with a margarita. Or fangirling at a soccer game. She's never met a dog she didn't want to hug. And if you have no plans for Thanksgiving, she'll probably invite you to dinner. Stacy is the mom of two boys and two poorly-trained rescue dogs who keep her on her toes in Los Angeles.

Facebook reader group: Stacy's Saucy Sisters

Super fun newsletter: https://geni.us/travisNL

Tiktok: https://www.tiktok.com/@stacytravisauthor

Website: https://www.www.stacytravis.com

Email: stacytraviswrites@gmail.com - tell me what you're reading!

facebook.com/stacytravisromance
instagram.com/stacytravisauthor
bookbub.com/authors/stacy-travis
goodreads.com/stacytravis
tiktok.com/@stacytravisauthor

ALSO BY STACY TRAVIS

The Summer Heat Duet

1. The Summer of Him: A Mistaken-Identity Celebrity Romance

2. Forever with Him: An Opposites-Attract Contemporary Romance

The Berkeley Hills Series - standalone novels

1. In Trouble with Him: A Forbidden-Love Office Romance (Finn and Annie's story)

2. Second Chance at Us: A Second Chance Romance (Becca and Blake)

3. Falling for You: A Friends-to-Lovers Romance (Isla and Owen)

4. The Spark Between Us: A Grumpy-Sunshine, Firefighter, Brother's Best Friend Romance (Sarah and Braden)

5. Playing for You: A Sports Romance (Tatum and Donovan)

6. No Match for Her - An Opposites-Attract, Friends-to-Lovers Romance (Cherry and Charlie)

San Francisco Strikers Series - standalone novels

1. He's a Keeper: A Grumpy-Sunshine Sports Romance (Molly and Holden)

2. He's a Player: A Second-Chance Sports Romance (Jordan and Tim)

3. He's a Charmer: A Brother's-Best-Friend, Forced-Proximity, Sports Romance (Linnie and Weston)

Buttercup Hill Series - standalone novels

1. Love You More; A Single-Dad, Grumpy-Sunshine Small-Town Romance (Jax and Ruby)

2. Love You Anyway; A Small-Town Billionaire-Next-Door Age Gap Romance (PJ and Colin)

3. Love You Truly; A Fake-Fiancé, Small-Town Romance (Dash and Mallory)

4. Love You Too; A Small-Town, Accidental Pregnancy Sports Romance (Beatrix and Ren)

5. Love You Always: A Small-Town, Grumpy-Sunshine Forbidden Romance (Archer and Ella)

Los Angeles Devils Series - standalone sports novels

1. Playing the Field; A Brother's Best Friend, Slow Burn Soccer Romance (Hunter and Gracie)